# PRAISE FOR **THE PROGRAM**

"Suspenseful and touching, *The Program* feels frighteningly real."
—Jay Asher, #1 *New York Times* bestselling author of
*Thirteen Reasons Why*

"Heartbreaking and chilling, *The Program* will leave you breathless."
—Kimberly Derting, author of the Body Finder series

★ "Readers will devour this fast-paced story that combines an intriguing
premise, a sexy romance, and a shifting landscape of truth."
—*Booklist*, starred review

★ "[A] powerful psychological drama."
—*BCCB*, starred review

# PRAISE FOR **THE TREATMENT**

★ "The reader will root for Sloane and James, and will feel
their star-crossed love . . . with romance, mystery, adventure,
and the complications of a suspense thriller."
—*VOYA*, starred review

"This jarring thriller looks at the cost of societal complacency
while lauding heroism and remembrance."
—*Kirkus Reviews*

## ALSO BY SUZANNE YOUNG

*The Program*

*The Recovery*

*Just Like Fate*
with Cat Patrick

## COMING SOON

*The Remedy*

# THE TREATMENT

## SUZANNE YOUNG

**SIMON PULSE**

New York London Toronto Sydney New Delhi

SIMON PULSE

An imprint of Simon & Schuster Children's Publishing Division

1230 Avenue of the Americas, New York, NY 10020

First Simon Pulse paperback edition March 2015

Text copyright © 2014 by Suzanne Young

Cover photograph of couple copyright © 2015 by Michael Frost

Cover background photograph copyright © by Thinkstock

Also available in a Simon Pulse hardcover edition.

All rights reserved, including the right of reproduction in whole or in part in any form.

SIMON PULSE and colophon are registered trademarks of Simon & Schuster, Inc.

For information about special discounts for bulk purchases,

please contact Simon & Schuster Special Sales at

1-866-506-1949 or business@simonandschuster.com.

The Simon & Schuster Speakers Bureau can bring authors to your

live event. For more information or to book an event contact

the Simon & Schuster Speakers Bureau at 1-866-248-3049 or visit

our website at www.simonspeakers.com.

Cover designed by Russell Gordon

Interior designed by Mike Rosamilia

The text of this book was set in Adobe Caslon Pro.

Manufactured in the United States of America

2 4 6 8 10 9 7 5 3 1

The Library of Congress has cataloged the hardcover edition as follows:

Young, Suzanne.

The Treatment / Suzanne Young. — First Simon Pulse hardcover edition.

p. cm.

Sequel to: The Program.

Summary: Working with rebels to bring down The Program, a suicide prevention treatment in which painful memories are erased, Sloane and James consider taking The Treatment to unlock their memories.

[1. Suicide—Fiction. 2. Government, Resistance to—Fiction. 3. Memory—Fiction. 4. Love—Fiction. 5. Science fiction.] I. Title.

PZ7.Y887Tr 2014    [Fic]—dc23    2013042326

ISBN 978-1-4424-4583-3 (hc)

ISBN 978-1-4424-4584-0 (pbk)

ISBN 978-1-4424-4585-7 (eBook)

*For Team Program*

*And in loving memory of my grandmother*
*Josephine Parzych*

PART I
# COME AS YOU WERE

THE EPIDEMIC

Over the last four years, suicide has reached epidemic proportions, killing one in three teens. But new studies have shown the incidence of suicide in adults has suddenly risen, debunking the myth that childhood vaccinations or overuse of antidepressants is the cause.

While The Program has been the only method of prevention, its scope is limited. But in reaction to the spread of the epidemic, officials have enacted a new law to take effect later this year. All teens under the age of eighteen will undergo behavior modification with The Program. Like any inoculation, the hope is to eradicate the disease from future generations. Through a combination of mood stabilization and memory therapy, The Program claims a 100 percent success rate among its patients.

Information about the mandatory treatment is soon to follow, but for now one thing is certain: The Program is coming.

—Reported by Kellan Thomas

.

# CHAPTER ONE

JAMES STARES STRAIGHT AHEAD, WITH NO IMMEDIATE reaction to what I've just told him. I think he's in shock. I follow his gaze out the windshield to the empty parking lot of the convenience store off the highway. The building is abandoned, plywood covering the windows, black graffiti tagged on the white siding. In a way, James and I have been abandoned too, our former selves boarded up and locked away while the world moves on around us. We were supposed to accept that change, follow the rules. Instead we broke all of them.

The streetlight above us flickers out as the sun, still below the mountains, begins to illuminate the cloudy horizon. It's nearly five in the morning, and I know we'll have to move soon if we want to stay ahead of the roadblocks. We'd barely beat the one at the Idaho border, and now there's an Amber Alert issued for our safe return.

Right. Because The Program is just concerned with our safety.

"It's a pill," James repeats quietly, finally coming around. "Michael Realm left you a pill that could bring back our memories"—he turns to me—"but he gave you only one."

I nod, watching as James's normally handsome face sags, almost like he's losing himself all over again. Since leaving The Program, James has been searching for a way to understand his past, our shared past. In my back pocket is a folded plastic Baggie with a little orange pill inside, a pill that can unlock everything. But I've made my choice: The risks are too high, the chance of relapsing too great to ignore. There will be grief and heartache and pain. Realm's sister's final words to me resonate: *Sometimes the only real thing is now.* And here, with James, I know exactly who I am.

"You're not going to take it, are you?" James asks, reading my expression. His bright blue eyes are weary, and it's hard to believe that just yesterday we were at the river, kissing and ignoring the world around us. For a moment we knew what it felt like to be free.

"The pill will change everything," I say. "I'll remember who I was, but I can never be her again, not really. All the pill can do is hurt me—bring back the sorrow I felt when I lost my brother. And I'm sure there are others. I like who I am with you, James. I like us together and I'm scared of messing that up."

SUZANNE YOUNG

James runs his fingers through his golden hair, blowing out a hard breath. "I'm never going to leave you, Sloane." He looks out the driver's side window. The clouds have gathered above us, and I think it'll be only a matter of time before we're caught in a downpour. "We're together," he says definitively, glancing back at me. "But there's only one pill, and I'd never take it without you. I'd never take that choice away from you."

My heart swells. James is choosing this life with me, a life I want except for the part where The Program is hunting us down. I lean over, my hands on his chest, and he pulls me closer.

James licks his lips, pausing before he kisses me. "We're going to keep the pill in case we change our minds later, right?"

"My thought exactly."

"You're so smart," he whispers, and kisses me. My hands slide up to his cheeks, and I begin to get lost in the feeling of him, the heat of his mouth on mine. I murmur that I love him, but his response is drowned out by the sound of squealing tires.

James spins to look outside. He begins to fumble with the keys in the ignition just as a white van screeches to a stop, barricading our SUV against the concrete wall of the highway behind us.

Panic, thick and choking, sweeps over me. I scream for James to go, even though the only way out is to ram them. But we can't go back to The Program to be erased again. James yanks down the gear lever, ready to floor it, when the driver's side door of the van opens and a person jumps out. I pause, my eyebrows pulled together in confusion, because there's no white jacket, no comb-smoothed hair of a handler.

It's a girl. She's wearing a Nirvana T-shirt and has long bleached-blond dreads flowing over her shoulders. She's tall, incredibly thin, and when she smiles, her bright-red lips pull apart to reveal a large gap between her two front teeth. I reach to put my hand on James's forearm, but he still looks like he's about to run her down. "Wait," I say.

James glances over at me as if I'm crazy, but then the other side of the van opens and a guy stands on the running board to peer over the door at us. He has two half-moon bruises under his eyes and a swollen nose. The vulnerability of his battered appearance is enough to make James stop, though, and he restrains himself from stomping on the gas.

The girl holds up her hands. "You can relax," she calls. "We're not with The Program."

James rolls down his window, the car still in drive and ready to launch forward—crushing her—at any second. "Then who the hell are you?" he demands.

The girl's smile widens and she tosses a look back at her companion before turning to James. "I'm Dallas," she says. "Realm sent us a message to find you." At the mention of Realm, I tell James to turn off the car, relieved that my friend is okay.

Dallas walks in front of the car, her boots echoing off the pavement, before she comes to pause at James's window. She lifts one of her dark eyebrows and looks him over. "Realm must have forgotten to mention how pretty you are," she says wryly. "Shame on him."

"How'd you find us?" James asks, ignoring her comment. "We went to the border for Lacey and Kevin, but there were patrols everywhere. We barely got through."

Dallas nods toward the car. "The phone Realm's sister gave you has a tracking device. Pretty handy, but you should probably ditch it now." Both James and I look in the center console at the black phone that was already in the car when we got in. There's also a duffel bag on the backseat, along with a couple hundred dollars Anna left us for provisions. But is this it? Are we part of the rebels now? If so . . . they don't look all that pulled together.

"Your friends," Dallas says, "never made it to the border either. We found Lacey, huddled in her Bug and crying. Seems Kevin didn't show. I think there's more to the story, but I'll let her tell it."

My heart sinks. What happened to Kevin? "Where's Lacey?" I ask. "Is she okay?"

"She's a firecracker." Dallas laughs. "She wouldn't talk to me, so I had Cas try and coax her out of her vehicle. She broke his nose. We had to sedate her, but don't worry, we don't steal your memories." She says it in a spooky voice, like The Program is just a monster living under our beds. I'm starting to wonder if she's sane. "Anyway . . ." She sighs, slipping her hands into the back pockets of her jeans. "She's already on her way to the safe house. And unless you're trying to get caught, I'd suggest you get out of the vehicle and come with me."

"In that van?" James scoffs. "You think we're less conspicuous in a big white van?"

She nods. "Yep. It's something a handler would drive. Not a group of people on the run. Listen—James, is it? You're super-hot and all, but you don't strike me as a real thinker. So maybe just follow orders and bring your little girlfriend into the van so we can get out of here."

"Screw you," I say, offended on so many levels it's difficult to pick just one. James turns to me, his brow furrowed.

"What do you think?" he asks quietly. I can see his indecision, but we don't have any other options right now. We were on our way to find the rebels, but they found us first. Lacey is with them.

"We have to get to Lacey," I say, wishing we could run off on our own. But we don't have the resources. We'll need to regroup.

James groans, not wanting to give in to Dallas. His aversion to authority is one of my very favorite things about him. "Fine," he says, looking back at Dallas. "But what are we going to do with the Escalade? It's a nice car."

"Cas is going to drive it back."

"What?" James asks. "Why does he get to—"

"Cas isn't on the run," she interrupts. "He's never been in The Program. He can drive through any checkpoint he wants. He's going ahead to scout the trip, get us to the safe house unscathed."

"Where are we going?" I ask.

Dallas casts a bored glance in my direction, looking annoyed that I spoke to her. "All in good time, sweetheart. Now, if you'd both climb out, we have a little business to take care of first."

James and I exchange a look, but ultimately we get out of the car. Cas starts toward us, and for a moment I have the fear we're getting carjacked. Especially when Cas pulls out a fistful of zip ties.

"What the fuck are those for?" James yells, grabbing my arm to pull me back.

Dallas puts her hand on her hip. "Cas had his nose broken today, and to be honest, you seem pretty volatile. This is for our protection. We don't trust you. You're returners."

The way she says "returners" makes us sound like we're abominations, like we disgust her. But it was probably just the right thing to say to catch us off guard, break us down enough so Cas could come behind us and slip the ties around our wrists, pulling them tight. Just then I feel the first drop of rain hit my cheek. I look sideways at James; he's angry, watching as Dallas and Cas go through the Escalade, take out our money, and toss the canvas bag onto the pavement. The rain starts to fall in a drizzle, and Dallas scowls at the sky. She walks around to swipe our bag from the ground, hanging it lazily over her shoulder.

I feel vulnerable, and I can't remember how we got here. We should have kept running. But now we hardly have a choice, so we follow behind Dallas as she leads us to the van and helps us into the back, slamming the door closed behind us.

*    *    *

James's shoulder is against mine as we sit in the backseat of the white van. I've become hyperaware of everything—the faint scents of gasoline and rubber tires that cling to my hair; the murmur from the police scanner too low to understand. James's fingers brush along mine, and I instinctively turn. He's staring ahead, his jaw set hard as he broods about the restraints. We've been driving for hours, and the hard plastic has rubbed my skin raw. I imagine it's doing the same to him.

Dallas glances in the rearview mirror in time to see James's hateful expression. "Don't worry, handsome. We're almost there. There's been a change of plans. Our warehouse in Philadelphia was raided last night, so we're going to our safe house in Salt Lake City."

Alarmed, I straighten up. "But Realm told us to head east. He said—"

"I know what Michael Realm told you," she snaps. "But then there's the reality of the situation. Don't be a child. The Program is hunting us; we're an infection they intend to cure. You should be happy we're helping you at all."

"I'll be honest, Dallas," James says in a shaky voice of barely contained rage. "If you don't take the ties off my girlfriend, I'm going to be a real asshole. I don't want to hurt you."

Dallas looks in the rearview mirror again, without even a hint of surprise. "What makes you think you can?" she asks seriously. "You have no idea what I'm capable of, James."

Her voice chills me, and I can see by James's posture that

he knows his threat didn't have its intended effect. Dallas is hardcore; I'm not sure she's afraid of anything.

We continue to drive and the landscape changes. Instead of the canopy of trees we left behind in Oregon, the sky here is wide open. But there are still flowers, rolling green hills. And then, towering over all of it, is a massive set of mountains. It's breathtaking.

Behind my back, the zip tie is biting into the skin of my wrists. I wince but try to play it off when I see how angry it makes James. He adjusts his position so I can lean against him and relax, and together we watch as the country fades to chain-link fences and old mechanic shops.

"Welcome to Salt Lake City," Dallas says, turning into the parking lot of a low-rise warehouse with crumbling brick siding. I expected a compound, and my panic begins to rise at the thought of being so exposed to The Program. "Technically," Dallas adds, pursing her lips as she looks around at the neighborhood, "we're on the outskirts. The city's much nicer. But we're more secluded here. It's dense enough to keep us hidden during the day. Cas did a great job."

Dallas parks behind the Escalade and cuts the engine. She turns in her seat, looking us over. "Will you promise to be good boys and girls if we cut the restraints?" she asks. "Because we've made it this far, and I'd like to trust that you won't cause trouble."

*Please don't say anything stupid, James.*

"All I do is cause trouble," James responds in monotone.

I turn to glare at him, but Dallas only laughs and climbs out. James looks sideways at me and shrugs, not all that apologetic for antagonizing the rebels who are basically holding us hostage.

The van door slides open with a loud metallic scrape and we're drowned in afternoon sunlight. We blink against it, and then Dallas takes my arm, pulling me from the van. I'm still adjusting to the brightness when Cas appears in front of me with a pocketknife. I suck in a frightened breath, but he quickly holds up his other hand.

"No, no," he says with a shake of his head, sounding offended that I'd think he would hurt me. "This is to cut the zip ties." He darts a look at James, who's moved to just inside the door, ready to pounce. "Here, seriously," Cas says, motioning him forward. "You're not prisoners, man."

James waits a beat, and then hops down onto the pavement. He turns his back to Cas, but keeps his gaze steady on me as Cas saws through the plastic binding. Dallas watches on, her high-arched dark eyebrows raised in amusement. It doesn't last long. The minute James is free, he spins and grabs Dallas's T-shirt in his fist, backing her against the van.

"If you mess with Sloane again," he growls, "I swear I'll—"

"You'll what?" Dallas asks coldly. "What will you do?" Dallas is nearly as tall as James, but she looks weak as her thin hand reaches to wrap around his wrist. She's calling his bluff. I watch as James's expression falters, and he lets her go. But before he steps away, Dallas's elbow shoots out, catching James in the chin with a sudden thud before her long leg hooks around his and she takes him to the ground. I yell his name, but James is still, lying there and staring at the sky. Dallas kneels next to him, smiling as she readjusts her crumpled shirt, the stretched-out material slipping off her shoulder.

"Such a temper," she says. "Too bad you didn't fight harder when they were dragging you into The Program." Her words shock me, hurt me, because it's such a cruel thing to say—as if it's our fault we were taken. James rubs his jaw, then pushes Dallas aside to climb up. He doesn't argue. How can we argue against something we can't remember?

"Now," Dallas says, making a loud clap, "we need to get inside." She walks toward the entrance of the loading dock. James mumbles that he's going to get our bag from the van.

The sun beats down on my cheeks. Without the shade of the trees, it's hotter than I'm used to. The lot next to this one is empty, and I think Dallas was right about the seclusion. It's quiet here.

Cas exhales and runs his hand through his long brown hair. On closer inspection, his nose doesn't look *that* broken. There's a small cut over the bridge, swelling in the nostrils, and of course the black bruising under his eyes. Lacey could have done worse.

"Dallas wasn't always like this," Cas says quietly. "She had a very different life before The Program."

"She was in The Program?" I ask, surprised. "She made it sound like she hated returners."

Cas shakes his head. "She hates what The Program does. Now she spends most of her time training."

"Training for what?" I ask, watching as James spits a mouthful of blood onto the pavement. Dallas hit him harder than I thought.

"Self-defense," Cas answers. "How to kill someone if she has to. Or wants to." He pauses. "Look, I know it doesn't seem like it, but we're on the same side."

"You sure?" I turn my shoulder so he can see the restraints still binding my hands. Cas apologizes, and gently holds my forearm so he can start cutting through the plastic.

"Who knows," Cas says from behind me. "Maybe in the end we'll all become friends." My wrists pull apart as the bond is cut, and I rub the spot where the restraints have left my skin raw.

"I wouldn't plan on that," James responds to Cas, and walks between us. He drops the duffel bag at our feet and then takes my hands to look over the red marks. He runs his thumb gently over the creased skin, then lifts my wrist to his lips to kiss it. "Better?" he asks, looking sorry even though this wasn't his fault.

I hug him, pressing my cheek against his neck. I'm not sure if our situation has gotten better or worse. "I'm freaking out," I murmur.

James turns his face into my hair, whispering so Cas won't hear. "Me too."

And somehow those words remind me of something, a

phantom memory I can't quite place. The pill in my pocket could change that—I'd remember everything. I pull back from James and see the look in his eyes, an uncertainty, as if he senses a familiar memory too. He opens his mouth to talk, but then Dallas calls to us from the front door.

"Unless you're advertising for handler intervention," she says, "you'd better get out of sight."

The mention of handlers is enough to make me move. James takes my hand, and we walk toward the empty-looking building, toward what's left of the rebels, and hope we're safe from The Program. Even if for only a moment.

# CHAPTER TWO

THE INSIDE OF THE BUILDING IS CLUTTERED WITH construction materials: large sealed buckets, piles of dusty bags, and flattened boxes of cardboard. I swallow hard, wondering how we'll live in an empty warehouse, when Dallas goes to the other side of the room and yanks open a door.

She gestures to the space around us. "This is just the front," she says. "We live downstairs. It's safer that way."

"Are there exits?" I ask, peering behind her to see a dark staircase.

She rolls her eyes. "Are you the safety inspector, Sloane? Of course there are exits, but I'd appreciate it if you didn't go out during the day. They've been running your story on CNN and I can't risk you being seen."

"Did they mention me?" James asks. His anger at Dallas

has tempered down, which I guess is positive, since it looks like we'll be stuck together for a while. My dislike for her hasn't eased up even a bit.

"You were mentioned," Dallas tells James. "But they haven't gotten ahold of your photo yet. Wait until they do; then we won't be able to hide you well enough."

James smiles at me and I slap his shoulder. "What?" he asks. "This is good. It means people must be questioning The Program. Why else would we be running from them?"

Cas chuckles and walks past us to make his way downstairs. Dallas stays, her hand on the doorknob, leveling her gaze on James. "Doesn't work like that," she says, and I hear the regret in her voice. "They're going to spin it. They always do. The Program controls the media, James. They control everything." Dallas seems unsettled about her comment, but she tries to cover it quickly, turning to hurry down the steps.

James watches after her like he's trying to figure her out, but if what Cas says is true and Dallas has been through The Program, she probably doesn't even know herself. So James is out of luck.

We descend the narrow staircase to the lower level, which I realize is barely below the street, to enter the first room. It has high windows, though they're covered with yellowed newspapers. The vents pump a steady flow of air as we pass, sending a chill over my arms. I'm not sure how they have electricity, but I guess the rebels aren't as ragtag as they look.

In the center of the room is a cracked leather couch and a

few folding chairs, but otherwise the space is lonely. Ominous. "Where is everyone?" I ask, worry starting to build. "I thought you said there were others. You said Lacey was here."

Dallas holds up her hands, telling me to calm down. "It's okay," she assures me. "They're all here." She heads back into the hallway, and it's long—impossibly long—until I realize it's the length of the entire building. Styrofoam peanuts have been swept into the corners. The fluorescent lights above flicker and hum.

"They're probably in the back," Dallas says. "This place isn't so bad, you know. It was the first safe house I came to after getting out of The Program."

"You went through The Program?" James asks. Knowing this about her seems to draw his sympathy, but Dallas turns on him fiercely.

"Don't feel sorry for me," she says. "I don't want your pity. The Program took everything from me—and not just from here." She taps her temple. Next to us Cas looks down, uncomfortable with whatever Dallas is referring to. "Let's just say," she starts again, "they owe me a whole hell of a lot." Vulnerability passes over her features and she wraps her arms around herself before turning to walk down the hall alone.

"What was that about?" I ask Cas, feeling like I might know more about Dallas's state of mind than I want to. It seems like a jump, but I think about the creepy handler Roger—how he bartered with the patients. And what they had to give him in return for a moment of their own memories.

"It's not my story to tell," Cas says seriously. "But I'm sure you'll hear about it eventually. Secrets are hard to keep in this camp."

"Sloane?" The voice is soft as it calls my name. I look up to see Lacey at the end of the hallway. She's standing there, her blond hair dyed a deep red, wearing a black tank top and a pair of camouflage pants. There's an explosion of relief and we both start forward, meeting somewhere in the middle with a hug. "I didn't think you'd make it," she says into my shoulder. "Your picture is everywhere." She pulls back, holding my upper arms as she examines my face. "Are you okay?"

I'm not sure how long I've known Lacey—can't remember my past—but since returning, she's been my constant friend. "I'm fine," I tell her. "Scared, but fine. James and I went to meet you at the border, but you weren't there." Dread slips in. "Dallas said Kevin was gone."

Lacey gives a quick nod, unable to hold my eyes. "He never made it to the rendezvous point," she says. "He was taken into custody, I guess. I . . . don't know where he is now." Her grip on my arms tightens, and I know there's more to her and Kevin's relationship than she ever let on. Whatever it is, she's not going to tell me right now. She pulls me forward into the room where Dallas and a few others are standing around.

In the middle of the dim space is an oval table with at least a dozen chairs. The wood is warped and some of the seats look like they might collapse, but Dallas grabs one, spinning it to sit on it backward. Her gaze is immediately drawn to the door when James walks in.

James scans the room, pausing when he notices Lacey. "I'm digging the red," he tells her, even though I think he really means to say he's glad she's safe.

Lacey smiles, her expression softening. "Why am I not surprised to see you here, James? Oh, that's right. Because you're a pain in the ass who constantly defies authority."

He reaches to pull out a chair for her. "Looks like we have a lot in common." After she sits, James pulls out another chair for me and then takes the next spot over. "So, Dallas," he calls, leaning his elbows on the table. "What's the plan here? What exactly do the rebels do?"

The three people around Dallas sit down, waiting for her to explain. They look normal—and not "returner" normal either; there are no collared polos or khaki skirts. Regular normal.

"Not all of us have been through The Program," Dallas starts. "Some, like Cas"—she points to him—"are here because someone they cared about disappeared, committed suicide. Or forgot them completely." The girl next to Dallas lowers her head. "The Program is everywhere, and it's becoming harder and harder to find people to fight with us. Especially adults. The rebels are trying to grow, to expand so we'll have the numbers to inflict real damage. But The Program is always one step ahead of us."

"What happened to the other rebels?" James asks. "The ones who were in your safe house?"

Dallas wilts slightly. "The place was raided," she begins, "and the ones who didn't get away were dragged back into

The Program. The official report said they were in recall—a side effect where memories crash back and drive a person insane—but that was a lie. The Program took them into custody to squash any rebellion. But they couldn't risk another incident." Her face grows pale. Suddenly she's not a rebel. She's just a girl. "The Program makes them disappear."

"What?" James asks, wide-eyed. "Are they killing them?"

"We don't know what they're doing to them. All we know is, certain patients disappear. They never contact us again; they never pop up on our radar. Basically, if The Program catches us . . . they'll end us."

"We have to save them," James says. "We can't let—"

"It's too late." Dallas waves her hand. "There's no way to break anyone out of The Program. We've tried."

"Maybe you're doing it wrong."

"Shut up, James," she says dismissively. "Like you know. We've tried, we've failed. It never ends well, so we've had to write them off. It's not like it was an easy decision."

"What are you going to do, then?" he demands. I can't believe Dallas would just give up. She seemed tougher than this.

Dallas takes a second to compose her thoughts, and it's like I can see her hardening herself against them. "They're the accepted loss," she says coldly. "For now, we're what's left. But I'm trying to find someone, something, to help us. When we gather everyone together again, we'll fight. I promise you we'll fight."

Dallas stands, pulling her long dreads into a high knot. She looks rattled by James's comments, and she can't hold his eyes. "I suggest you get some sleep," Dallas says in our direction. "We have plans later, so I'll need you back here at four." Before we can ask any more questions, she leaves the room, taking the conversation with her. It's quiet for a moment, and then James leans over to whisper to me.

"If I ever get sent away, Sloane, I expect you to save my ass. Is that clear?"

"And vice versa," I say. He gives a definitive nod and then turns to study the others in the room. Lacey is sitting quietly, her arms folded over her chest. This may be the most subdued I've ever seen her. It worries me. My stomach growls loudly, and James glances at me before calling to Cas.

"Hey, man," he says. "Do you have any food in this place? This one"—he hikes his thumb in my direction—"sounds like she's on a hunger strike."

Cas laughs. "Yeah. Let me show you around." I get up, but Lacey is still sitting there, rubbing her forehead like she has a headache.

"You okay?" I ask, reaching to touch her shoulder.

She lifts her gaze, and her eyes are out of focus, as if she's staring through me. "Stress. Rebels. Who knows?" She smiles weakly. "It'll pass."

Her response does little to placate my worry. "James," I say, turning to him. "I'll catch up with you in a second." He leans forward as if asking if everything is all right. When I nod that it is, he walks out into the hallway with Cas. I move closer to Lacey.

"We've been through a hell of a lot," I tell her. The other rebels eventually filter out, and in the quiet, the sadness starts to fill the air. "I'm sorry about Kevin."

Lacey closes her eyes. "Me too."

Kevin was the handler assigned to me right after The Program, and Lacey was my only friend. I had no idea they even knew each other until Realm's sister mentioned it. "How did you get involved with the rebels?" I ask Lacey. The room is empty, but I keep my voice hushed—paranoia engrained at this point in my recovery.

"It was Kevin," she says. "I met him at Sumpter High, weeks before you ever showed up. There was something about him that told me he wasn't like the other handlers. We met a few times at the Wellness Center. Talked outside. And then we went out for coffee—in another town, of course. He told me he could see I was a fighter. He asked me to be part of the rebels. Then you appeared, and you were like me—a natural trouble-maker, I think." We both smile at this, but I ache at the loss of Kevin. He was my friend.

"He called me before he disappeared," Lacey says, swiping under her eyes to catch the tears. "Kevin thought he was being followed and told me to go ahead without him to meet you and James. He said he'd see me at the rendezvous point. I waited so long. I waited until Cas and Dallas showed up, and I fought them when they tried to make me leave without Kevin. I even punched Cas in the face. I fought like hell, but they shoved me into another van and one of the guys swept me away to here—just a few hours ahead of you. I think Kevin's gone, Sloane," she says. "I think he's dead."

"He could be in The Program," I offer, although I'm not sure what sort of consolation that's supposed to be, especially now that Dallas has told us that rebels disappear. "When this is over, we can find him."

Lacey wipes roughly at her cheeks, clearing away the tears she couldn't catch. "No," she says. "He's over eighteen and he knows too much. They've killed him. I know they have."

"Don't think that way," I start. "There are so many other—"

"Sloane," she says, cutting me off, "I'm actually really tired. Can we talk about this another time? My head is killing me."

"I'll be here," I say. "It's not like I'm going anywhere." I try to make her smile, but Lacey only thanks me and hurries from the room. Alone, I glance around the barren space, processing the fact I'm actually here. I'm a rebel.

The kitchen is a revamped office with a small counter and sink, a white refrigerator, and an old cooktop. "What did this building used to be?" I ask, looking around.

"Don't know," Cas says. "This place has been here for a while, but Dallas couldn't remember exactly where it was. I tracked it down for her; it's in pretty good shape. A lot better than some of the other places I've lived in."

Cas pulls a couple of burritos out of the freezer and pops them into the microwave. I murmur my thanks and take a seat at the round table while James leans against the counter. Now that there's actual food, I realize how hungry I am.

"So," Cas says, motioning around, "I know it doesn't look like much, but at this location there are ten of us—twelve now. We had about thirty members in Philadelphia, but that includes the ones who were taken back to The Program. We're not sure how many we've lost yet." He lowers his eyes. "We're starting to have more safe houses than people."

The microwave beeps, and Cas puts the burritos on a paper plate and sets it on the table. James sits next to me and immediately grabs a burrito. He quickly mumbles around the food in his mouth that it's too hot to eat.

"I was never in The Program," Cas says conversationally. "But I lost my brother to the epidemic."

I look up, a sharp ache in my chest. "Me too."

"And my little sister went missing a while back," Cas adds. "Presumed dead. After Henley died, she kind of lost it. Became really paranoid, said our phones were tapped and that she was being followed. She disappeared, but it turns out she was right about The Program. I watched the handlers from the road as they showed up at the house looking for her."

"How old is your sister?" James asks.

"She'd be fourteen now."

A wave of nausea hits me with the thought of someone so young doing something as desperate as running away, possibly killing themselves. "I'm sorry," I say, pushing my burrito toward James.

Cas sniffs hard. "Thanks. I keep thinking one day she'll just show up. I'll give her a big hug, and then I'll ground her for the rest of her life." He laughs, but he doesn't look like he believes his words. He doesn't think his sister will ever come back.

Cas pushes off the counter and lets out a shaky breath. "I should go," he says. "I'm exhausted from the drive, and I need some sleep before our meeting."

"Thank you," I tell him quickly. "I really appreciate your help."

"We're going to help each other," he responds. "Otherwise none of us will make it. Now, the room at the end of the hallway is yours. But I'll warn you," he adds with a smile, "it's not much."

"Damn," James responds. "I was hoping for little chocolates on my pillow in the morning."

"Next stop. Promise."

After Cas leaves, James resets my food in front of me, motioning for me to eat. After we're both done, we grab a couple of bottles of water from the floor next to the fridge. Even though it's still daytime, it feels like it could be midnight—our days and nights are twisted around now that we're on the run.

When we get to the room, James pushes open the door and actually laughs. The small room has a twin bed and a shabby wooden dresser. There are no windows, only a naked bulb hanging from the ceiling as a source of light.

"Whoa," James says, glancing sideways at me. "I sure hope I'm up to date on all my shots."

I walk inside, relieved to see clean-looking sheets on the mattress. James closes the door and throws the lock before tossing the duffel bag on the dresser. He stands there, looking about the room and I go to sit on the edge of the bed.

"Could use a woman's touch," he says, glancing at me. "You up for it?"

I smile, knowing he's not exactly talking about my decorating skills. But I'm still bothered that Kevin is gone, that Lacey isn't feeling well. I'm still bothered by everything.

James's eyes slide over me, reading my expression. "Let's crash," he says softly. "We haven't had any real sleep in days, and I think we should be clear for what comes next."

"And what's that?" I ask.

James shakes his head. "I wish I knew." He exhales and climbs onto the bed. He slaps the flat pillow a few times and then curls up behind me. When he's quiet, I look down at him. His eyes weaken slightly. "Want to snuggle?" he asks.

We've been through so much the past few days, few months, few years, I'm guessing. It's too great to even put into words, so I nod and settle down next to him.

James moves until his mouth is at my ear. "We made it," he whispers, the curve of his bottom lip grazing my skin. His other hand slides up my thigh, and James pulls my leg over his hip. Wrapped around him, I feel safer—like I can hold on to both of us.

But as James kisses my neck, I think about the pill in my pocket. We haven't had time to discuss it, not fully. "James," I say, my voice hoarse. "We should talk about the orange pill."

He stops abruptly, his breath still hot against my neck. "Okay." He trails his lips over my skin for another moment and then moves to rest his head next to mine on the pillow. His eyes read serious, even though he's trying for calm. "What's up?"

It confirms my suspicions. "Would you want your past back, all of it—including the bad stuff—if it could make you sick again?"

"Sloane," he says, "It doesn't matter. We've—"

"If I wasn't here," I interrupt. "If I wasn't a consideration at all, would you take it?"

"Where the fuck are you going?"

"Just answer me."

James pauses and then nods. "Yes." He breathes out. "I guess I would."

"No hesitation?"

He scoffs, getting on his elbow to look down at me. "Sure I'd hesitate. This is dangerous stuff. But The Program took my life—*our* life together. It couldn't have been all bad. I want to know who I was, and I want to know what happened to land me in The Program."

I close my eyes, ready to cry. "Then you should take it," I whisper. James wants his life back, even if it means he could get sick again. He's willing to run the risk, so who am I to hold him back? I'm giving him the same choice Realm gave me, right or wrong.

SUZANNE YOUNG

"Sloane," James says, putting his hand on my cheek until I look at him. "I can't take the pill. Not without you. And if you weren't here, well . . . I don't think I'd give a shit about anything at all. So let's stop dreaming up stupid scenarios in which one of us evaporates and the other has to soldier on. If you want to take the pill, then let's talk about the risks. Otherwise, we're just going to hold on to it and see how this whole rebellion thing works out. Deal?"

James's skin is flushed, his eyes wide with vulnerability. He's lying; he wouldn't hesitate before taking the pill. He'd swallow it down dry, to hell with the consequences. But he's also stubborn—he would never take my choice from me. And for that, I love him madly. So I press my lips into a smile and draw him next to me once again, snuggling close until we both drift off.

# CHAPTER THREE

THOUGH THERE ARE NO WINDOWS, THE HARSH
overhead light from the bulb slowly draws me awake. James is
turned away, calm and quiet with sleep. I'm not sure what time
it is, but my body is restless. I get up and take the pill from my
back pocket, staring at it through the plastic Baggie.

If there were two, would we take them? How could we
when a possible side effect is death? Besides, aren't James and
I happy now? Would memories really be worth the risk of our
lives? If only I could talk to Realm, I think I'd understand more.
But Realm ran away; he left me.

I close my eyes and compose myself, shaking off the bad
vibes. I stride over to the dresser and stuff the pill in the top
drawer, tossing in a few pairs of underwear on top of it. Then I
grab a knit sweater and leave to wander alone down the hallway.

The place smells like cardboard and packing tape, but it's better than the medicinal smell of The Program. I pass the kitchen and see Dallas standing at the counter, pouring a cup of coffee. I stop, and then make a point of shuffling my feet so I don't startle her.

"Hello, Sloane," she says without looking up. "If you need to take a shower"—her dark eyes drift to mine—"and it looks like you do—there's a bathroom off the main room."

I nod a thank-you and take a seat at the table. Dallas sips slowly from her coffee before smiling, the gap between her front teeth charming, her lips a natural bright red. She takes out another cup and fills it, then sets it front of me. I'm surprised, and touched, that she'd make even this small offering. I know I'm not imagining the tension between us. She takes the chair across from me and scrolls through her phone, resting her elbows on the table.

"So how long have you and Prince Charming been together?" she asks without looking up.

"We just—" I pause. "I don't know, actually. I can't remember."

Dallas lifts her head, an apology crossing her lips. "I know how that is. When I first came back, I didn't feel right. My hair"—she picks up a dread—"was dark and thick—sort of like yours now. My clothes were stiff and scratchy. My mother died right after I was born, I still knew that, but my dad's an asshole. You'd think The Program would have changed *him* if they wanted my return to be successful." She stops to take another drink. "And when he punched me in the face after he came home drunk one night, my tooth wasn't the only thing to fall out. So did a few memories."

I nearly drop my cup. "Wait, your dad . . . You have memories?" I'm not sure which question to ask first, but Dallas holds up her hand for me to wait.

"My father went to jail," she says. "I got extra therapy. I didn't tell the doctors about the memories because it dawned on me where they were from. How I kept them." She waits a long moment, reading my expression. "I take it you've met Roger too."

"Roger was the handler who took me," I say, lowering my voice as shame—shame I know I don't deserve—sickens me. "And in The Program he was making trades. I gave him a kiss in order to keep a memory, one that led me back to James."

"A kiss?" Dallas laughs bitterly. "Roger is the epitome of everything evil in this world. Everything I despise. He was in my facility too. But he didn't ask for just a kiss." Red blotches dot Dallas's chest and neck as she starts to wring her hands in front of her. "Bare skin or nothing," she says, mimicking his voice so perfectly it chills me.

"Oh my God," I murmur. "Dallas, I'm so sorry—"

"By the time it was over," she continues, ignoring my condolences, "I had six memories. But that's not enough. I want more; I want all of them. Sometimes I'm not sure if I'm a real person—I don't like what's left." She smiles sadly. "And I'm so damn angry. I want them to pay."

SUZANNE YOUNG

"I'll help you take down The Program," I say seriously. "I won't go back there, and I'll destroy them to make sure of it." Dallas's story has resonated, awakening the desperation I left Oregon with. We're fighting for our lives here. The Program will never stop.

Dallas seems surprised by my response. "There just might be more to you than I realized, Sloane," she says. Weirdly, her approval validates me somehow. Then, after sharing her secrets, Dallas gets up and walks out, leaving her half-drank coffee on the table.

My stomach is still twisted from thoughts of Roger, and I dump Dallas's coffee down the sink and rinse out the cup before setting it in the strainer. When I was in The Program, Roger propositioned me. He asked me for a kiss in exchange for a pill that would save one memory. His touch, his taste—I don't think I'll ever forget it. I cried the entire time his hands were on me, his mouth on mine. Just thinking of it now, I feel a shiver of helplessness and I wrap my arms around myself. The things he would have done given the chance. But I had Realm. He kept me safe from Roger, breaking his arm and getting him fired. No one saved Dallas.

The bleakness of our situation—on the run with nowhere else to go—is not lost on me. But at least we're free. There are no handlers tying us down. There are no doctors interfering with our memories. In a way, we're lucky. As I look around at the small room, our dire straits, I try to remind myself of that. We're lucky to be alive.

* * *

"Why do I smell soap?" James murmurs from the bed when I enter the room. He turns and looks over at me, blinking heavily with the drowsiness of sleep. "And coffee?" he asks. "Dear God, Sloane. Do you have coffee?"

I grin. "Are you going to be sweet to me?"

"Are you kidding? I'll kiss you right now if you have coffee. And, baby, if you have a cheeseburger, I'll get down on one knee."

I laugh and hold out a cup to him. James climbs out of bed, yawning loudly. He reaches to take a strand of my still-damp hair. "It's curly," he says, raveling it around his finger. "And clean. How'd you manage that?"

"I showered," I say like it's a huge achievement.

"Fancy."

"Next time I might try to get my hands on some styling products." Without a blowdryer and straightener, my hair has been getting curlier by the day. Makes sense considering there are old photos hanging on my parents' living room wall of me with ringlets.

"Okay, cover girl." James sips and then makes a face before setting his cup on the dresser. "Horrible coffee."

"Yeah, and I couldn't find any creamer."

James stretches as he takes in the room. "So we're really here. Find out anything interesting while you were out getting pretty and ruining coffee?"

"I had a long talk with Dallas," I say, feeling like I'm betraying her for even mentioning it. James crosses the room and starts sorting through the bag of clothes.

"Any hair-pulling?"

"Not yet," I say. "I think I'm starting to understand her. I also think she may have a tiny crush on you." James shrugs apologetically, and I go to wrap my arms around him from behind, resting my chin on his shoulder. "No idea what she sees in you," I whisper.

"Me either." James spins me, and then I'm pinned against the concrete wall. "I thought you were the only one delusional enough to be with me."

"Oh, I am," I say, licking my lips. "So I wouldn't bother with those other girls. Out of your league."

"Mm . . . hmm." James kisses me, and my pulse climbs as his hand glides up my back toward my bra clasp.

There's a soft knock at the door, and I groan. "Don't answer it," James says, kissing my jaw, then over to a spot near my ear. I smile, letting him get in a few more kisses before I finally push him back.

"It's not like they don't know we're in here."

"We're busy," he calls out, and then tries to kiss me again.

"I need to talk to you guys," Lacey calls from the other side of the door.

James stops, concern crossing his features when he glances at the entrance. Then to cover it, he looks me up and down, false confidence filling in his worry. "We're not done with this, Barstow," he says, then heads for the door. I pick up his coffee and take a sip, scrunching my nose at the bitter taste. James lets Lacey in, and the minute I see her, my stomach drops.

"What's wrong?" I ask. She doesn't answer right away. She goes to sit on the bed, resting her elbows on her knees and her head in her hands. Her red hair is slicked back and wet, and as I watch her, I can see from here how she trembles. James must notice too, because he closes the door and then comes to stand next to me, crossing his arms over his chest.

Lacey looks up suddenly. "Something's wrong with me," she whispers. "Can you see it?"

Her question catches me off guard, and I immediately try to normalize it. "Is it a migraine?" I ask. "Maybe we can—"

"My mother would get migraines," she interrupts, her voice taking on a distant quality. "One time—during a really bad episode—she sat me down and told me she was going to ask my dad for a divorce. She cried until she choked on her own tears, and I kept telling her to stop before she made my father mad. Her headaches were always worse when he was angry."

James shifts, and drops his arms. "That's horrible. Why didn't The Program take that memory?"

He's right. The Program should have erased that tragic thought. Could they make mistakes like that?

Lacey continues like she didn't hear him. "My dad came home with roses," she says. "He took one look at my mother's puffy face, and promptly grabbed her arm and walked out of the room. My mother never mentioned divorce again. She never smiled again either. But she had a migraine almost every day."

A small trickle of blood begins to leak from Lacey's nose, trailing red down over her lips before dripping onto her lap. I call her name and she reaches to touch the blood with her fingers. Her eyes begin to stream tears when she sees the crimson streaked across her hand. "Fuck," she says, blood sputtering from between her lips.

James moves quickly, sitting next to her on the bed. "Here," he says. "Press here." He puts his fingers on the bridge of her nose and then guides her shaky hand to the right spot. When she's pinching, he has her rest back against the headboard. Lacey meets his eyes with a helpless look, but James only smiles at her, smoothing her hair. "It's just a nosebleed," he says. "You're going to be just fine."

"You're such a liar," she whispers.

His expression doesn't falter, doesn't even show one crack. "Shut up. You're fine. Say it."

"Shut up?"

"You're fine, Lacey."

She closes her eyes, resigned to trusting James. "I'm fine," she repeats.

And when James relaxes next to her, putting his arm over her shoulders so she can rest her head against him, I realize he's the biggest liar I've ever known. But he does it with the best of intentions.

When Lacey's nosebleed stops, she goes to wash up, not mentioning the memory that surfaced even though it shouldn't have. She didn't know Roger. This is an actual memory; it's recall. In The Program they told us too much stimulus could lead to a brain-function meltdown. Dallas mentioned it as a side effect too. I don't want to believe anything of the sort, but at the same time, I'm terrified it might be true—our memories might kill us.

"Hey," Cas says from the doorway, pulling me from my daze. His long hair is tucked behind his ears, and he's wearing different clothes from earlier. "It's four. We're meeting up in the living room. You coming?"

"Oh . . ." I look to where James still sits on the bed, and he gives me a quick nod. "Yeah," I say. "We'll be right there."

Cas glances from James to me, and his sharp jaw hardens. "Something wrong?" he asks. His voice drops a tone, and the hint of seriousness in it sounds more authentic than the let's-all-be-best-friends guy I met this morning.

"No," I answer quickly. "Still a little tired, I guess."

There's a slight pause as Cas studies our appearances, but then he smiles broadly and I can't help thinking it's false. "Well, you'd better hurry," he says, casting a glance around the room. "One of the guys brought back pizza, and that kind of luxury never lasts around here."

James crosses his arms over his chest. "Like she said," he begins, "we'll be out in a few minutes."

Cas's smile fades. "I'll see you in a bit, then." He starts for the door, but I see the way he takes in every aspect of our room, every object placement, as if trying to determine what's off about us. I don't like how observant he is. I don't like that he doesn't trust us, even though we certainly don't trust him.

What's changed is Lacey. Something's wrong with her, but we can't tell the rebels until we figure out what it is. They might want to kick her out if they think she's become infected again, or if she's a liability. We have to protect Lacey, because in this world, you can't know who to trust. All we have is each other.

When James and I finally get up the nerve, we go to find the others. Everyone is gathered in the main room, even a few I hadn't seen before. But it's how they're dressed that really alarms me. The rebels are no longer in T-shirts or tank tops. They're wearing black—a color rarely worn in public anymore—and their makeup is dark and dramatic, even the guys. The entire scene is so stereotypically emo that I'm utterly confused.

"What's going on?" I ask.

Dallas smiles broadly from the other end of the table. Her dreads are pulled back behind a black headband, and she's wearing a leather corset with red ribbons laced through the shoulders. "It's a special night," she says, lifting her plastic cup in cheers. "The Suicide Club just reopened."

# CHAPTER FOUR

"THE SUICIDE CLUB?" I ASK, GLANCING AROUND
the room. The others look downright gleeful, smiling and
laughing, but I have a horrible feeling I've crossed into some
hideous version of reality. "I don't understand."

Dallas grins, taking a long sip from her cup before answering. "We're not going to kill ourselves, silly."

*Silly?* I wonder what's in her plastic cup.

"It means we're going out. You should be happy to leave
this dreary place for a while." She glances to the side. "Are you
happy, James?"

There's a pinch of jealousy. She's not just asking if he's happy
about going out, she's asking if he's happy with me. James looks
her over, trying to gauge the situation.

"Yes," he answers dismissively. "Now, what exactly is the Suicide Club?"

Dallas's smile falters slightly under the authority in James's tone. She turns to me instead, her posture taking on an irritated quality as she sets her drink down. "You remember the Wellness Center?" she asks. "This is the opposite. It's like a place for those of us who don't want to wear polo shirts and khakis. For those who want to celebrate choice—the choice to kill ourselves if we damn well please." She shrugs. "We don't want to die, but it's fun to explore our dark sides when the rest of the world is intent on burying it."

"That's the stupidest thing I've ever heard," James says. "And it sounds dangerous."

Dallas shakes her head. "Not even. It's actually the safest you'll be from The Program's influence. You can be yourself, James. When's the last time you were that?"

"Fuck off," he mutters, examining a hangnail on his thumb. I can see her words hurt him and it infuriates me. James is always himself. He may not remember his life, but he wasn't *changed*. He's still him. That's what I believe, anyway.

"I think we'll pass," I say, reaching to slip my hand in the crook of James's elbow. "Thanks, though."

"You'll go," Dallas says, then softens her voice. "You should go. It's a great place to recruit new members. That's where I met Cas." She looks over at him. "You were so handsome," she teases. "Those big brown eyes and long hair, I think I would have brought you home even if you were depressed."

"Let's not share all our secrets now . . . ," Cas replies, fighting back an embarrassed smile. I can't tell if they've had a thing or not, and frankly, I don't care.

"So we're on the run from The Program, but we're going to a club?" James asks, pointing out the obvious flaw in this plan. "Why not just call the handlers ourselves and ask them to meet us there?"

"You're so funny," Dallas says with a mock laugh. "Sure, the Suicide Club has risks, but the proprietors are careful. It's never in the same place twice—completely underground. Only those of us in the know hear about it, and even then only the day of. It's not like they advertise." Dallas leans her elbows on the table. "Not everyone wants to be well-behaved all the time, so they go to the Suicide Club to let loose for a while. And when it comes to rebels, this is the best place to find them. We get to see what they're really like. We just have to pick through the really disturbed to find the fighters. Isn't that how Realm found you, Sloane? Because of your bad attitude?"

At the mention of Realm, both James and I turn to her defensively. I don't take Dallas's bait. Whether her words are meant to hurt me or to come between me and James, I won't give her any more opportunities than she already tries to take. She does hurt me though, and I try to squash the memory of Michael Realm and how desperately I miss him, worry about him. Dallas watches with a sort of satisfaction—the girl who told me her secrets is hidden behind makeup and whatever booze is in her cup. She takes our silence as agreement.

"We leave in an hour," she says. "I'll get something appropriate for you to wear and I'll send it to your room, Sloane. They won't let us in with you looking so bland. James"—she smiles—"you're fine the way you are."

James and I stand there like a couple of idiots, staring at her, and Dallas goes back to laughing and drinking with the other rebels as if we don't exist at all.

James looks me over skeptically. "I'm supposed to be okay with you going out like this?" he asks, rubbing his chin as he circles me. "I think I can see your womb."

"You can not." I laugh and turn to follow his slow assessment.

He looks at me doubtfully. "It's short."

"Not that short. The boots are kind of hot, though." I lift my foot, modeling the spiked black leather boots Dallas sent over. They're a little big, but I'm hoping that will stop them from hurting me too much.

Neither me nor James had been interested in going out, but now that I'm dressed in this short black skirt, ripped T-shirt, and enough makeup to make me unrecognizable to my family, I feel sort of . . . good. Like I can be someone else for tonight.

"With you dressed like this, I'm probably going to end up in a fight," he says.

"I know." I smile. "Dallas and the others are waiting in the main room, so we should probably hurry before she gets even more pissed off."

"Is that possible?" he asks, walking to the dresser. He pulls a T-shirt from the duffel bag and then turns to me. His cheeks are scruffy from not shaving; light shadows are painted under his eyes. "Sloane," he asks softly, "are you sure this is a good idea?"

Anxiety knots in my stomach. "I'm pretty sure this is a terrible idea," I say. "But I don't know what else to do. We could refuse, or even take off with Lacey—but the truth is we have nowhere to go. We can't leave without getting some answers or we'll end up defenseless, getting dragged back into The Program."

James pauses, absorbing my words, but he must not have a better plan because he just yanks off his shirt before pulling the clean one over his head. I wait at the door, but then I notice I'm still wearing my ring, the plastic ring James gave me at the river. It looks childish next to the very grown-up clothes I'm wearing, so I slip it off and set it on the dresser. James lifts one eyebrow, questioning my motives.

"It's too sweet," I say with a smile. James scans my clothes once again, and with a heavy sigh, he agrees. I'm someone else tonight.

In the front room I find everyone gathered, the scene so out of place I'm starting to think it's just a hallucination. Dallas stands there, a gothic vision in black and red. Cas is next to her, his long hair wild along his face, black liner around his eyes. Everyone looks like they just walked off some trashy version of *The Addams Family*, and that includes me.

"I'm underdressed," James says.

"No," Dallas says with a smile. "You're perfect. I was hoping you'd drive us tonight. We need someone normal-looking behind the wheel. Not that you could ever be average."

I roll my eyes and turn away. It seems petty to tell her not to notice my boyfriend, and I'd like to believe I'm above that. But if she does it again, I might just scratch her eyes out.

"Where is this place?" James asks.

"The club's on Kelsey, about twenty minutes away. I'll navigate."

James nods, but then something catches his eye. I follow his gaze to where Lacey is standing in the doorway. She's not dressed for the Suicide Club. Instead she's wearing baggy sweats and an oversize sweatshirt that reads OREGON DUCKS.

"I'm not feeling well," she says, her makeup-free skin startling in a room of painted faces. "I'll go next time."

Cas immediately crosses to Lacey and touches her arm. He leans in to whisper in her ear, and after a moment Lacey pulls back to stare at him before she nods slowly. I want to know what Cas said, what he knows about Lacey that I don't. She's my friend—he's just the guy whose nose she broke. Cas puts his arm across her shoulders and begins to lead her out, but I'm quick to jog after them into the hallway.

"Lacey," I call to her. She glances back at me, her eyes weary.

"Please don't worry about me, Sloane," she says. "It's not

good for you or James. I just need a little sleep, that's all. Go have fun—we'll talk tomorrow."

"I'm going to stay with her," Cas says. "I've been to the Suicide Club enough times. Dallas can do without me for one night." He turns to smile gently at Lacey, but she doesn't return it. Instead her eyes drift toward her room like she wants nothing more than sleep. Solitude.

"I don't think I should leave you." I start toward her, but Lacey's posture straightens with agitation.

"Sloane," she says, "I love you, but please, it's nothing personal. I promise. I'm just tired, and I haven't been alone since leaving Oregon. I want some space." She turns to Cas, shrugging his arm off her shoulders. "And that includes you, Casanova. I don't need you hovering over me or trying to get into my pants."

Cas laughs loudly and then bites back his smile. I'm not sure if he really was going to hit on her or if Lacey just knew how to embarrass him so he'd back off. He holds up his hands in a show of surrender, and Lacey thanks him. She starts toward her room, disappearing around the corner before I hear the click of her door shutting.

I'm still for a moment, unsure of what to do. Other than the nosebleed and wanting to be alone, Lacey doesn't seem to be falling apart. There are no signs of real depression—dark eyes, spirals, erratic behavior. After all, she's been cured. She lost Kevin—*Kevin*—and maybe she needs a little more time to come to terms with that. We all do.

Cas walks back into the main room, and I decide to let Lacey have a night of peace, vowing to harass her tomorrow. She'll have to talk eventually. We'll get through this together. I reenter the room and scan the area for James. I find him sitting on the table with Dallas standing close by, talking animatedly. James says something I can't hear, and she laughs, leaning in to casually touch his knee. The tingling burn of jealousy spreads through my chest.

Dallas glances up, sensing my presence, and then lets her hand fall from James. She faces the room. "Well," she announces with a loud clap. "Now that we're all back, it's time for a little fun." She motions to the stairwell and quickly, the room starts to empty. James turns and finds me, taking in my outfit like he's just remembered how scandalously I'm dressed. He bites his lip as he approaches, and my earlier jealousy fades when he takes my hand.

Cas appears next to us and Dallas starts in our direction. "I think I'm going to stay behind," Cas says, exchanging a look with Dallas. "Keep an eye on things here."

"If this is about Lacey, I don't think she wants you to bother her," I say quickly.

"What's wrong with Lacey?" James demands.

I shrug. "She wants some space." James tries to discern any hidden meaning in my words, but there is none. "I think she's just tired," I say seriously.

"Is that your diagnosis, doctor?" Dallas asks. I clench my teeth and turn to her. "Even if you're right," she adds, "we don't leave people at our safe houses alone—depressed or not. They can inadvertently set us up, or maybe even on purpose. The suicidal aren't at all predictable."

"She's not suicidal," I snap.

"Sure," Dallas says. "Either way, Cas is staying behind. And we have a club to get to, so if you two wouldn't mind moving your asses . . ."

I look up at James, but he's lost, turning over the situation in his head, analyzing our options. After a second his light-blue gaze falls on me. "What do you want to do?" he asks.

"I need you, James," Dallas cuts in, more sober than I had guessed. "Lacey will be here in the morning and the three of you can play psychologist. But right now the rebels need you. We're not exactly deep in muscle around here." She glances at Cas. "No offense."

"None taken." He buries his hands in his pockets, but he doesn't seem disappointed to miss out on the Suicide Club. In fact, I think he's itching to get out of his black clothes and wash off the eyeliner.

Dallas grows impatient with James's silence, and her hardened layers begin to unravel. "Please come with us tonight," she says. "I need backup, whether for incoming rebels or handlers. I can't do this alone. And Cas gets his nose broken too often. There's something about you, about both of you," she allows, "that's inspiring people. We're dying off here. We need more members and I don't know when the next Suicide Club will happen."

Her plea must hit James in the right way because, without consulting me first, he nods. James isn't a fighter, not really. But he has a good heart, and even pretending to be a dick half the time can't mask that. I love that about him. And now, with a mix of anxiety and outright fear, I let him pull me away to leave for the Suicide Club.

The building is unmarked. Its gray stone front is menacing with iron bars over the windows, dead bougainvillea crawling up the side. The defaced sign above the door used to belong to a tattoo shop, and a sketchy one at that. Dallas directs James to the back, and we park near the other cars at the entrance. It's so strange to be out, a group of teenagers without any sort of supervision from a handler. The taste of freedom is overwhelming, like I'm spinning out of control, drunk on life.

There's a bouncer at the entrance of the Suicide Club, a scary-looking guy with a studded bracelet and an affection for overly tight tank tops. He studies each of us, flashing a penlight in our eyes. They say when the sickness—the depression—takes hold, our eyes actually change. And that if you know what to look for, you can see the deadness there. It's been only a short time since I met Liam outside of the Wellness Center. He'd gotten sick, spewing horrible words at me. I saw him in the thrall of the epidemic, the way his eyes weren't quite right.

I guess that's what the bouncer is checking us for now, making sure we don't spread our thoughts of suicide to the others. When James is cleared ahead of me, I actually let out a relieved breath. And when I'm in after him, I finally stop shaking.

# CHAPTER FIVE

THE INSIDE OF THE SUICIDE CLUB IS HAZY WITH cigarette smoke. There are large rooms with stucco walls painted a deep purple, and black lights mingling with the neon, creating a shadowy kind of depth. The people float by, their chatter muted by the music—the beats are transfixing, heavy, and soul-scratching. I'm swayed by it, by something I forgot was there—something dark. A part of me that used to be sad and maybe still is.

James's hand touches the small of my back as he motions to an empty bartop table. I sit down, and he stands next to me, surveying the room. "This isn't really my idea of fun," he says. He doesn't seem to feel it the way I do—the sadness. He's not drawn to it, and I think again about our missing past, and what this moment says about it. Maybe James was never sad. Maybe

I always was. For a fleeting moment, it's like I'm slipping away, and I reach for his shirtsleeve to tug him closer, bringing me back to reality.

I must hide my insecurity well, because James kisses the top of my head, brushing his fingers along the black netting on my knee before whispering he'll be right back. I don't want him to leave, but I say nothing as he walks away. This place makes me feel vulnerable, exposed. Across from me a couple is in a booth, pressed against each other as they kiss, seemingly oblivious to the people around them. I avert my eyes, but then I notice the lost looks in the crowd. I've read The Program pamphlets, the ones my mother used to leave by the phone. The Program says those who are infected exhibit all sorts of uncharacteristic behaviors, including promiscuity, anger, and depression. Maybe it never occurred to the good doctors that sometimes a couple might just be hot for each other or angry or sad. It's not always sickness.

Just as I think this, I notice a guy leaning against the stucco wall, a ring through his lip and another through his eyebrow. His black hair is half in his eyes as he searches the room. I'm not sure if it's his posture, or just the setting, but his desperation is palpable.

I'm reminded of where I am, the music suddenly too loud, the air too smoky. I lean my elbows on the table and put my face in my palms. I'm barely able to shake off my newly heightened anxiety before I feel someone next to me.

"You're kind of a downer, Sloane," Dallas says. She's holding a clear plastic cup filled with bright-red liquid. The club probably doesn't trust its patrons with glass. Dallas takes a slow sip of her drink, running her gaze over me and pausing at the red scar slashed into my wrist. Her pupils are pinholes and I wonder what she's on—if it's just alcohol or drugs. "How many times have you tried to kill yourself?" she asks.

A hurt sound escapes my throat as her question brings up pain I can't associate with any specific memory. But suddenly I hate her. I can see exactly what she's doing, how she's trying to provoke me.

"You know damn well I can't remember," I tell her. "But I can assure you I'm not going to kill myself now—if that's what you're hoping for."

Dallas chuckles, sipping again from her drink. "Why would you think I'd want that?"

I glance over to where James is waiting at the bar, handing cash to the tattooed bartender before swirling the red liquid in one of the cups with a doubtful look. Dallas makes a *tsk* sound.

"Oh, please, Sloane," she says, leaning closer to me as we both watch my boyfriend. "If I wanted James—really wanted him—I wouldn't need you dead to take him."

I'm about to slap the drink out of her hand and tell her to sober up before I punch her lights out, when James is there, setting a cup in front of me. He doesn't even acknowledge Dallas.

"No idea what this is," he says to me. "But it's the only drink they serve."

"It's called Bloodshot," Dallas says. "It makes you *feel*

things." She grins when James glances over his shoulder at her, her lips tinged with the red liquid. She reaches to run the backs of her fingers over James's bicep, and rather than flinch away, he stares at her like she's lost her mind. "I'll see you later," she murmurs intimately to him before strolling away, earning a few eager looks from the other guys in the club—including the pierced one who's still against the wall. When Dallas is gone, James sits.

"What the hell is wrong with her?" he asks, picking up the cup and smelling it before taking a tentative sip.

"She's psychotic," I say, and take a long drink to block out the doubt and worry. The taste is unbearably sweet at first, and I make a face after I swallow it. I don't believe Dallas. She couldn't have James—not even if I was dead. James blows out a hard breath, examining the drink.

"This is strong," he says, pushing it aside.

I nod, taking another sip. Heat crawls down my throat, spreads through my chest—but I like it. I like how quickly it makes my body relax, my thoughts blur. I finish my drink, observing the room until James leans closer to talk next to my ear, his arm casually over my lap.

"I think that dude is on something a little heavier," he says, motioning to the guy I'd been watching. But I've lost interest in the suicidal kid.

My mind swirls with comfort, and as James's fingers draw patterns into my skin, desire. He's midsentence when I turn and kiss him, catching him off guard for only a moment before his hand is my hair and his tongue is in my mouth. The world fades away and it's just us, murmuring I love yous in between kisses. I'm feeling so much and thinking so little. Soon I'm out of my chair and dancing in the middle of the crowd, James pressed against me as the music builds walls around us.

Red drinks. Sad eyes. I kiss James, threading my fingers through his hair, wishing we were anywhere else. And then we are. James is leading me through a dark maze before he backs me up against a cool wall. I'm out of breath as he pulls my thigh up around his hip. He kisses my neck, my collarbone. "James." I breathe deeply, ready to be lost completely, when a bright light floods my vision.

"Hey!" a deep voice calls. James stays against me but turns toward the light, lifting his hand to block the glare. "You two can't be in here," the man says.

It takes too long for my focus to clear, to find we're in some back room next to crates and boxes. My palm touches the exposed block wall behind me as light from the club filters in the open door. I'm not drunk. This is something different, something better.

"I think they put something in my drink," I murmur as James steps back. I try to straighten my clothes, but James has to catch me by the arm when I nearly trip on my high-heeled boots. James, still flushed, takes a second to realize what I've said.

"You sure?" he asks. Confused, he glances around at where we are, at me, and then curses under his breath. "Yeah, they did," he agrees. I let him walk me to where the bouncer is holding the door open. When we pass him, he shakes his head, looking more annoyed than angry.

"Keep it in the club or take it home," the bouncer calls after us. James chuckles and tells him he'll try his best.

When we escape into the smoky room, James pauses to look around. Low voices and loud beats surround us, and they sway me once again. I'm in a hyper-reality where nothing is wrong, nothing hurts. I like this.

"Do you feel okay?" James asks, his eyebrows pulling together in concern. I want to touch him, and I reach to put my hand on his cheek. I think about how much I love him, and before I can tell him, I get on my tiptoes and kiss him again.

"I want you," I murmur against his lips. I'm suddenly convinced I need him, need that closeness in a way I never have before. The intensity of our touch, his mouth against mine—

"Sloane," James says, taking my hands from his body. He leans down so his eyes are level with mine, smiling. "Although I'd like nothing more than to tear off those ridiculous clothes, I'd prefer to do it in private." He nods his chin to the scene around us, and I'm reminded we're still in public. I touch my forehead, trying to make sense of my feelings. I blink quickly and look back at James.

"Ecstasy?" I ask.

"I'm guessing. But I'm not sure why they'd put it in the drinks. Either way, we should get out of here. Let's find Dallas."

I curl my lip at the mention of her name, but we begin searching the club for her anyway. Faces are a blur, and the harder I try to concentrate on them, the more difficult it becomes. Features upon features, voices all around—inside my head. I'm slowing us down, so James plants me against the wall.

"Wait here," he says. "I'll be right back." I watch him disappear into the crowd, and then I lean the back of my head on the wall and close my eyes. The sweetness of the red drink has faded into a metallic, chemical taste.

"Gross," I say, wishing for a bottle of water.

"It's phenylethylamine," someone next to me says. "Among other things." I'm not entirely surprised to see the pierced boy from earlier. He turns to face me, and his eyes are even darker up close, but not nearly as dead. It's like he's wearing contacts. "The drugs are meant to give euphoria, mask the depression," he says. "But really they just fuck us up."

"I've noticed," I say, fascinated by his face. I want to touch one of the rings, but then I clench my hand into a fist to bury the thought. "Is it legal for them to drug us?" I ask him.

"It isn't legal for us to even be here, so it's not like we can turn them in."

"Good point." Although I know I'm not myself, I still like this feeling—this careless freedom. The sadness I came in with is gone. Now it's like I'll never be sad again. I feel invincible. I wonder if it's done the same thing to this guy. "What's your name?" I ask him.

"Just call me Adam."

"You make it sound like that's not your real name."

He bites his lip to hide his smile. "It's not. You know, you're pretty clever for someone who drank an entire Bloodshot."

"Or maybe you just hang around a lot of stupid people."

He laughs, moving closer to me as he does. When he sighs, it occurs to me his lips aren't red—don't have that slight red tint Dallas's (and probably mine) have from the drink. Did he have a Bloodshot?

"We should get out of here," Adam says, gesturing toward the door. "I have a car, a pretty nice place. Where are you staying?"

He doesn't say it creepily, even if he is asking me to leave with him. And maybe I would have waved it off, mentioned how James would probably kick his ass, but I'm bothered by the fact he's not giving me his real name. I am about to ask him when my boyfriend suddenly appears, walking from the crowd with Dallas trailing behind—holding hands with a guy with purple hair and way-too-skinny jeans.

James casts a suspicious glance from me and Adam. "And this conversation's over," he mutters, and pulls me away from the wall. I hadn't noticed how much it was holding me up. "You really shouldn't talk to strangers," James adds quietly, shooting another look in Adam's direction.

Dallas finally catches up and steps in front of us, letting go of her companion. "I'm not leaving yet," she states. I'm about to protest, but she grins widely and holds up the keys, dangling them from her finger. "But you two go on," she says, looking positively wasted. "I'll get another ride back." She nods to the guy next to her.

That seems completely reckless, but at this point, I'm not going to argue. This place is overwhelming, vexing . . . alluring. James takes the keys from her hand and then starts toward the door. As we leave, I hear Adam's voice.

"Have a good night, Sloane," he calls after me. I turn and wave because he wasn't a total jerk or anything.

"Yeah, you too."

I follow James out, occasionally taking his arm as we pass through the bottlenecked crowd waiting to get in. It isn't until we're in the cool night air that I stop to look back at the building, a chill running over my skin. Because I realize . . . I never told Adam my name.

# CHAPTER SIX

**THE WAREHOUSE IS QUIET WHEN WE ENTER. EVERY** movement I make sounds too loud—every step. Every breath. Lacey's door is shut, and the lights buzz as we make our way down the hall. We're barely inside the bedroom door when James's hand grazes my hip, moving me aside, but I grab him by the shirt and pull him to me.

As if we're starving for each other, his mouth is on mine and he backs me against the door, closing it. We've slept together only once—that I can remember—and I'm feverish for him now. My hands slip under his shirt before yanking it over his head, and I hear my T-shirt rip more as he pulls away the fabric in his fist. When it doesn't come off entirely, he growls, and then we're moving toward the bed. I push him down and then climb on top of him, forgetting everything outside of us. Our layers of clothes begin to evaporate, and his skin is hot against mine. I whisper his name, and then he rolls me over, his weight heavy but perfect. He's reaching for his pants that lie in a heap next to the bed, when I feel something under my back. I shift, thinking it's a tag from the sheets, but when I reach to pull it from behind me; I see it's a folded piece of paper.

James takes a condom from his wallet and then notices I'm holding something. He pauses. "What's that?" he asks, his voice hoarse.

"I don't know," I say. Panic begins to bubble up as James moves off me to get a better look at the paper. I start to unfold it, seeing through the sheet that there's something written in ink—it's a note. In Lacey's perfect print, there is a single word that means nothing to me, and yet I hitch in a ragged breath.

## Miller

"Sloane?" James's voice is a million miles away as I drop the paper, my chest heavy with a grief I can't understand. James grabs the note from my lap and reads it. He tosses it aside before taking my shoulders. "Who's this from?" he asks.

My panicked eyes find his as I begin to shake all over. "Lacey." In my head I can think only *Miller. My Miller.* But I don't know what it means.

"Goddamn it," James says, jumping to grab his pants from the floor and pulling them on. He tosses his shirt in my direction and then he's out the door, running barefoot down the hallway. I slip on his shirt and chase after him.

*Why would Lacey write that note? Why would she put it on my bed? Oh, God.* I start running faster. *Where's Lacey?*

I catch up with James just as he stops in front of Lacey's door, not knocking before bursting through. The room is dark, and as I look in, he's in the middle, swiping his hand through the air looking for the chain for the light.

"What's happening?"

I turn and see Cas stalking toward us, pulling out his switchblade. His face is swollen with sleep, his clothes wrinkled, but he's as alert as if he'd been waiting for handlers all night. Just then light floods the room, and my heart leaps with hope. The room is stark and the bed is empty. Lacey is gone.

Cas pushes past me into the room, pulling back the covers as if Lacey is somehow hiding. He spins to face James. "Where is she?" he demands accusingly.

James looks devastated, shocked. "I don't know."

Cas yanks open the dresser drawers, cursing when he finds them empty. I'm still in the doorway and any trace of the drink at the Suicide Club is gone, replaced instead with disbelief and panic. Cas pulls his phone out of his pocket and begins to pace as he dials. James still stands under the swinging, naked bulb, his head lowered, his chest heaving.

"James?" I say weakly. He looks over, and I'm struck with an image so familiar, I'm not sure how to process it. James's eyes are red, his skin blotchy, like he's about to cry. I think Lacey is gone, and then mingling with that is the thought that "Miller" is gone too. James's expression fits the thought somehow, like he's replaying a memory from my head.

James coughs out the start of a cry but then crosses the room and gathers me into a hug. His lips press a hard kiss against my forehead, his muscles rigid as I grip his arm.

"Dallas," Cas says into the phone. "You need to come back." James and I both look at Cas as he continues to pace. "I don't give a shit," he snaps into the receiver. "Lacey's gone. We're compromised." James and I exchange a glance, fear spiking within me. "I'm on my way," Cas tells Dallas, and then hangs up.

"What's going on?" James asks.

"Get your things," Cas says, storming past us. "We're leaving." He pauses in the doorway and turns to look back at me. "I'm sorry about your friend," he says. "I really am. But a returner is always a threat, and Lacey is gone. It'll be only a matter of time before The Program comes for the rest of us."

"Do you think they have Lacey?" I ask, frantic.

"Yes," Cas says in a quiet voice. "I think Lacey is with The Program. Now get your things and meet me at the van."

Cas leaves, and I turn to James, waiting for him to tell me Cas is wrong. But James just stares after him. "I tried," he whispers, mostly to himself. Then he lowers his eyes to meet mine. "I tried to help Lacey, but it wasn't enough."

"We have to get her back," I say, nodding to get James to understand. "We have to find her and get her back."

James can only mumble his agreement, but he's not here with me. His eyes look unfocused and he starts out of the room. I follow, the floor cold on my feet, while I search my mind for other places Lacey could be. Maybe she decided to go to the Suicide Club after all. Maybe . . . anything. This can't be the end.

Guilt attacks my conscience when I think about how Lacey acted just before we left for the Suicide Club. I should have done more, but I thought I'd see her tomorrow. I thought there was more time. I was so stupid. She recalled a memory she wasn't supposed to—and I just left her.

James is already in the room when I walk in, stuffing clothes into the duffel bag. I grab a pair of jeans and pull them on before crossing to the dresser. I take out the pill, and at that moment James looks over. "If we find Lacey," I say, my body trembling, "we could give her the pill. Maybe it could help. Maybe it could cure her."

James lowers his eyes. "It was her memories that hurt her, Sloane. I'm not sure giving her more of them is a good idea."

I look down at the pill, ready to debate the point, but Cas is yelling from the other room for us to hurry. I shove the pill into my pocket and finish packing up our stuff. Before I worry about what to do with the pill, we have to find Lacey.

Once packed, we head toward the door. James staggers to a stop and picks up the note from the floor to examine it one last time. "What does this mean?" he asks. "Who's Miller?"

"I don't know," I say, moving beside him to read the word again. "But it hurts."

"I know," James says, crushing the paper in his fist. "It's like grief, a pain right here"—he taps his heart—"for someone I don't know."

But I can tell what he's thinking—we must have known Miller.

It's twenty minutes later when James is driving the Escalade we'd left Oregon with, Cas following in the white van. We're picking up Dallas and the others at the Suicide Club, but as we drive, I watch the streets, hoping to catch sight of Lacey wandering or lost. I don't want to believe she's gone.

Lacey—snow-blond hair she dyes red just because. Lacey who ate cupcakes for lunch and questioned *everything*. I could have done more to help her. I could have stayed behind tonight. But she ran away, took her stuff—where would she go? What did she remember that was so awful? I touch my chest as the hurt starts again, the name Miller haunting my thoughts.

As we pull up to the Suicide Club, the bouncer straightens, looking alarmed. He immediately takes out his phone and presses it to his ear. Cas parks and jogs over to him as James and I wait in the SUV. We're silent. Anxiety and worry twist in my gut, and I don't know what to do. I almost want another Bloodshot from the club.

"I'm sick of losing," James says in a low voice. "And I'm sick of running." He turns to me, and the fire is back in his eyes, the sadness replaced with anger. "We're going to take down The Program, Sloane. And we'll get Lacey back."

"Promise?" I ask, wanting to believe his words even though I know James doesn't have the power to make them come true. But I'll believe them if he tells me. I have no other choice.

"Yeah," he says, looking past me toward the club. "I promise."

I blink back the tears that are starting and then follow his gaze to the Suicide Club. Dallas and Cas rush out, with the others, including the guy with the purple hair, close behind them. The bouncer nods as they leave, but I'm surprised to see another person, lingering near the door as he smokes a cigarette. It's Adam—watching with careful regard. It strikes me then that he's not like the other people from the club. And as Dallas climbs into the van, telling us to "Go, go!" I watch as Adam turns toward me.

He smiles, and it's not sinister, it's not threatening. It's almost apologetic. He lifts his hand in a wave as James peels out of the parking lot, and I know The Program can't be far behind.

# CHAPTER SEVEN

"HAVE YOU SEEN HER?" DALLAS ASKS INTO THE PHONE. Her words are slightly slurred, but she seems otherwise pulled together. In fact, she's taking charge in a way that makes me trust her. "Is that so?" she asks, hardening her tone. "Where?"

James tightens his grip on the steering wheel, turning his knuckles white. The minute we'd pulled away from the Suicide Club, Dallas had started making calls, while Cas took the others in the van. Dallas said she had contacts within The Program and that they could tell us if Lacey had been picked up. I turn to look back just as Dallas lowers the phone. When her eyes meet mine, they're stunned.

"She's gone," Dallas says.

"What do you mean?" I ask, my voice cracking over the words.

"She's alive," Dallas says, as if that's the bad news. "But she's back in The Program. They're saying she had a brain-function meltdown, and she's hospitalized within their facility. They found her at a bus station, set to head back to Oregon." She shakes her head, absorbing her words. "She must have cracked. It happens sometimes. I'm sorry, Sloane. But . . . she's never going to be the same. Even if they can put her pieces together again, The Program isn't going to just let her walk out of there. They're going to take whatever's left of her. They probably already have our location and are raiding the warehouse now." Dallas reaches to rub her eyes with the heels of her hands, smudging her makeup.

"What are you saying?" I ask.

"I'm saying Lacey no longer exists. And there's no way to bring her back."

There's a flurry of motion next to me and the SUV swerves. James pounds his fist against the steering wheel. Then again. Again.

"James, stop," I say, reaching over to grab his arm, but he yanks it away and squeals the tires as he slams on the brakes. We all pitch forward, and behind us we hear the van skid to a stop.

James opens the driver's door and jumps out to begin walking. I scramble behind him, confused by his behavior and horrified by the news we've just received. "Wait!" I yell, chasing after James. Before I reach him, he spins and startles me. He pulls at his blond hair, knotting his fingers as his face contorts with anger and misery.

"We can't trust them," he says, motioning toward the cars. "We can't trust one fucking person, Sloane. Do you understand that?"

"Yeah, but—"

"Contacts in The Program," he says, as if the idea is ridiculous. "Are you kidding?" He reaches to take my upper arms and pull me closer. "Listen to me," he says. "We trust only each other from here on out. I don't give a shit what they tell us; it's me and you. No one else. For all we know, they could have *sent* Lacey to The Program."

The thought hadn't occurred to me, and I instinctively turn to look back at the Escalade. The doors are wide open, flooding the dark street with light. Dallas is leaning between the front seats, waving for us to get back inside the SUV. James puts his hand on my cheek and turns me toward him; his touch is gentle, so serious. When I meet his eyes, my body relaxes slightly. James draws me into a hug, resting his chin on the top of my head, his arms tight around me.

"It's just us," I whisper into the fabric of his shirt. "Forever, just us."

"That's the idea," he responds. The horn beeps, making us jump. James looks me over one more time before smoothing the curls of my hair away from my face. In this moment of calm, the disappearance of Lacey is crushing. But it's no longer panic, it's loss. Heavy, terrible loss covers me in a shadow. Rather than cry, I take James's hand and go back to the waiting car. There's no time to mourn. There's only time to run.

*　　*　　*

I've never been to Colorado before, and when we cross the state line, the sun is shining. It does nothing to comfort me though, and I lean my head on James's shoulder in the backseat as Dallas drives. I've been checking the CNN feed on Dallas's phone—hoping for word on Lacey, but at the same time, terrified of what an article would say about her. But there are no updates, save for an older one about James and I running away.

James asks me to check the *New York Times*, and when I do, my stomach drops. "Oh my God," I murmur, scrolling through an interview. This can't be real.

"What is it?" James asks. From the front, Dallas flicks her gaze to the rearview mirror. The date on the interview is from a few days ago, and when I meet Dallas's eyes, I see she already knows.

"What's going on?" James demands. I hold the phone out to him and watch as his expression falters. It's an in-depth interview about us. And James's dad is doing the talking.

"He's claiming it's your fault," Dallas says quietly, looking at me in the mirror, "like you're some sort of vixen. You'd think he'd be more concerned about getting his only son home."

James is still reading, and every second that ticks by makes his posture tighter, his hands curl into fists. I'd only skimmed the interview, but James's dad claimed I was the mastermind behind our disappearance. There's even a picture of him posing with a framed photo of James from middle school. It's absolutely absurd.

"Propaganda," Dallas calls back, even though James and I have fallen silent. "They baited him into that interview to gain public support. I wouldn't let it bother you too much."

I scoff. "Right, Dallas. I'll just put it out of my mind." I look at James, trying to gauge his reaction. Eventually he turns the phone screen off and hands the cell forward to Dallas. I start to chew on my nail, waiting. But James just crosses his arms over his chest like he might never talk again.

"James?" I ask when his nonresponse nearly sends me over the edge.

"My dad's an asshole," he says quietly. "Let's just leave it at that for now."

But I can't drop it. I don't know how James's father feels about me—or at least I can't remember. He could have a reason to hate me, or like James said, he could just be an asshole. Either way, the fact that this is news shows the reach of The Program. Using his father is another layer of betrayal. They knew it would hurt James. They wanted it to. It's proof they won't stop. They won't let us go. "What are we going to do?" I whisper.

James turns toward me. "We hold on," he replies. It's not the give-them-hell response I need to hear, but James is only human. We're all vulnerable. Like Lacey.

The reality of our situation is crushing, and we ride in silence—James lost somewhere next to me. I watch out the window as we pass a park. There are children playing in bright-colored shirts, running around while their doting mothers look on. For an instant, I miss my parents in a desperate way I haven't felt in a long while. For an instant I wish I could go home.

But then I think of James's dad sitting down for that interview and know it just as easily could have been my parents. I close my eyes until I'm back to now, on the run with James and Dallas.

"I think you're going to love Denver," Dallas calls from the front, startling me from my thoughts. "There won't be any Suicide Clubs for a while, though. The last one got raided after we left. In a way, Lacey saved my ass by taking off."

"How did they find out about the club?" I ask.

Dallas begins twisting her blond dreads absently. "A handler probably," she says, watching the road outside the windshield. "Those bastards are embedded everywhere."

Embedded handlers—the thought hadn't occurred to me. My memories from last night at the Suicide Club are hazy, but I remember Adam. Was he a handler putting on an act, pretending to be depressed? That's so wrong, so unethical. If he was a handler, then . . .

Fear crawls up my back and arms, a devastating reality I can't even tell James. Not yet, not when he's still feeling guilty about Lacey. But Adam knew my name—he knew who I was. If he was a handler, why didn't he take me right then? What if I was the reason the Suicide Club was raided?

"Hold up," Dallas tells us when her phone vibrates. James's eyes narrow as he watches in the rearview mirror as she answers it. "Seriously?" Dallas says into the phone. "Goddamn it, Cas.

Fine," she growls, and hangs up, dropping her phone into the cup holder. The Escalade zooms past us, but we turn right.

"Cas says we need to split up," Dallas tells us. "The place in Denver won't work for you, and it's too risky to continue driving right now. Apparently they're doing a *Dateline* special about the two of you. The media has totally latched on to your runaway-lovers story—and the scanner is going crazy with possible sightings. This is a total clusterfuck."

"So where are we going, then?" James asks, his mood still dark from reading about his father. "Don't you have any friends here?"

The dig makes Dallas flinch, but she smiles, brushing her hair behind her shoulder. "Oh, I have friends, James. But they won't exactly welcome me in with the rebel poster children in tow. Too bad your handsome face couldn't be a little less memorable." She says it like she hates him for it.

"Yes, too bad," I respond sarcastically. James chuckles, side-eyeing me. His angry expression softens, and then he shoves my shoulder playfully.

"Hey!" I push him back, to which he retaliates until I'm finally smiling. I love how we can do that—break through the misery to always find each other.

Dallas interrupts. "We're heading to Colorado Springs. There's a small house where Cas used to crash. He told us to head over while he drops off the others. He's going to stay with us, though. The four of us," she mumbles. "Won't that be cozy?"

"Lovely," I respond. Because spending more time with

Dallas is what I need. I rest against James; he braids strands of my hair between his fingers as I watch the passing street out the window. The blue sky and the white-capped mountains.

And when the moment of normalcy fades, I'm haunted once again by thoughts of Lacey—and how I could have saved her. I go to twist the ring on my finger and become alarmed when there's only naked flesh. I hold up my hand and hitch in a breath. I spin to James, tears ready to spill over.

"I left it behind," I say. At first his expression is a mixture of concern and confusion, but then he looks at my hand and realizes I'm talking about the ring. His shoulders slump, hurt crossing his features.

A few weeks ago I'd found a ring hidden in my bedroom. I'd placed it there for when I got out of The Program, and it eventually helped lead me back to James. Just last week he'd gotten me a second ring—a new promise. But I was careless enough to lose it. It's starting to feel like a pattern: losing things I care about. People I care about. I curl against James, my face buried in his shirt while he murmurs he'll get me another. It was just an object; it's replaceable. But as he talks, I rub absently at the empty space on my ring finger, thinking about replacements. And wondering if I'm just a replacement of the girl I used to be.

The house is a skinny two-story with peeling yellow paint and a broken wooden fence. I take a quick peek around as we pull into the garage behind the house. Dallas leads us toward a sagging back porch and picks up a key from underneath a coffee can filled with old cigarette butts that's just outside the door. James and I survey the yard, and he points to a dilapidated doghouse in the corner.

"Can we get a puppy?" he asks, grinning at me. I want to say yes and then really get a dog. We'll give it a stupid name and take it everywhere with us. But our situation isn't permanent. We may never find permanence again. We may never find Lacey again. When I don't respond, James's smile fades and he puts his arm around me as we wait for Dallas to get the door open.

I was in the school cafeteria the first time I met Lacey. She was wearing the same sort of clothes as the other returners, but on her they didn't seem so bland. She told me not to eat the food because they put sedatives in it. She told me this even though it could have gotten her in trouble. She sat with me—a hollowed-out, confused girl—until I started to feel less lost. She made me laugh. She tried to protect me from The Program. But I let her down. I should have taken the nosebleed more seriously. I'm not sure what I could have done for her, but I should have figured something out. If Realm had been here, he would have known what to do.

"Sloane?" James asks, startling me from my thoughts. The door is open and Dallas is gone, but I'm still on the back porch while James looks at me from inside. "You coming?" he asks.

I think about the doghouse again, a symbol of the normal life we'll never have, and then follow James into the house before bolting the door behind us. The entryway leads into the

SUZANNE YOUNG

kitchen, which although old-fashioned, seems to be perfectly intact. There are appliances, and dishes in the open cupboards. It's like a real home, but that doesn't offer me much comfort. Instead I'm reminded of my home back in Oregon, of my parents who I haven't spoken to since the day I left. Are they sick with worry? Are they okay?

"I think I want to lie down," I say to James, my chest constricting when I think of my father waiting for me to come home. My mother looking out the front window, wondering if I'm alive. James asks Dallas where the bedrooms are and she motions toward the stairs. I don't wait for James and start up them, noticing small nails punched into the walls without pictures hanging from them.

There are three rooms, and James lets me decide which one I want. I pick the one with the biggest bed, and James drops our bag onto the dresser. The room has a dormer with a chair set in the space, along with a little table. The walls are a grayish-white and the furniture is old but still useable. The blankets look decent and I lie on top of a faded green comforter. When I curl up in the fetal position, James comes to lie next to me, rubbing his hand over my back.

"We'll get through this," he says. "You're stronger than anyone I know, Sloane. We'll keep each other safe."

The words ring hollow, words I'm sure I've heard before. If I dwell on the negative thoughts any longer, I'm afraid I'll get sick. It's like the depression is always there, threatening to pull me under. I turn and wrap my arm around James, my cheek on his shoulder. He strokes my hair, comfortable and innocent, but it's not enough for me. I get up on my elbow and look down at his handsome face, his trusting eyes.

I kiss him. "Make me forget," I murmur between his lips, sliding my hand under his shirt. James is quick to respond, moving me on top of him, and the negative thoughts are leaving. The faces—real or imagined—are fading away.

I try to strip away his clothes, but my hands are too shaky and tears sting my eyes. It's all so overwhelming and I'm not sure I can bear even one more loss. I just want all my feelings to go away. Why can't they just go away?

James grabs my wrists and stops me, pulling me against him for an embrace.

"Make it go away," I whimper. James swallows hard, his grip on me loosening. My hands once again search his body, but the passion is gone. When I finally meet his eyes, they pin me in place.

"I don't want you like this," he says. "I don't want us like this."

Emptiness tears through me, curling around my toes. I am a black hole of doubt and misery. I glide my fingers over James's jaw, his full lips. He gently takes my hand and kisses it.

"We'll get through this," he says, a cry threatening to break the sternness of his statement. He waits until I agree, and when he pulls me closer, I just lie against him—and let the darkness swallow me up.

# CHAPTER EIGHT

WE'RE LIVING OFF GAS STATION CUISINE UNTIL CAS shows up a few days later with a bag of nonperishable goods he snagged from the food bank. Dallas eyes him but doesn't ask where he's been. But soon after he returns, they're leaving for long stretches—hours at a time—with no explanation of where they're going. Because of my and James's high-profile statuses, we're left behind to wonder about them.

The days begin to blur together, and cut off from the outside world, James and I are falling into a routine. I start to think that maybe we could actually get a dog—but then my rational side reminds me that this is all pretend. At least for now.

"You should wear an apron," James calls out playfully from the kitchen table as I wash the last of our dishes. I've never thought of myself as very domestic, and if my cooking proves anything, I'm not. So James cooks, and I clean, and Dallas and Cas wander about like rebel leaders and make jokes about how James and I are playing house.

I shut off the water and then, instead of drying my hands on the dishtowel, I walk over and wipe them on James's face as he tries to fight me off. We're both laughing, wrestling in a way that will surely end in kissing, when Dallas walks in, taking in the scene.

"Cute," she says, as if she doesn't find it even the least bit endearing. "Did you get the hot water heater working?" she asks James. He bends his head back to look at her as I sit on his lap.

"Not yet. I'm not very handy." He smiles. "My talents lie elsewhere." I swat his chest and he laughs, turning back to Dallas. "The Internet on your phone is spotty here, so I can't download a how-to video or anything. Is Cas good at fixing stuff?"

"No," she says immediately. "Cas is good at gathering information, not evaluating it."

James straightens and helps me off of him as he stands. "What sort of information? What exactly are you and Cas doing all day, and why won't you tell us?"

"We're collecting intel, monitoring the safe houses, looking for new recruits. And we don't tell you because we don't trust you. While you and Sloane are living in some delusion, there are people killing themselves. It's an epidemic out there, James, and The Program is using that to further their agenda. First step is getting rid of all of us."

"And how do I know you're not the one leading them here?" James asks, calling her on the suspicions that have been festering.

Dallas's normally pretty face hardens, her jaw tightens. "You want to know why I don't work for The Program?" she asks him. She pushes up her sleeves and holds out her arms, a wide scar, light pink and healed, wraps around her wrists. "This is from the restraints," she says. "I kept pulling out my hair, so they tied me down. But that made fighting off the handler pretty difficult."

"Fuck," James murmurs as he looks over her scars. A shudder races through me, knowing the story, and hating Roger even more for it.

"'The first one's free,' he told me," Dallas says, her eyes dark and cold. "He stuffed a pill inside my mouth and said to focus on a memory. I focused on my mother. I nearly choked to death on my own vomit, but he wouldn't take off the restraints. Said I was a danger to myself."

James reaches for the chair to steady himself, but I'm watching Dallas with both sympathy and understanding. She can't be part of The Program—after what Roger did to her, she could never work for them.

"They kept me sedated for close to three weeks," Dallas continues. "And for those three weeks all I remember is his hands on me. His body on mine. He said he only liked the willing, but when the choice is him or eradication, I'm not sure there is much willingness in that. I gave in to him. I had no choice. But he stopped giving me the pills, said I couldn't remember too much or The Program would realize what he was doing. He lied to me. He took everything from me.

"The minute they removed my restraints, I grabbed a Taser and nearly killed him. I wanted to." Her hard expression cracks long enough for a few tears to streak from her heavily lined eyes. "I'm going to kill them all," she says quietly. "I'm going to burn that place to the ground."

"I didn't know," James says to her. "I'm sorry." Then to my surprise, he reaches for Dallas and draws her into a hug, brushing his hand over her arm in a moment so tender, I can't help but feel jealous. "We'll find him," James whispers. "And we'll kill him."

Dallas doesn't look at me. Instead she closes her eyes, squeezing them tight as her arms come around James, turning her face to rest on his shoulder. She's completely stripped down and broken, and James is the only thing holding her up as she starts to cry.

"Shh . . ." He strokes her blond dreads. After a few minutes I leave to go back to our room, giving them some privacy. Because even though I don't trust Dallas, I trust James completely.

In my bedroom I go to the closet, where I set the pill on the top shelf behind an old book of children's Bible stories. I pull the string connected to the light and then sit on the floor of the closet, examining the pill through the Baggie. How hard both Dallas and I must have fought to keep our memories. Roger preyed on us. And now here I am with a key I would have given anything for.

Now I can take it. But it's been only a few days since I felt the darkness, and only seven weeks since I left The Program. Am I truly cured? Wasn't Lacey?

*Lacey.*

I close my eyes, crumpling the Baggie in my fist. Lacey's memories drove her crazy; I can't risk that. I can't get sick again; I can't let James get sick again. The girl I used to be is dead— The Program killed her. And for better or worse, I'm what's left. I'll never take the pill. I never want to know. Resigned to this, I stand and put the pill back in its place. Then I turn off the light and close the door behind me.


James and I are in the backyard, lying shoulder to shoulder in the dying grass, tanning our skin. We've been inside so much, we're starting to look like vampires. We never did see the *Dateline* special, but it seems that since then we've been replaced with more tragic stories about the spreading epidemic. We're trying to make the best of our situation here, but staying in the house is making us stir-crazy. So we came to lie in the backyard, pretending we're on the grass beach in Oregon again.

The Escalade turns into the driveway, and I shade the sunlight with my palm, watching the car pull into the garage. I'm annoyed Dallas and Cas are back—annoyed this isn't just all ours. I wonder what James and I would do if they never came back at all. Would we stay here?

"I hope they brought food," James says from next to me, his eyes still closed. "If not, we're stealing the car and making a McDonald's run."

"Deal." I turn over, curling against James as the heat of the sun beats down on my cheek and arm. If I could, I'd live this moment forever. Birds chirping, sun shining. James opens one eye to look over at me, and I smile broadly.

"Adorable," he says, and gives me a quick kiss. When the garage door closes, James groans and sits up. "Dallas," he calls. "What's for dinner?"

Dallas walks from the garage with a brown fast-food bag in one hand, and a canvas satchel in the other. She looks us over, her face more serious than I'd expect on a beautiful summer day. "I have something for you," she says to James. Cas comes from the garage, his face downturned, and immediately James is on his feet.

"What's happening?" he asks, meeting them at the back door. "What's wrong?"

Dallas leans against the railing, the wood creaking like it might break. Cas tosses a weary glance in my direction. I climb up, suddenly out of breath. Are the handlers on their way? Did they hear something about Lacey?

Out of the satchel Dallas pulls a black accordion file, stuffed with papers, their edges fraying. My gut sinks, and I walk over to put my foot up on the stair, waiting to hear what they've found.

"It's your file, James," Dallas says. "From your time in

The Program. I got access to it from a source—she stole the whole damn thing. It's"—she looks at me—"an interesting read."

"You read my file?" James asks, but his voice is choked as he stares at the papers. Dallas is about to give him what I wouldn't . . . his past. My body begins to tremble.

Dallas shrugs. "I didn't read the entire thing," she offers. "Just the good parts." She flashes her gap-toothed smile. "And sorry, Sloane. I couldn't get my hands on yours. They're keeping that one on lock."

James stands frozen, as if he can't believe this is really happening. When he takes the file from Dallas, he turns to me, wide-eyed. "Let's check it out."

"James"—Dallas holds up her finger—"maybe you should read it alone first." Her gaze flicks to me for a second, and from behind me I hear Cas shift. I swallow hard.

"Thanks for the advice," James says, then points to the fast-food bag Dallas is holding. "That for us?" Dallas nods, and James plucks the bag from her hands and disappears inside, calling my name from the kitchen.

I climb the rest of the stairs, dread seeping from my pores. I pause in front of Dallas when I get to the top. "What's in his file?" I whisper. Her expression is both fascinated and smug.

"Guess you'll see," she says. She holds the door open for me, and I narrow my eyes at her before walking in.

"Tattoos," James says the minute I'm through the kitchen

door. He's got a cheeseburger to his lips, the open file spread out on the table. "These scars were tattoos. Can you believe it?" He slaps the page down and pulls up his shirtsleeve to show the white lines. On the table is a photograph, and I take in a sharp gasp when I see the first name.

"Brady," I say. Surprised, James looks down and sets the cheeseburger aside.

"I tattooed your brother's name on my arm," he says quietly, and looks up. "I must have cared a lot about him." The thought brings me comfort, knowing Brady wasn't alone even though Realm had told us as much. But I'm glad they were friends. It tells me a lot about the kind of person James must have been, and it reassures me. Maybe I never needed to be afraid of our past together.

James leans forward suddenly and pokes at the picture. "Holy shit. Look."

I sit next to him, and when I see it, I turn to him. "Miller." The name Miller is the last on James's list, but it's not tattooed like the other names. It's a cut, jagged and scabbed over like he . . . carved it into his arm. I grab his bicep, inspecting the space, trailing my thumb along the scars.

Miller. *Miller.* My eyes flutter closed, something itching behind my skull, a thought cracking through the smooth surface of my memories until it shatters open.

*"Would you mind moving over?" a guy says, coming to stand next to me at the lab table. "I'm kind of an expert at this." I glance*

up and back away from the Bunsen burner, which I couldn't manage to turn on.

"Golly gee, thanks," I say sarcastically. "I didn't know they were sending in the professionals."

The guy's mouth twitches with a smile as he reaches to turn the gas all the way up, the hissing barely audible over the sound of the other students' conversations in the chemistry room. "Name's Miller, by the way," he says. "In case you want to write a thank-you letter."

"I'm drafting it in my mind as we speak. Um . . . are you sure the gas should be turned up that high?" I look around the room, but my teacher seems preoccupied with his computer screen. "Miller," I say, feeling funny using his name when we've only just met. "Please don't burn up my homework."

He turns to me, the igniter dangling from his fingers. "Are you kidding?" he asks. "I could do this with one hand tied—"

He clicks the igniter and the minute there's a spark, all I hear is a giant whoosh before a bright-blue flame explodes over the Bunsen burner. I yelp and Miller drops the igniter, sending more sparks over the lab table, igniting the homework I'd just specifically told him not to burn up!

The girl at the lab table in front of us looks back and then points a panicked finger at our now-flaming table. Miller reaches quickly to turn down the Bunsen burner, and then, with complete calm, he picks up my half-empty can of Diet Pepsi and douses the fire, putting it out with an unceremonious sizzle.

"Well, shit," he says, staring down at the soggy, smoking, withered paper. "That didn't go the way I planned it in my head."

*I put my hand on my hip and turn to glare at him. But the minute his dark brown gaze meets mine, we both start laughing.*

Miller. I open my eyes, feeling the tears rush over my cheeks. What happened to Miller?

"I remember him," I whisper. "I have a memory of him." James grips my forearm, squeezing tight, even though I'm sure he doesn't know he's doing it. I shouldn't have this memory. Is this recall? Will I end up like Lacey, broken and crashing? My heart is pounding so fast, I'm afraid it might just quit. "I think Miller was my friend, and I remember him."

James gathers me into a hug. "What have they done to us?" he whispers, mostly to himself. I replay the memory over and over like a sad song on repeat, familiar and comforting even though it's scratchy and painful. "Look at me," James says, pulling back to examine my face. "Headache?"

I shake my head, and he takes another second to make sure I don't spontaneously combust. He waits while I tell him the memory, smiling likes it's a good story and not some forgotten piece of my past. When I'm done talking, I'm calmer.

"Better?" James asks softly.

"Yeah. There's nothing else trying to break through. It was just a blip—a spike and then back to flatlining. This isn't like Lacey," I say. Even though James didn't bring up the connection, I know it must have crossed his mind.

"Of course it's not," he says dismissively, his jaw tight. "But that memory—we're not going to tell anyone about it. Maybe you'll have others, maybe you won't, but this is our secret." He looks at me. "Right?"

"I'm fine," I assure him. I quickly assess myself and realize I'm telling the truth. I do feel fine. A little stressed, but I don't feel like I'm about to fall apart or anything. This isn't at all like Lacey.

After a moment James picks up the photo of his tattoos again, checking it against the scars on his arm. "What happened to all these people?" he asks.

"They died." I think about Brady. My brother's final days were erased from my memory, and this could be our only chance to find out what really happened to him. "James," I say, reaching past him to spread out the files, looking for my brother's name. "See if there's any mention of Brady."

He helps me sort through the file, picking out papers that he thinks look promising. "How about this one?" he asks, sliding out a page. "It's minutes from my sessions with Dr. Tabor." I look sideways at James, surprised he remembers his doctor's name. I remember Dr. Warren, but James has never mentioned anything about his time in The Program, nothing beyond that it's all a blur.

"It's the only one," he says, examining the print on a few other papers before he gives up the search. He settles back in the chair with a quick look at me to make sure I'm listening, and then he starts to read from the page. "Session one," he starts. "Patient 486: James Murphy. Doctor: Eli Tabor. The patient refused medication for targeted recall and was therefore injected." James tenses at the line, and I lean down to read over his shoulder.


    Dr. Tabor: Why are you here, James?

    Patient 486: What? They didn't tell you? What sort of a seedy operation is this?

    Dr. Tabor: Are you depressed?

    Patient 486: Not that depressed. Maybe I'm just tired.

    Dr. Tabor: Tell me about Brady Barstow.

    Patient 486: Fuck you.

    (Patient becomes uneasy and another injection is given.)

    Dr. Tabor: Better?

    Patient 486: No.

    Dr. Tabor: I see. James, teens in your position are always combative; this isn't a new feeling. But you need to understand that we're here to help you. To cure you. Do you want to live?

    Patient 486: Not after you're done, I won't.

    (Note that patient's speech is slurred.)

    Dr. Tabor: Is it because of your girlfriend?

    Patient 486: Don't have one.


I pause at the line and look at James. The minute he reads it, his breathing changes, but he doesn't turn to me. A new sort of worry begins, and I read on, hoping it's just a lie.


                                         **SUZANNE YOUNG**

Dr. Tabor: You're not dating Sloane Barstow, Brady's sister?

Patient 486: I wouldn't call it dating.

Dr. Tabor: What would you call it then?

Patient 486: Pity.

My stomach drops at the word *pity*. I don't believe it, but inside, a seed of doubt has been planted.

Dr. Tabor: We have extensive research on you and Miss Barstow. We know you've been in a relationship for years now.

Patient 486: Her brother asked me to take care of her. I have been. But the minute she's eighteen, I'm done. I'll be done with Sloane and you won't have to worry about her ever again.

Dr. Tabor: But we are worried. She may not be carving names into her arm, but she's high-risk, James. We want to bring her in.

Patient 486: You're wasting your time. She doesn't love me. I don't love her. Sure, we sleep together sometimes, but that should be expected. I'm a pretty good catch.

Dr. Tabor: James—

Patient 486: Are we done here? Because I'm done talking.

Dr. Tabor: No. I want to—

(Note that Patient 486 charged the desk and grabbed my coat to attack me. Handlers were brought in to sedate him. He will sit in isolation for three days before his next session.)

Additional notes: Patient 486 attempted to terminate his life following his session. After waking from his sedation, he used his sheets to try to hang himself in his room. Dr. Arthur Pritchard has been called in for a consult.


I stand up from the kitchen chair, bumping it back against the wall. James is motionless, still staring down at the papers. He tried to kill himself. He said he never loved me. I can remember Miller.

Suddenly my head *is* pounding, my heart racing. I touch my temples just as a wave of dizziness hits—I shouldn't mess with my memories, but I can't stop myself. I'm trying to piece together what I know for certain.

When I first returned from The Program, I met James outside of the Wellness Center. A guy named Liam had called me a freak, and although we didn't know each other, James stood up for me. As we got closer, James always held back. Is this why? Would he have really left me when I turned eighteen?

Tears start to sting my eyes, and I rub them roughly as I back away from the table. I need a minute to figure out what's happening. I leave the kitchen, heading for our room . . . and James doesn't stop me.

# CHAPTER NINE

I WALK INTO THE BEDROOM AND BEGIN PACING. MY mind is in overdrive, imagining the worst—making up elaborate scenarios where James was my unrequited love. Is this what Realm said I wouldn't want to find? He'd told me I loved James madly, but he didn't say James loved me back. Could that be why I got sick?

I cover my face, begging myself to stop, stop the negative thoughts that are feeding on me. But I can't. Something I'd accepted as fact, this love story between James and me, might not be true. When I think about it, there were plenty of signs. That day he came to my house to talk about Brady—he walked out on me when I hugged him. And later he even told me I was imagining our relationship in my head.

"Sloane." James's voice startles me, but I don't respond.

James pulls my hands from my face, and I start to sob. It's not just because of James's file. I've lost Lacey. I've lost Miller. I'm completely falling apart and I'm scared. I'm so scared!

"You're spinning out, Sloane," James says, his voice hurried. "I need you to pull it together right now. Right fucking now." I start to shake my head, but James takes my wrist to pull me up, hugging me tightly against his chest. "Stay with me," he murmurs next to my ear. "Stop thinking and stay with me. Everything is going to be okay. Everything is just fine," he soothes in his liar's voice.

It comforts me though. Those words ease down my skin as James strokes my hair, telling me we'll be all right. I measure my breathing until it settles into a normal pattern, the tears dry on my cheeks. James is right: I'm spiraling, and I need to pull myself out.

"Do you think you were lying to the doctor?" I ask, my voice thick from tears.

James holds me away from him so I can see his face. "Yes, Sloane. Obviously, I wasn't telling him the truth. Do you think I'd really tell The Program about us? There's no way."

"But how do we know?" I ask, hitching in a breath. "How do we know what's real anymore?"

James puts his hand over his heart, anguish on his face that nearly kills me. "Because I can feel it here, and I could read it in my words. I was protecting you. I would have died to protect you had they not stopped me. We're fucking mental for each other—but maybe that's how we survive from

SUZANNE YOUNG

here. We just have to be crazier than The Program."

I choke out a small laugh, and James hugs me once again. "I'm tired of running," I whisper.

"Me too," he says. "But this is when we have to fight the hardest. This is all that's left of us—this right now. We have to make it count." James brushes my hair behind my ear. No matter what the file says, lies or not, who we are now matters.

"I still love you madly," I whisper.

"I love you too." He says it so honestly that I can't believe there's any other way for him to feel. My doubt begins to fade, and James buries his face in my hair. Gliding my hand up his arm, I stop over his scars—his tattoos—tracing patterns until I feel him kiss softly at my neck.

A soft sound escapes my throat, and I turn my face to kiss him. He professes his love again, his hands gripping my hips. I back us toward the bed, kissing, whispering. I'm quickly losing layers of clothing, but James is still dressed as we lie on the bed. When I try to undo his belt, he stops me.

"Don't," he says. He looks down at me and laughs. "I can't handle the temptation."

"Then stop resisting." I lift my head to kiss him again. He returns the kiss, but then quickly flops over onto his back.

"I can't, Sloane," he says. "I forgot the condoms back in Phoenix."

I freeze for a moment, and he turns to me, smiling sheepishly. "Are you kidding?" I ask.

"No. But believe me—I'm pretty pissed about it."

I groan, but then I realize I'm better. The distraction worked, and my head doesn't hurt as much—although there's still a tiny ache behind my eyes. But James made me forget the pain. I throw my leg over his, and put my head on his chest. "At least we're building some anticipation," I say with a smile, content to feel well again.

"At the very least," he mutters.

I slide my hand under James's shirt to rest it over his heart, feeling its rapid beats. They say stress brings on the meltdowns, so I block out the thoughts of Brady, Miller, and Lacey. If there's one thing The Program made us experts at, it's repression.

"I mean it, you know," James says quietly. "I love you like crazy, and I don't give a goddamn about anything else."

We're quiet for a long while until James has to sit up because his arm fell asleep. "Should we check out the rest of that file?" he asks tentatively. "You'll have to take it easy, but this could be our only chance to find out what happened. Pretty sure The Program isn't handing them out like greeting cards."

I'm worried, but I agree, letting him take the investigative lead. This was a fluke—I'm not breaking down. There's nothing wrong with a few memories, so long as I don't let them control me. I can handle this. I'm strong enough.

Dallas is in the kitchen, pouring water into the back of the coffeemaker while Cas sits at the table, looking exhausted. When we come down, he presses his lips into a smile, seeming relieved that we're joining them. Dallas tosses a curious glance over her shoulder but doesn't say anything as James and I each take a seat.

"So what happened to my file?" I ask as the coffee begins to percolate.

Cas shrugs, answering only after Dallas stays silent. "I've called every contact I have," he says, "but your file is gone, or at least, not accessible. They tried to pull James's, too—probably after you ran—but I got to it in time. I think they're trying to cover their asses in case you turn up dead or on an *Oprah* special."

"That's the next stop on our publicity tour," James says with a grin. Dallas turns, flashing him a smile before grabbing two coffee mugs and setting one in front of James. He thanks her, then starts going through his file again. I can't look at Dallas. She read the notes from James's session, and whatever doubts I had are probably magnified by a thousand in her mind. Luckily, I don't have to dwell on her possible thoughts before James holds up another paper.

"Look at this," he announces. "Says here I assaulted a handler." The paper is an incident report and apparently, after his blackout session, James attacked a handler in the hallway. It reminds me of when Realm took down Roger, and I turn to James, thinking for the first time that he and Realm have a lot in common—more than just me.

Dallas tops off James's coffee, her hand shaking. She asks Cas if he wants a cup, but he passes. She never offers one to me. She clinks the pot back in place just as James calls my name.

"Here it is," he says. He looks to me immediately and then points to a page clipped to the file. It's an entrance form, and in the bottom box is a handwritten note in blue ink. The first word I recognize is my brother's name, and I prepare myself for what comes next.

Patient 486 was first infected after the self-termination of Brady Barstow (drowning), and was later triggered by the self-termination of Miller Andrews (QuikDeath). Under the influence of his medication, Patient 486 admitted to witnessing Brady Barstow's death at the river, where his attempts to rescue him failed. He has since been struggling with depression, kept hidden with the help of Sloane Barstow, the deceased's sister.

"You tried to save him," I whisper. Then, before James can reply, I lean over and kiss him, my hands on his cheeks. My brother wasn't alone when he died, that I knew, but the idea of James trying to save him fills me with a comfort I can't explain.

I pull back, smiling at how brave James must have been. Across the room, I notice a figure standing in the doorway. His shoulders are slumped, his head downcast. I hitch in a breath when he lifts his dark eyes to mine. It can't be. . . .

"Realm?" My voice cracks and I scramble to my feet. Realm

is thinner, his clothes hang on his tall frame. His dark hair is now a brassy shade of orange, as if he'd dyed it blond not too long ago. The shadows under his eyes are deep and dark, and I think he's been through something. I step toward him. "You're back?"

A small smile pulls at Realm's lips, and I'm absolutely over-come with relief. Dallas chuckles, standing at the sink, but nothing else matters as I rush over to Realm and throw myself against him, wrapping my arms around his neck. He's alive. "I've missed you," I whisper into his shirt.

"Ah, Michael Realm," James calls out, still sitting at the kitchen table. "What a surprise. I'd give you a hug too, but I think I'd rather punch you in the face."

I don't bother reacting; I just hold on to Realm. I didn't think I'd ever see him again. He touches gingerly at my shoul-ders and then glances past me to James. "You're not really my type, James," he says. "So I think I'd prefer the punch anyway."

"Good to know." James darts a look between me and Realm, smiling but obviously tense by our proximity. It wasn't that long ago that he saw me kiss Realm, back before we got together. And he knows about the time I went to Realm's house in the middle of the night. He knows we've been more than friends.

I feel a touch on my cheek and turn to Realm as he glides his finger over my skin. "You look good," he says softly. "I was worried."

"*You* were worried? I haven't heard from you. I thought you were . . ." I stop, not wanting to finish the thought.

"Dead," James finishes for me.

Realm ignores him, still looking at me with a sort of reverence. "So you're happy to see me?" he asks, as if he's scared of the answer.

"Yes. What kind of question is that?"

He smiles, dropping his hand. "Of course. You didn't take it."

My expression falters when he mentions the pill. Realm doesn't know I told James about it. He doesn't know we've kept it secret from the others. Dallas slams the cabinet door under the sink, and my heart jumps. When I look up, she's walking over with a small box in her hand, focused on Realm, and I relax.

"Hey, blondie," she says with a big grin. "Was wondering when you'd get here. I picked this up for you earlier." She slaps a box of hair dye against his chest. "I've always liked you better as a brunette anyway."

Realms smiles at her, something affectionate and familiar. "Thank you, Dal."

She shrugs as if it was nothing, grabs a kitchen chair, and spins around to sit on it backward. "You really shouldn't sneak up on us," she says teasingly to Realm. "Have you gotten my messages?"

"I apologize," he tells her. "But yes, I got them. That's how I found you, actually. We shouldn't stay here. We'll need another safe house."

"Working on it," Cas says, getting up to grab a backpack from the closet. "Didn't expect you for another week at least."

They exchange a look before Cas tosses the pack in Realm's direction. Realm immediately opens it, sorting through its contents. "We've found a basement apartment," Cas continues, "but I don't think it's a good choice. Not enough exits."

"Keep looking," Realm says, taking out a cell phone. "This clean?" he asks.

"Just got it today. Why?" Cas smiles. "You want to order a pizza?"

"I need to call Anna and thank her. Let her know I'm okay."

Anna, Realm's sister, is the one who told us to run, gave us a car and some money. She helped us get away before The Program could catch us. And she did it all just because her brother asked her to.

"Tell her thanks from me, too," I say, reaching to touch Realm's arm. He flinches but then looks down at where my hand is on him. He seems a little lost, and I want to ask him where he's been all these weeks, but I don't. Not yet.

"I'll tell her," he replies.

"Hey, Realm," Cas says. "I'll drop your stuff in my room. I think I'd rather sleep on the couch anyway. Place is getting a bit claustrophobic." He gives Realm a fist bump before leaving.

Michael Realm smiles at me, somewhat sheepishly, and then he dials a number on the phone and walks into the living room. I stand, looking after him, and when I hear him choke out a cry, promising he's okay, there's a familiar warmth for him. I like how he cares about his sister. He reminds me of Brady.

"I'll be upstairs," James mumbles, and leaves. His file is still spread open on the table, but I know he's distraught. Realm is his insecurity, and I was jerk for not being more sensitive to it. I glance at Dallas, who is leaning her elbows on the back of her chair, looking self-righteous.

"A boyfriend and a lover?" she asks. "Would have never thought you the type."

"Shut up," I reply, although I feel my cheeks redden. Then, with my pulse still racing from Realm's return, I hurry up the stairs toward James.

# CHAPTER TEN

**THE SILENCE IS DEAFENING ON THE LANDING LEAD-**ing to the bedrooms. I expect James to be jealous, angry—instead I find him in the chair at the window, staring out at the street. Looking so lonely.

I'm such an idiot. "James . . ."

"He's your friend," he says, keeping his eyes trained outside. "I get it. I'm even glad he's not dead."

"You don't mean that."

"Which part?" He turns then, the dim light making his normally crystal-blue eyes darker. I cross the room and sit on the bed, pulling my legs under me as I watch him. James isn't pouting, exactly. He just seems hurt, and maybe a little confused. "What can I do?" I ask.

It's quiet at first, and then James lowers his head. "What

does he want?" he asks. He looks up and his face is absolutely miserable. "Why is he helping you like this?"

"Realm?"

"Yeah. Why does he keep risking his life for you?"

I shrug, but I know the answer. Realm is in love with me, even if I don't feel the same way about him. But my non-response does little to console James.

"There's something I need to know," he says, "although I might not like the answer."

"Oh God. What?"

"That night . . . the night we argued and you went to Realm's house? What happened between you two exactly?"

"Does it matter now?"

James exhales, leaning back in the chair like he's exhausted. "A little."

"We didn't sleep together."

He closes his eyes. "The fact that you jumped immediately to that as your defense isn't comforting."

"I was upset."

"You kissed him."

I nod, feeling ashamed. James and I weren't even a couple, but I knew how I felt about him. My hookup with Realm was completely reactionary.

"And more?" James asks.

I nod again, and I look out the window at the tree branches as they sway in the wind. I think I can actually hear the sound of James's heart breaking.

"Did you touch it?"

"Touch what?"

"It."

I laugh and shake my head. "No. No, I did not."

"Did he touch yours?"

"James!"

"Did he? I'm trying to get a handle on what 'and more' means."

"No." I stand up and walk to his chair. "James, no. He didn't . . . do that."

"How about those?" He points to my chest. He must see my expression change because he nods. "So he got to second base."

"Really, James? Second base?"

He turns away from me. "I don't blame him," he murmurs. "They're nice."

"Thanks."

"Besides, it was my fault anyway. I was an asshole. I practically gave you to him." And although he's trying to sound like he's being reasonable, a tear spills over onto his cheek and he wipes it quickly so he thinks I won't notice.

I drape my arms over his shoulders, and he turns his cheek against my shirt, his hands on my hips. "I'm sorry," I whisper, wishing I could take away the betrayal he must feel. "Realm knew I wasn't into it. He knew I was nuts for you."

James sniffles and pulls back enough to look up at me with a small smile. "You didn't like it?" he asks.

"No."

"Because you love me?"

"Yes."

"And you won't kiss him again?"

I smile. "Never."

He licks his lips. "But you'll kiss me now?"

I answer by bringing my mouth to his, kissing him softly. He's slow to respond, his body tense. I can feel his arms shaking as he wraps them around me. He's all raw nerve endings, and then James, my James, practically collapses and cries into my hair, saying how sorry he is for almost losing me.

I go downstairs for dinner as James runs to the store for supplies with Cas, opting to skip the meal. Really I think he's avoiding Realm, but at the moment—considering what we'd talked about earlier—that's probably a good idea.

I make it into the kitchen and Dallas is the only one there, frying up something that smells like charcoal in a pan. When she notices me, she shrugs. "I burn everything." She lifts the pan. "Chicken?"

"Uh . . ." I peek into the skillet and shake my head. "No, thanks. Do we have any mac 'n' cheese left? James isn't cooking for us tonight."

Dallas sets the burned food aside. "I figured." She reaches into a cabinet to pull down a box of macaroni and cheese and then grabs a pot and fills it with water. Once it's going, she turns to me. "Is he okay?" She sounds truly concerned.

"He's not a huge fan of my and Realm's friendship."

"I suppose not. And I'm guessing from the reaction to the file, your past wasn't exactly what you thought it was."

"James was trying to protect me," I say defensively. "And if you're going to gloat—"

"Gloat? Sloane, I don't want you to be miserable. And I definitely don't want James unhappy. Do I personally think the two of you together is a bad idea? Yes. I think you love each other to a fault, but in a world like this, being one half of Romeo and Juliet is stupid. I'll take my chances staying single."

I can't help it. I laugh. I take a seat at the table, and Dallas grabs a couple of sodas from the fridge and gives me one. Sometimes I don't totally hate her.

"Realm's the one who told me James and I were together before," I start. "I mean, I had guessed it because I found a picture of James with my brother, but I didn't know for sure. It was tortuous, because James would switch between hot and cold, flirting and ignoring me on a daily basis. We worked it out, though," I say. "So I call bullshit on that file."

"Huh," Dallas says, sipping from her drink. "Sounds like it. James would lie to protect you. Which leads me to my next question." She twists the tab on her soda can until it pops off. "How do you know Realm?"

Heat rises to my cheeks. "We met in The Program."

She laughs. "Well, obviously. But are you friends?" She pauses. "The kind with benefits?"

I pick up my drink, trying to look casual. "We're just friends."

But even I detect the tightness in my voice, the obvious pitch of lying. She chuckles, and I look up to see her smile.

"Yeah," she says sarcastically. "Me too." Right then the niceties slip away, both from my face and her posture. "But my friendship comes with benefits," she adds, grabbing her soda as she walks back over to the stove where the water has begun to boil.

She leaves me sitting here with a mix of jealousy and embarrassment. It had never really occurred to me that Realm was with anyone else, that he had a life outside of The Program. But he did. He does.

And Dallas made it clear it doesn't really include me anymore.

I sit on the unmade bed of my empty room, the window cracked open to let in a breeze. James is showering in the bathroom down the hall, the steam slipping out from under the door. I'm still on edge from my talk with Dallas, my brain and my heart at odds about what I should be feeling. Realm didn't come to dinner, it was just me and Dallas—eating in silence except for when she asked me to pass the hot sauce.

I just don't understand why Realm never told me about her. All that time in The Program, all the nights playing cards. He never mentioned her name. Why? And what does it mean now? Is she his girlfriend? Is Dallas his James?

"You're not falling asleep already, are you?"

Startled, I glance up and see James standing in the doorway, a towel tied around his waist, his blond hair wet and brushed back. He's smiling wryly, a sort of infectious smile that seems to burn through me. "So guess what I got earlier," he says.

I'm overwhelmed with the sight of him, the way his eyes hold me in their gaze—wicked and loving at the same time. I watch as he comes toward the bed, leaning in slowly but confidently. He's no longer cautious of me; he's given himself up to me completely. And so I kiss him hard, digging my nails into his skin as I pull him down onto the bed. We're addicted to each other—no matter what the consequences.

"I think I need another shower," James says from next to me. I laugh, rolling over to rest my face on his shoulder.

"Shh . . ." I say, putting my finger over his lips. "Don't ruin it."

"I'm the one who's ruined."

"Shut up, James."

"I'm like . . . corrupted."

"You are not."

"I think you have to marry me now."

I laugh, but when he doesn't keep going, I look over at his face. A grin pulls at his lips, but his expression is far more serious than I expected. There's a cool draft from the window where it's barely nudged open, but neither of us are in a hurry to get up.

"You might as well marry me now," he says. "You know you will, anyway."

Tingles spread over my skin. "Will I?" I ask.

He nods. "On the beach. After you learn how to swim."

I wince. "You had me until you said 'swim.'"

"Aw, come on," James says. "You can't be scared of water for the rest of your life." When tell him that I sure can, James puts his hand behind my neck, pulling me into a soft kiss. "Say yes to me," he murmurs. "Say yes now so I'll never have to ask again."

His mouth, his taste—it's all so familiar and exciting. It's heavy and suffocating, it's then and now. "Yes," I whisper finally, closing my eyes as I snuggle against him. "I'll marry you someday, James. I'd do anything for you."

I can feel his jaw shift as he smiles, taking my hand to squeeze his fingers between mine before kissing my ring finger.

# CHAPTER ELEVEN

BREAKFAST IS ALL SORTS OF AWKWARD AS I SIT across from Realm, James next to me with his body turned slightly away. I would have figured James to be more of the possessive type, somehow claiming me in front of Realm while crunching on his Frosted Flakes. But instead he has only a small smirk that I notice between spoonfuls.

"You're happy today," Realm says, eyeing him as he drinks black coffee from a Styrofoam cup. Dallas glances over from where she sits on the counter, studying James's expression until she understands, and then turns away.

"I am so very happy," James replies to Realm, not looking up.

"It won't last," Realm snaps. "You know that."

James smiles broadly, finally meeting Realm's suspicious gaze. "You have no idea how long I can last," James says with a little laugh. He pushes back from the table, grabbing his bowl. He kisses the top of my head before walking to the sink, pats Dallas's leg, and then leaves the room—smiling the entire time.

Realm's dark stare flicks to me; the quiet guy who showed up yesterday is gone. "See the two of you made up," he says.

I've suddenly lost my appetite. The first time I introduced Realm to James, they nearly killed each other, because Realm was being a dick to me. Right now this is feeling pretty familiar. "When were James and I fighting?"

"Before you left Oregon. When you came to my house and kissed me. Unless you forgot about that."

There's the clink of a bowl before Dallas hops down from the counter. "That would be my cue to exit," she says. "Realm, I'll catch up with you at the site later."

Realm reaches for her as she starts past him, touching her hand. There's a slight twinge in my stomach. "Just give me a few minutes, Dal," he says kindly. She considers, but then after an annoyed look in my direction, she nods and walks out.

The weight of an impending argument floods the room— even though I'm not entirely sure what Realm and I have to fight about. Yes, I kissed him, but that was because of The Program. They tried to erase James, but I still loved him. Even Realm saw that.

"If you're going to be a jerk," I start. "Then—"

"What did you expect, Sloane?" Realm puts his elbows on the table, leaning forward like he's ready to pounce. "I told you to stay away from James—that he'd make you sick again.

And yet here you are on the run because of him, because you were being reckless and The Program was called. Do you think I should applaud that? What the hell do you want from me?"

"I don't know," I say. "For you to go back to the way you were in The Program."

"You mean the way you want me to be."

"That's not what I'm saying."

"It doesn't work like that. You don't get to dictate how I act, how I feel."

"I'm not trying—"

"You're not?" he shouts, and I straighten up, alarmed by his harsh tone. "Why didn't you take the pill, Sloane? Why can't you remember?" I immediately look toward the door, afraid someone might have overheard. Realm's mouth opens, a knowing expression on his face. "It's because of him, isn't it?" he demands. "You didn't take it because of James."

"It was an impossible choice! There was only one pill—how could I choose?"

"Easy. I gave it to you."

I shake my head. "And what about the danger? How was I supposed to take that leap of faith while people are going crazy from their memories? That's what happened to Lacey!"

"The pill isn't like recall. It's not a stress fracture. It brings back what The Program locked away, and sure, it hurts, but it wouldn't have killed you."

I lean toward him, trying to keep my voice hushed, but I'm failing. "Oh, that's very comforting. But this wasn't just about

James. Your sister told me I might not like what I found in my past. I don't know who I was, Realm. But I know who I am now. What's wrong with wanting to live in the now?"

Realm's expression softens, and he stretches his hand in my direction, just short of touching mine. "There's nothing wrong with it," he says. "Was that all Anna told you?"

"She said I might not forgive you. Why? What have you kept from me?" I don't remember much of my time in The Program. There are fragments, bits where I was playing cards or laughing with Realm. But my past is gone, as are the pasts of others. Somehow Realm held on to my history. He didn't tell me right away, not until I demanded it. I can feel he has more secrets; his sister all but confirmed that he does. Yet . . . I still trust him. I trust him even though I know he's lying to me.

"Anna never wanted me to remember. She said the past would be too painful. And to be honest, I can understand where she's coming from. But I've told you everything I can, Sloane," Realm says, clearly frustrated. "That has to be enough. If you take the pill, you'll know the truth."

"And if I don't take it? If I give it to James, what will he remember?"

Realm's eyes narrow at the thought of me giving his gift to James instead. "Maybe he'll realize you don't belong together."

I try to retract my hand, but Realm grabs it. "I'm sorry," he says quickly. "I'm sorry, sweetness. Don't leave."

"Like you left me?" The words hit me, and the grief and

worry I felt about Realm's sudden disappearance crashes down. "You gave me a stupid pill and then you left me," I whisper.

Realm winces and brings my hand to his lips. "I know," he murmurs into my skin. "But I love you so much." He kisses my knuckles. "I wanted you to have a chance to remember." My wrist. His touch radiates over my skin, twisting me up, confusing me. "Tell me that you missed me too."

My breathing deepens as Realm kisses my inner forearm. He's inside my head—I know it. But I can't deny that I missed him. I did. I really, really did.

"I missed you," I whisper as his hand slides up my arm, cupping my shoulder to pull me close enough to kiss. In front of me, Realm's deep brown eyes are earnest but dark. Dark and tortured. It brings me back to my senses, and Realm must read it in my expression because his jaw hardens.

"James doesn't love you," he says slowly, his breath warm across my lips. "If he did, he would have *made* you take that pill."

There's a sound, and both Realm and I turn to see James standing in the doorway. He's still, his expression unreadable. I push Realm's hand away and jump back from the table, but I know it's too late. James saw—heard—all of that. He doesn't look at me again, only continues to stare at where I was sitting. And then, without a word, James turns and leaves.

The walk to the bedroom seems endless. My heart thuds, my mouth is dry. James heard my and Realm's conversation, saw

Realm close enough to kiss me. How could I have let that happen?

"James?" I call softly as I push open the door to our room. The closet door is ajar, the chain for the light still swaying.

"Do you think he's right?"

I spin and find James in the far corner of the room. He doesn't sneer, or do anything even remotely hateful. He just looks heartbroken, unable to meet my eyes. In his fist he clutches the plastic Baggie.

"About the pill?" I ask, wanting nothing more than to fix the damage I've inflicted. James would never have let another girl get that close to him, and Dallas sure tried.

James looks up, his blue eyes rimmed in red. "About me," he says. "Do you think I should have made you take the pill?"

I start to say no, but James has already made up his mind. Realm's words have shaken him, made him doubt everything. It's as if Realm knows exactly how to hurt us.

James holds out the wrapped pill, but I can't even look at it, so he shoves it into his back pocket. "James—" I start.

"No more lies," he interrupts. "Right now, with Realm, what was that? Christ, Sloane. Did you sleep with him?"

"Of course not!"

"I heard you. You missed him." His lips pull apart in anguish, his eyes weaken. "You nearly kissed him. I . . . I saw all of it, and not once"—he jabs his finger in my direction—"did you tell him to stop."

Tears drip onto my cheeks, but there's nothing I can say. I have no excuse. I did miss Realm; I didn't lie about that. There's

SUZANNE YOUNG

an unspoken bond between us that doesn't seem connected to any specific memory. I trust Realm with my life. And sometimes he uses that against me.

"I don't know you right now," James says. "Because to me"—he motions toward the hall—"it looks like he's your boyfriend. And I'm jealous! God, I'm a fucking jealous asshole and I hate it!" He groans, tugging roughly at his hair. "I thought it was me and you, Sloane. It was me and you forever or not at all."

"I want forever too."

"He gave you a pill," James says. "He gave you a way to bring back all your memories. I don't have that power, and who the hell knows how I would react if I did. Maybe he's right. Maybe I should have made you take it."

There's a sound, and James and I both look over to see Dallas standing in the doorway, holding a can of Coke. "What pill?" she asks, not even trying to pretend she wasn't listening to our conversation. Her dark eyes flick to James, but he only seems annoyed at her interruption. When I don't respond, Dallas steps into the room. The click of her boots is loud in the small space as she sets her soda on the dresser. "What pill?"

"Ease off," Realm says. My gut sinks when Realm walks in behind her, shooting a cautious glance at James before addressing Dallas. "I gave it to her."

Dallas spins on him, but before she can react, James is moving. He crashes into Realm and the two slam into the bare white wall. Realm gets in the first punch, his closed fist connecting high on James's cheek with a loud *thwack*. I scream, rushing forward, but then they're on the ground, a flurry of movement I can't untangle.

"Stop!" I scream, reaching to grab James's arm as he pulls back to punch Realm, but he only shakes me off before getting hit again and knocked sideways. Realm scrambles on top of him, but James blasts him in the face, blood spurting instantly from Realm's nose. Dallas exhales, finally coming over to help. I'm yelling for both guys to stop, but they seem bent on killing each other. Blood is pouring over Realm's lips as he sputters out random bits of rage; James is swinging at whatever he can hit.

Realm falls to the side and James gets to his knees, fist raised to smash down on Realm's face, until Dallas pulls something out of her pocket. The switchblade flashes, and then she's got the knife to James's throat, stopping him cold. My eyes are wide as Dallas has her arm twisted around James's neck, the blade biting into his skin. He lifts his eyes to where she is, his chest heaving and a trickle of blood coming from the cut on his cheekbone.

"I can't let you kill him," she says. "Sorry, James."

For a moment we're all quiet, and then Dallas lowers her knife, and James—watching her the entire time—climbs to his feet. He glances in my direction before walking out. I want to check that he's okay, but I decide to give him some time to cool off.

Realm sits up, resting his elbows on his bent knees as he lets the blood continue to run down his face. Drops tap on the wood floor. Dallas looks between us, her expression darkening before she goes over to grab her drink, taking a long swig.

I'm in shock, unable to utter a word, until Dallas throws her half-filled soda at Realm, hitting him in the shoulder before the can falls to the ground, sending out a sticky spray of Coke. I yelp and step back, staring at her as soda foams from the mouth of the can.

"So you got ahold of The Treatment," she snarls at Realm, "and you gave it to *her*?" Dallas glares in my direction and I shrink away with immediate guilt.

"Not the time, Dallas," Realm says. "We'll talk about this later."

"Don't dismiss me. I swear to God, I'll—"

Realm jumps to his feet, the bottom half of his face still awash with blood. He looks insane, and for the first time I can remember, I'm scared of him. Realm balls his hands into fists, but Dallas doesn't back away.

"Get out," he says through clenched teeth.

"Not until you tell me how you got it. Not until you tell me why her!" Dallas is coming undone, her lips quivering like she might cry. I expect Realm to reach for her, call her "sweetness," and soothe away her anger. But he doesn't.

"You don't matter, Dallas," he says seriously. "You don't matter the way she does and you know it. I love her. And that's all I'm going to say about it."

A terrible silence falls over the room, and Dallas lowers her eyes, injured by Realm's words. In them I feel betrayal, and the emotion strikes me as familiar—even though I can't place where it's from.

"I hate both of you," Dallas murmurs, not lifting her head as she leaves.

I don't care if Dallas hates me—the feeling is mutual. But when Realm's posture sags, I know there's more to their relationship than friends with benefits. And yet he was so quick to send her away, crush her. Is that how he cares? When I no longer matter, will he dismiss me, too?

Neither Realm nor I make a move to clean the mess of soda Dallas left behind. My body is still shaking with adrenalin, but underneath I'm drowning in the deep darkness, aching everywhere.

"What's going on, Realm?" I ask. "What is The Treatment?"

He drags his forearm over his chin to clean off some of the blood. "That little orange pill you've been hiding," he says, "is the cure for The Program—they call it The Treatment. There were only a few prototypes, but after The Program found out about them, they destroyed the laboratory. They destroyed the scientist who made them too. But there was one pill left."

I don't deserve this, not when Dallas or James or probably a hundred others would give anything to take it. "Why did you give it to me?"

"Because you needed it," he says simply. "You went off the grid, broke their rules. The Program wants you back, Sloane. And this was the only way I could protect what's left of you."

"But how—"

"I'm sorry to interrupt." Cas stands in the doorway, his hair pulled into a ponytail and his chin unshaven. He darts an uneasy look around the trashed bedroom. "We have a visitor," he adds.

Realm's hand immediately grips my elbow, pulling me to stand behind him. "Who is it?" he asks quickly. "And how did they find us?"

"Looks like Dallas got ahold of the doctor after all."

Realm curses under his breath, but I'm freaking out, terrified of the word *doctor*.

"Has he said anything?" Realm asks, wiping his bloody hands on the bottom of his T-shirt as if it'll be enough to make him presentable.

"Just that he's here to talk. He asked for them," Cas says, motioning to me.

I take in a sharp breath. "No," I say. "Realm, are they going to take me?"

"No, sweetness," he says. "Dallas has been searching for this man for a while—against my objections." He shakes his head, a mix of annoyance and anger. "I don't think he's a threat. He's not with The Program." Realm and Cas exchange a look before Realm starts for the door, muttering under his breath: "At least not anymore."

I'm a total mess as I walk downstairs, fearful of the doctor, guilty for what I've put James through, ashamed I've taken Realm's gift for granted—Dallas's reaction proves it. I walk into the living room and Dallas's scowl from the couch radiates white-hot hatred. I move to the other side of the room. Realm stops to wash his face, and then he meets me in the room. Cas walks past us toward the kitchen, where I assume the doctor is waiting.

I expect James to come in, but the minutes tick by without him. I shoot a few cautious looks in Dallas's direction, but she seems unconcerned with his absence. I, however, am beginning to freak out.

"Where's James?" I murmur to Realm. He shrugs, annoyed I'd even pose the question to him. I'm about to call to Dallas, when there's movement from the hallway and I startle as a man strides into the room, not waiting for Cas to introduce him.

The man is tall and thin underneath his charcoal suit. He has a gray beard and mustache. He looks like someone's rich old grandpa, but when he speaks, his voice is crisp as it cuts through the quiet room.

"You're completely vulnerable here," he says. He searches until he finds Dallas. "What if I was a handler?"

"Then you'd be wearing white."

He doesn't crack a smile. "You know that's not what I mean, Miss Stone. All of you," he motions around the room, "are accessories. One slipup will land you in jail, or worse, in The Program. I suggest you keep your guard up. I won't be able to save you if you're caught."

Dallas's hard exterior wanes and she begins to chew on her thumbnail, averting his eyes. Everyone else is calm as this man stands in front of us like he's in charge. James is missing and I'm suddenly alone.

"Who are you?" I ask the man finally.

The doctor slides his hands into the pockets of his suit and presses his lips together in apology. "I'm sorry it's taken us so long to be introduced," he says somberly. "I've been following your case for some time, Miss Barstow." He takes a step toward me and extends his palm. "I'm Dr. Arthur Pritchard, and I'm the creator of The Program."

# PART II
# THE TREATMENT

## THE PROGRAM TIGHTENS CONTROL

With the increasing restrictions put forth by The Program, teens have turned to a new form of expression. Suicide Clubs have cropped up all over the country—illegal underground parties where drugs, alcohol, and depression are commonplace.

Authorities worry Suicide Clubs will lead to a spike in self-termination, and they're expending considerable resources to track down the proprietors. A recently raided club in Utah touched off a manhunt spanning several states, but The Program isn't providing any further details about the suspects at this time. However, they're asking for the public's help in reporting any and all suspicious behavior.

With the rise of Program-related arrests, the concern of government interference in personal matters has come up again and again. But as the epidemic rages on, inquiries into The Program's methods continue to be ignored. The focus remains on the success rate of returners and containment of the worsening outbreak.

—Reported by Kellan Thomas

# CHAPTER ONE

I SWAY, COMPLETELY STUNNED AS PINPRICKS OF fear inject me with panic. Having the creator of The Program know your name is a bit like Death calling out to you. But here he is, the man who ruined our lives, standing in front of me. No one is reacting the way they should. I scoff at his outstretched hand and then look accusingly around at the others. Everything about the world is upended from what it should be: James isn't here, but the creator of The Program is. This can't really be happening.

Cas calmly goes to sit next to Dallas, but Realm has angled his body so he can step in front of me if he has to. Although I appreciate it, I'd think he'd want to stop the madness happening right now. But he's just standing here.

"Why are you here?" I demand from the doctor. He looks

at his hand and lowers it. My body begins to tremble, and I'm sure he can see it. "What more could you possibly want from us?" I ask.

"First let me assure you that I have no intention of harming any of you. In fact, as Dallas can tell you, I'm here to help. We all want the same thing, Sloane. An end to The Program."

"You expect me to believe that?" I snap. "You ruined my life. You're a monster!" I spin, looking around at the others in the room. "What is wrong with all of you?"

"Hear him out," Cas says. "You don't know the whole story." I shake my head in complete and utter disbelief.

"Thank you, Mr. Gutierrez," the doctor tells him, and turns back to me. "My dear," he continues, and I cringe under his caring tone, "you are the perfect example of why The Program can never truly work. It's in your personality to fight for what you believe in, what you love. The Program will fail because, although it can erase memories, the basic personalities remain unchanged. This leads to repeating the same behaviors, and ultimately, the same risks and mistakes."

What he's describing sounds like my and James's relationship. It reminds me that if we fought before and failed, we were stupid enough to try again. "There's no way I'd ever trust you," I tell Dr. Pritchard. "I don't want your help."

"I'm afraid you don't have another choice." He looks at Dallas. "I know you contacted me in hopes of better news, Miss Stone, but your intelligence was correct. The epidemic has spread. There's a call to action, and The Program is using this to further their agenda."

It feels like the world has dropped out from under me. Before he killed himself, Liam had told me about his cousin—an adult—who committed suicide. He was raving about the epidemic spreading, but I attributed it to his depression. I thought he'd gone crazy. But Liam was right.

Dr. Pritchard takes a stark white handkerchief out of his pocket and wipes the sweat that has begun to gather on his brow. He loosens his tie. He sits on a stool in the front of the room as if he's a teacher and we're his class. I'm ready to run, find James, and get out of here.

"There have been several incidents of termination just this morning," the doctor says. "Young men and women in their early twenties, no known exposure to stimulus. Now The Program is evolving to combat the worsening epidemic. There was a story that ran a few weeks ago, but it was quickly buried."

"What are you going to do?" I ask. What sort of action is The Program proposing? How much more can they take from us?

"No," the doctor states. "Not me. I may have created The Program, but I lost control of it months ago. It's a corporation, bought and paid for by the U.S. government—and they expect results."

Could The Program be worse than we thought? Is that even possible? Next to me Realm remains quiet, but his turned shoulder looks less like protection now. He doesn't want

Arthur Pritchard to notice his face. Secrets. Realm is full of secrets, and I don't think I can take any more at this point.

"What are they planning?" I ask the doctor. The fight has gone out of my voice, replaced with fear.

"Mandatory admittance," Dr. Pritchard responds. "Everyone under the age of eighteen will go through The Program. That means, before graduation, every person will be erased and re-created as a well-balanced, well-behaved individual. Complacency. An entire generation lost—as I'm sure you feel now, Miss Barstow."

Mandatory admittance for people who aren't even depressed is like mass brainwashing. Some sick and twisted version of utopia. There's no way the public would let that happen. Right?

The doctor continues. "The Program is trying to jumpstart new polices. They've shown they are one hundred percent effective, proven their preventative measures work. And so now everyone under eighteen will be changed—for better or for worse—against their will. Think of what they can do with that much control," he says. "Think of what they can create from a society without any experience, any learned mistakes. People without connections."

"Then stop it," I say forcefully. "If you tell the government what's really going on with The Program, they'll put an end to it."

"And there lies my dilemma," the doctor says, clasping his hands together under his chin. "Like everyone who works for The Program, I have a gag order—a binding contract that gives them the right to take my memories—to wipe the slate clean if I violate the confidentiality agreement. Only they won't stop there—not with my security clearance. They'll lobotomize me," the doctor says. "The Program considers some returners, and others like me, beyond help. When brought back into The Program, a patient's evaluated. And if erasure isn't an option, they're subject to a lobotomy. It's the last resort of an otherwise flawless operation. It's how The Program keeps their success rate at one hundred percent."

Realm's hand closes around mine, but I can barely feel him. It's like the edges of my reality are breaking apart. "Then what?" I ask weakly.

"Their entire personalities are stripped and they're institutionalized. They're wiped off the map, my dear. Evaporated into thin air."

No, it's too cruel. It's too cruel to be a real possibility. "How can any rational human being inflict this on another? How can this happen in a civilized world?" I ask.

"Haven't they done it before?" the doctor asks. "Years ago, when physicians didn't know how to treat the mentally ill, they began shock therapy, and in extreme cases—lobotomies. They would poke holes in their brains, Miss Barstow. Human beings are cruel creatures. And what we don't understand, we tamper with until we destroy it. The epidemic is forcing the world to focus on mental disease, but they've twisted it into something to be feared, rather than treated. I'm afraid the public support is not behind you on this. We're in the middle of an epidemic killing our children. You have no idea how far the world will go to stop it."

He's right. I know he's right, but all I want to do is scream that he's a liar. I want James to burst in and call, "Bullshit!" and punch him in the face. But that doesn't happen. Instead loneliness and terror bind together to consume me.

"We make no difference compared to the many they can save," Arthur Pritchard says. "And if I go to the press, give The Program any indication that I'm no longer on their side, they will neutralize me. I need to complete my work before they do."

I lift my eyes to his, my vision hazy from the gathering tears. "What sort of work is that?"

"A pill," he says. "One that can counteract the effects of The Program and prevent erasure. It's called The Treatment."

My hand slips from Realm's and I immediately glance at Dallas. She has no noticeable reaction as she twists a dread around her finger. *Oh God. Please don't say anything, Dallas.*

"I need to locate The Treatment," Dr. Pritchard says. "I plan to analyze it so it can be reproduced. If I can prevent The Program from erasing others—then it will be obsolete."

My mouth has gone dry and I feel as though there's a spotlight on me. Does he know Realm gave me the pill? Is that why he's here?

"Say you do bring all the memories back," Realm says quietly. "Not everyone can handle them—what will you do to stop them from killing themselves?"

The doctor's eyes narrow slightly as he looks Realm up and

down. "People will still die, son. I can't claim otherwise. But after we restore the original memories, we'll treat the depression as best we can with traditional therapy. We'll work through the issues, rather than avoiding them."

I can't believe what I'm hearing. He's actually making sense, but I'm scared this is all an act. No, I'm sure it's all an act. But how can he say these things and not see the truth in them? At the same time, how did the doctor know about the pill? Realm said it was the last one and that The Program thought it'd been destroyed. Who's the bigger liar here—Realm or Arthur Pritchard?

"They tried that," I say, facing Dr. Pritchard. "In the beginning they tried regular therapy, but it didn't work. Why should I think yours will be any different?"

"The problem was that they didn't—I didn't—give therapy enough time to be effective. We moved forward too quickly. And now it's time to set things right. I believe The Program itself is adding to the pressure, leading to more suicide attempts. You live in a pressure cooker. It's not right."

"It's not," Dallas agrees, drawing all our gazes. "But tell me more about this pill you're looking for, Arthur. Where did it come from? I've heard only rumors."

*What the hell is Dallas doing?*

The doctor crosses his legs, resting his folded hands on his thighs. "Dr. Evelyn Valentine never believed in The Program," he starts. "While working there, she created a pill and tested it on several returners. There had been various incarnations, but eventually she found one that worked. It restored all their memories, and with it, their depression. One terminated himself immediately, and before Evelyn could properly treat her patients, she disappeared. Her files were destroyed, and the records of her patients went missing. The Program never found them. That's why I think there's still a pill or two out there. I'm looking for it. Evelyn's cure is gone, but I'd like to create another one in her absence."

My heart thumps; I expect Dallas to point one of her bony fingers in my direction, telling the doctor that I'm the person who has it. But her face remains neutral, loyal to Realm. Despite what he said earlier, she won't betray him. I think Dallas loves him.

"I don't understand," I say, shaking my head. "Why do you need the actual pill? The formula can't be that complicated to figure out. Wouldn't that be easier than hunting down what might not even exist?"

Dr. Pritchard's eyes lock on mine, and I feel myself wilt under their heavy suspicion. "No one knew the formula other than Evelyn, and she was a better chemist than any of us. Do you think I haven't exhausted all other options? I've spent everything I have trying to buy scientists to help me, but they're all with The Program—or scared of them. There's no one left to fight with me. Except those of you here. I don't think you realize how dire our situation is. I don't think you realize how truly alone we are.

"If The Program finds the pill before we do," he continues, "the formula will be lost. They plan to extract the ingredients, patent them, and make their production illegal. At least now we can continue testing. But once they have control of the substances, then no other treatment—nothing The Program doesn't approve of—will ever be made."

It's all around me then, the pressure, suffocating and absolute. When the only person left to trust is the creator of The Program, all is lost. Realm reacts, walking swiftly from the room without a word, the doctor's eyes following him the entire way. When he's gone, it's like I can't get in a full breath—like a panic attack. Arthur Pritchard continues to talk, but soon I'm heading for the door.

"I need you, Sloane," he calls to my back. The use of my first name startles me, but I don't turn. "Together we can change the world."

He's offering hope where there is none. But isn't that a form of brainwashing in itself? Hope in place of change? I shake my head, a small whimper caught in my throat, and leave—desperate to find James.

Outside of the room I'm able to breathe again, even though I'm still trembling. The house is eerily quiet as I pass through the kitchen, not finding James, and I head upstairs toward the bedrooms. Mine is empty, and it's like I'm engulfed in isolation. James might not sleep here tonight. It'll be the first time we've been apart since leaving Oregon.

I put my palm on my forehead, trying to steady myself. I can't start thinking of the negative. I can't afford to lose my sanity right now. I'm a fugitive, and I have to be smarter.

Realm's room is down the hall, and when I walk in, I find

his bed pushed next to the window. He's sitting there, staring into the dark beyond it. He reminds me of a lost little boy, and for a second I want to hold him and tell him it will all be okay.

"I don't trust the doctor," Realm says, startling me. He turns, and his cheeks and neck are a blotchy red. "I think he's lying."

I obviously don't trust the doctor either, but I'm curious as to Realm's reasoning. I go to sit beside him, gnawing on the inside of my lip as I wait for him to explain. This is the first time I've been in his room since leaving The Program. There's nothing here beyond the scratchy blue blanket and the hard mattress of his crooked bed. There's nothing that says who Realm is. Even I have a few possessions, and I've been on the run since leaving school weeks ago.

Realm exhales, glancing outside once again. "I moved the bed next to the window because otherwise I start to feel claustrophobic, locked up. I check the pane at least three times a day, just to make sure it's not sealed." He looks at me. "Just to make sure I'm not locked in."

"Side effect of The Program?"

"Among other things. And having Arthur Pritchard here doesn't exactly help to ease my anxiety. I don't trust him, and I need to get as far away from him as possible."

Realm is always full of secrets. But this one he'll have to share. "Why?" I demand.

"Because," he says with a shrug, "Evelyn was a friend of mine. And I'm one of those patients she cured."

# CHAPTER TWO

REALM'S WORDS SMASH TOGETHER AND FALL AROUND me, heavy as stones. His secret is so much bigger than anything I could have imagined. Realm has been cured. *When did this happen? What else hasn't he told me?*

Realm searches my expression. "What do you think of that, Sloane? How do you feel about the fact that I have all of my past but never told you?"

"I think you're a dick." Only I'm in such shock that I'm not sure how I feel about it. His sister had said he was saving it for after The Program, but he was already cured. He was lying to her, too.

Realm smiles, but there's no humor in it. "I wish you really did hate me," he says. "But I know you don't. Not yet."

He reaches to touch my hand, a movement too intimate

while we're on his bed, and I pull away. Realm opens his mouth to speak, but then he promptly shuts it as his gaze moves past me to the door. My heart leaps and I expect James, but instead I find Dr. Pritchard standing there.

"May I talk to you, Miss Barstow?" he asks. Terrified, I look at Realm. He rubs his palm over his face, then meets my eyes.

"I'll be right outside, okay?" he says quietly. "Nothing will happen to you."

"You're going to leave me here with him?" I whisper back fiercely. I'm trying to gather my nerve, but it's not easy when the doctor is standing behind me. Because either he knows I was given the pill, or he knows Realm has taken it before. Which means Realm shouldn't leave me alone with the Program doctor! I'm not like him or James—I can't just lie my way out of everything.

"You'll be fine," Realm whispers, widening his eyes as if asking me not to reveal what he just told me. Oh, sure. I haven't even had time to process it, but let's pretend I don't know. I'm hiding so many things I'm starting to lose track.

Realm touches my shoulder as he gets up, and once he's gone, the doctor comes to sit next to me on the bed. I feel him watching me, and slowly I lift my head, petrified of what he's here to say. Rather than continue pleading for my help, he takes out his wallet to remove a photo. When he hands me the picture, I see tears gathered in his eyes.

"I'm sorry for all that's happened to you, Sloane." He pauses. "May I call you Sloane?" I shrug, a noncommittal answer, and then gaze down at the picture. "I think it's time you hear the reason," he continues. "The purpose behind it all. I want you to know why I created The Program."

The words are too big for me to comprehend. It's as if God has just shown up to tell me the meaning of life—only it's not God. It's the disturbed doctor who stole who I was. And now he's going to tell me why.

Arthur Pritchard taps the corner of the picture I'm holding. "She was seven when this was taken," he says with a faint smile. "My daughter, Virginia." For the first time I study the picture in my hand. There's a little girl wearing a princess crown, a feather boa wrapped around her neck. She's yelling or laughing, I'm not sure which. But the picture is sweet and sad and oddly lonely. The doctor takes it back from me.

"She had just turned fifteen the day I came home early from the office," he says. "I found her hanging from a wooden beam in the attic. The rope was poorly tied. I imagine she struggled to breathe for quite a while."

I blink quickly against the sick image of a girl suffering. I can feel her desperation, her isolation. It strikes me that I was probably suicidal once, suffering and alone. I'm alive now. Had I changed my mind in my last moments? Had my brother? Had Virginia?

"She left a note," Dr. Pritchard continues. "A page of scribbles and nonsense. Virginia's mother passed away when she was just a baby, and so it'd just been the two of us for so long. My daughter was among the first of the epidemic."

I want to tell him I'm sorry, but I don't. I don't know how to tell the man who ruined our lives that I'm sorry for his loss, not when I can't even remember all that I've lost.

Dr. Pritchard tucks the picture back into his wallet, running his index finger over the plastic where the photo has started to fade. "I used to work with the pharmaceutical companies," he says. "I would prescribe medications for depression. But after Virginia's death, and after the news started to break that antidepressants were a possible cause, I threw myself into finding a cure. I lost six patients in one week. I couldn't keep them alive."

"What caused the epidemic?" I ask him. The thought of finally knowing the answer makes my body electric in anticipation.

"It was a combination of factors," he says simply. "Side effects of medications, news coverage, behavioral contagion. The government is about to pass a law banning stories about suicide from the news networks. They claim it's contributing to the outbreak—the cases of copycats. We'll never know exactly where it started, Sloane. We can only guess. But we tried for a cure right away. I got a committee together—ones who were fearful enough to volunteer their own children as test subjects. We experimented with a mix of counseling and medication, intense psychotherapy. We even lobotomized one at his father's insistence. We tried everything. But then we found that if we take out the behavior, the contagious part of the epidemic, then the patients could retain most of their personalities. It became the trick of how to target them.

SUZANNE YOUNG

"Some of the smartest minds of our time came together to create The Program. I'm the one who created the black pill, the last step in locking away the memories—the final pill you take. It was meant to be a permanent solution. Of course, it was all to be followed with extensive world-building, slow integration into society. But after a few months, we weren't at one hundred percent and the committee made it clear that perfection was the ultimate goal. They began to turn up the pressure—they brought in handlers, embedded others. They will stop at nothing to get the results they want—and that comes at the expense of your lives. Even if you take The Treatment now, you can't really go back to who you were, Sloane. Too much has changed now. You see that don't you?"

"Maybe I don't want to be who I was," I say, a familiar ache at my words. "I just want The Program to leave me alone."

"Yes, I suppose that's true. But it's not that easy. The Program has many flaws, and one they're starting to discover is with the returners themselves. The brain is smarter than any therapy can be, and trauma and overstimulation are affecting rehabilitation. Mandatory resetting is inevitable for someone like you—a person in a high-stress situation. It's the only way to keep you sane."

My stomach takes a sick turn. "Are you saying my memories will come back?"

"No." He shakes his head. "Not all of them. Bits and pieces out of place, sometimes skewed. It occurs only under extreme duress: tragedy, grief, joining up with rebels, say. These cause cracks in the otherwise smooth surface The Program created. I can imagine it would be very traumatizing to have these unfamiliar thoughts. People have gone crazy from them." He pauses to study me. "Have you had this problem, Sloane?"

"No," I lie. It happened when I remembered Miller. I saw what it did to Lacey. Dr. Pritchard's telling the truth about this. Could he be telling the truth about everything?

"That's good," the doctor says, smiling. "That means it's not too late. If I had the pill, I could clear the fog and treat the real problem. The Program's locked away your memories, like those of your brother, to keep you from killing yourself too. What I'm suggesting is that they let patients keep the painful stuff—and no, life won't be happy and normal. But then again, none of you were really happy, even after your transformation. You wouldn't have joined the rebels otherwise."

"You already told us the public won't be on our side. So why should we risk working with you?" I realize I actually want him to give me a reason.

The doctor folds his hands on his lap. "What's your alternative?"

It wasn't the answer I needed to hear. He thinks he knows best, and that makes Arthur Pritchard just like my parents. Just like The Program. "I can still run," I say.

His jaw hardens and his careful facade begins to fall away. "Don't do that," he snaps. "Don't spend the rest of your life running. You'll never be safe. You'll never have a home."

I had a home with James, even when we were running. I have to find him and apologize, make this right. I'm sick of all the lies and secrets. James and I can leave the rebels for good, and it'll be just me and him—the way we wanted it. I stand, about to find James so we can plan our escape, when the doctor reaches for my arm.

"Sloane, I need that pill," he says. I don't turn back right away, his fingers a vise around my wrist. "We can't let The Program get their hands on it." Heat creeps into my cheeks as I falter for an answer.

"I don't have it," I say as calmly as possible, glancing over my shoulder. The Program is looking for The Treatment—that's what this is. He's still working for them.

"Do you know who does?" he asks.

"No."

He studies me, trying to detect if I'm lying. "Sloane," he says. "The pill is—"

"I get it," I interrupt. "It's the key to saving the world. But I can't help you."

He lets my arm fall, taking a moment to collect himself. "Listen," he begins again, softer. "I know you're angry, but we have a common purpose here. The Program is after you. You and your friends are fugitives, and in my book that makes you my ally. I've told you my plan, put myself at risk. You should take that same leap with me, Sloane. You have nothing else left."

"You may be right," I say with a quick nod, my resolve to

find James overwhelming me. "But I'm still alive, Arthur. And as long as I live, I won't forgive you for what you've done to us." Then, before he can stop me again, I stride toward the door and open it, waving my hand for him to leave.

Realm is standing in the hallway, and he glances between me and the doctor before moving next to me like backup. Arthur Pritchard sighs heavily and gets up. He looks defeated, but I can't trust him. I can't trust the man who created The Program.

"It was nice to finally meet you in person, Sloane," the doctor says. "Please tell James I said hello."

A shiver runs over me, a cold realization. In James's file it mentioned that Arthur Pritchard had been called in for a consult. He knows James. He did this to James. I turn abruptly and start down the hall—desperate to find James and warn him about Arthur.

"James!" I yell just as I get to the stairs. Cas is coming up from below, a crease of concern between his eyebrows.

"Sloane," he starts, sounding pained. I push past him, still calling for James.

*Where is he?*

"Sloane," Cas says again, but this time I can hear in his voice that something's wrong. I stop near the bottom step and turn toward him. He holds up his hands helplessly, and the world around me starts to close in. "Sloane," Cas says, "James left. When Arthur was talking to us, he grabbed the keys and took the Escalade. He said . . ." He pauses, lifting his eyes to

Realm, who nods for him to go on. "He said there's no one he can trust anymore. Then he left."

I reach out to catch the wall as I stumble back, my sneaker slipping off the last stair. James left me. Oh my God. James is gone.

# CHAPTER THREE

**I'M IN A DAZE AS ARTHUR PRITCHARD WALKS PAST** me on the stairs. He doesn't mention James again, even though he clearly heard Cas's admission. Maybe he can see the devastation on my face. When I hear the front door close, I slowly make my way back to my room, not crying, too shocked to cry.

On the dresser is James's file—he left it behind. I wish I could read my file, read about my brother, my friends. I'd know the truth about James. Was he really lying to protect me? Did I love him? I love him now, and yet, I didn't run after him. I *let* him leave.

I lie on the bed and fold my hands over my chest as if I'm dead—in a coffin and rotting. I miss my father, memories of him taking me for ice cream still clear in my head. But the time surrounding my brother's death is gone. How did my father act then? How did he behave when they took me into The Program? I wonder if he even tried to stop them. I wonder if he still loved who I was at that point.

My thoughts are becoming distorted and I curl up on my side, burrowing my cheek into the pillow. I miss James. I miss my home. I miss the memories I no longer have. It's so empty here. I'm so empty.

Cas appears in the doorway, his face filled with the pity I feel for myself. "Can I get you anything?" he asks. "We're a little worried about you."

Realm probably sent him in here to gauge my sanity. Now isn't a good time for my friend to tell me he loves me, to try to take advantage of the situation. Even he knows that. But I won't be a creature to be pitied. I'm not helpless. I can still fight.

"I'm fine," I tell Cas, trying to block it all out. "I just have to stop feeling for a while. Isn't that what The Program wanted in the first place?"

"Jesus, Sloane," Cas says, taking a step inside the room. "You're going a little dark."

But I'm on my feet and past him before he can worry anymore. For a minute I'm better. My chest feels hollow, but the ache has dulled. The respite slips when I get to the kitchen and find Realm sitting at the dinner table, eating ramen noodles. Dallas is behind him, staring daggers at the back of his head while she twirls noodles around her fork.

"Is there any food left?" I ask, motioning toward their bowls. Dallas hitches up one of her eyebrows in surprise, and

Realm looks astonished to see me out of the bedroom so soon. Cas goes to fill a bowl from the counter before setting it in front of an empty seat. He watches me cautiously as I sit down. I take a bite and the food is tasteless, a soggy mass of noodles that I don't want to consume. But right now survival is key.

I can't bring myself to look at Realm. He's the reason James left. He's been lying to me. He's had his memories this entire time. It doesn't make sense, though. How many times has he been through The Program? How can he still remember? My suspicions start to gnaw at me, but when I pick up my head, Dallas has turned her hatred to me.

"So he left you?" she asks.

She might as well have punched me. Water floods my eyes, and I grip my fork so tightly the metal bites into my skin. "Please don't," I murmur, setting down the utensil. Realm continues eating.

"Don't what?" Dallas asks innocently. "I'm just making dinner conversation."

"He'll come back," Cas says, drawing my attention. "Don't pay attention to Dallas—she's just being a bitch. We all know James will be back."

"Shut up, Cas," Dallas sneers. "You don't know what you're talking about. Besides, we're not staying here. Sloane's got The Treatment. She's had it this entire time."

Cas's eyes go round and his breathing catches like he's been struck. But I immediately look at Realm as a realization hits me: I don't have The Treatment. James does. Oh my God,

James put it in his pocket. Will he take it now that he's not with me?

"We can't leave," I say to Realm, my pulse racing. "We have to wait until James gets back."

Realm exhales, pushing his bowl aside. "Your love life is the least of our concerns, Sloane. I'm sorry, but we're leaving as soon as night falls."

"I'm not going without James!"

"Well, then I'll drag you out of here!" Realm says, raising his voice. "Unlike your boyfriend, I'm not scared to do what's right for you. We're not risking you or The Treatment because he's throwing a temper tantrum."

I slap my hand down the table, making the forks rattle in the bowls. "Stop it," I hiss. "Stop always trying to break us up. It's not going to work no matter what excuse you put behind it!"

Realm reacts immediately, jumping up from his chair and knocking it to the floor. His cheeks are glowing pink and he looks completely crazed.

"He left you!" he shouts.

"So did you!" But the damage has been done. Realm's words cut me, piercing my vulnerability. I grab my bowl and fling it at the wall, sending bits of ceramic and wet noodles everywhere. I'm so sick of this! If Realm wants a fight, he's got one.

Cas curses under his breath and pushes back from the table. "I'm done," he says dismissively. "You two can go ahead and kill each other." He looks over his shoulder at Dallas, and motions for her to follow him.

Dallas smirks, and then she takes one more slurp of cold noodles before tossing her folk on the table with a clank. "Do kiss and make up, kids," she adds. "It's going to be a long car ride otherwise."

When they're gone, I find Realm watching me. "You're being horrible," I tell him. "You know I'm hurt and you're still being cruel. What's wrong with you?" I'm angry, feeling a deep resentment toward him I don't fully comprehend. Or maybe I just don't remember.

"If you're waiting for me to tell you how to fix things between you and James," he says, "that's never going to happen."

"I don't expect you to. I . . . I thought you were my friend, but we keep ending up like this." I motion to the chaos around us. It's clear to me that if anyone is toxic, it's Realm.

"Friend?" Realm laughs, patronizing me. "Sure, sweetness, we're friends. But if I'm being honest, there's a bigger part of me that just doesn't want James to win. You could have come out of The Program and restarted your life. You could have been happy. But instead you went back to him and now look. You have nothing. You have no one." His eyes weaken a little. "How long before you get sick again? Has it started?"

I feel my expression fall because I know it has. The dark thoughts, the isolation, it's all there under the surface. Waiting. Realm swallows hard, reading my reaction.

"I won't lose you, Sloane," he whispers. "I'll kill him if I have to."

"I'd rather die."

Realm turns away. "That's what I'm afraid of."

He's quiet for a moment; his posture slumps. With complete exhaustion, I sit down in my chair, too tired to fight with Realm anymore. Too tired to make excuses for our behavior. "What do I do now?"

"We have to leave," Realm says. "Right now, before the doctor, The Program, whoever comes back. We'll leave this place behind us."

I pause, his intentions becoming clear. "Us?"

He looks up. "Just us."

He isn't listening, not about James, not about what I really want. "Realm, I don't have The Treatment anymore," I say quietly.

His lips part, and he looks absolutely stunned. He runs his hand through his hair. "Well, fuck," he mutters. "Did you take it?"

"No. James has it. When we were in my room, he put it in his pocket. He still had it when he left. I . . . I don't know what he's going to do."

Realm looks around the room like he's trying to gather his thoughts. After a quiet moment he nods his head definitively. "James won't take the pill," he says. "Of course he won't take it."

"I just want him to come back," I say, holding up my hands helplessly. "I don't care about The Treatment."

"You should care about it," he says, righting his chair and collapsing into it. "The Program does. Arthur Pritchard does. It changed my life." He glances away, and I can't tell if he's feeling nostalgic or tormented. "Sloane," he says. "When we met, it wasn't my first time in The Program. Evelyn Valentine had been my doctor, and she chose me to go through the testing—she gave me The Treatment. You see, the depression had started creeping back in, and she'd thought she found the answer. But there is a drawback to the pill. Only the truly strong can survive the crash of memories. Evelyn got me through it with therapy, but she couldn't save all of us. I don't think she could handle the loss.

"She disappeared soon after. I showed up at her office and it'd been ransacked. Evelyn was gone—along with her research, our identities. She kept us a secret from The Program, saving me one last time. As a precaution, they put every patient she'd come in contact with back through The Program, but the pill protected my memories, cemented them. There are only four people who know I've taken The Treatment—no one else, not even my sister. It nearly drove me insane. I wish I could tell you that getting it all back was worth it, but you have no idea how awful it is to remember, Sloane. You have no idea how cancerous it can be."

I've seen the scar on Realm's neck from when he'd tried to kill himself. But I never had to picture it before. It always seemed like it happened to someone else. Now I imagine what it must be like to have all of your dark thoughts descend on you at once. Even if Realm thinks I am, I'm not sure I would have been strong enough to handle that.

"How did The Treatment protect your memories?" I ask. Everyone is so bent on getting this pill, and I still don't even know how it works.

"It made my brain like Teflon," Realm says with a somber

smile. "The dye The Program used couldn't stick. It just slipped away. None of my memories could be targeted for erasure, but of course, the doctors couldn't see that. I learned to become a very talented liar. The good news is: I'll never forget. The bad news is: I can never forget."

"Protection against The Program," I say, a small glimpse of hope finally breaking through my otherwise gloomy existence. What would it be like to have that worry gone?

"They could still lobotomize us," Realm says. "But I can't imagine they would want to do that. It'd be a PR nightmare for them to send you—a recognizable face—back as anything other than well-behaved and complacent."

"What about Arthur? Would he really mass produce it?"

Realm shakes his head. "Evelyn was a smart lady. I don't know what she put in the pills, I really don't, but I'm not sure it is reproducible. Thing is, she never meant for The Treatment to go public. She wouldn't want Arthur to get his hands on the pill; be responsible for the mass suicides she'd been trying to prevent. It broke her heart when Peter died."

The house is eerily quiet around us, and I lean my elbows on the table, glad Realm is finally sharing his secrets with me. "Peter?"

Realm presses his lips into a sad smile. "Peter Alan was my friend, but his memories—he couldn't survive them. He ingested QuikDeath." Realm looks down. "Evelyn destroyed the files after that. She said the risks were too great—one in four. She didn't like those odds."

A new worry spikes as I consider James's reaction to The Treatment. *If he takes it . . .* I swallow hard, unable to finish the thought. I have to find him.

"What about the others?" I ask, hoping for better news. "Who were the others patients?"

Realm bites down on his lip. "Well, you've met Kevin."

"My handler?" Kevin was supposed to be here with us, but he disappeared. Lacey thought The Program got to him, and I know she's right. But if he took The Treatment, then they can't erase him. He'll be okay. Thank God he'll be okay.

Realm's brown eyes are so sorry when he mentions the next name. "And Roger."

All the air seems to whoosh from my lungs, and I slap my hand over my mouth. Realm knew Roger? Roger who bartered for sexual favors in The Program with intimidation and sadistic threats. Roger who ruined Dallas, destroyed her trust in people. Realm knew him and never once mentioned it while we were in The Program together?

"How could you keep that from me?" I demand. Roger is a monster and Realm *knew* him. All the lies are dragging me down, plunging me into a darkness I can't swim out of.

"I'm sorry," Realm says, reaching to take my hand. I don't pull away because I'm starting to drown. "I'm so sorry, Sloane." He pauses, looking down at my hand. "I need you to promise me something: When we get The Treatment back from James, you have to take it. You'll be fine—I swear. But I want you to be protected when The Program finds you."

"*When* they find me?" I get up and stumble back from the table. Roger, Kevin, Realm—they all know each other. There's a hint of something beneath that knowledge, like a memory fighting to surface. Fluid trickles over my lip and I sniffle, wiping my nose. My mouth floods with a metallic taste, and when I glance down at my hand, I see blood.

I hold out my red fingers to Realm, terrified. He quickly comes over and tips my head back, pinching my nose. I'm too shaken to stop him, too shaken to tell him that I want James and not him. Instead I think of how James helped Lacey when this happened to her. And how he told her she would be fine.

Lacey wasn't fine. And I know I'm not either.

# CHAPTER FOUR

I'M SITTING ON THE EDGE OF THE TUB AS REALM dabs a cold washcloth under my nose. Any anger he had is gone, replaced only with concern. For a moment I see him how he was in The Program: sweet, understanding, devoted to me. I want to believe that's the real him, but my mind is spinning, leaving me dizzy.

"Am I going to end up like Lacey?" I mumble under the edge of the washcloth.

"No," he says. "Not unless you have more breaks. It's stress—not normal everyday stress—but this emotional roller coaster you've put yourself on is messing with your head. You're fracturing your memories, but in a scattered way. It can make you crazy, Sloane. You need to take it easier."

"I'm a runner," I say. "It's not like I can kick back on the couch, eating cookies. Things aren't going to calm down any-time soon. If anything, they're just getting more complicated. Why did Dallas have to bring Arthur Pritchard here? Does she buy into his story?"

Realm laughs. "Dallas doesn't trust anybody. She's a really good actress when she needs to be. She wanted to find out what Pritchard knew about The Treatment." He lowers his eyes. "I didn't tell her I had it."

"Yeah, I got that," I say. Dallas pretty much hates us both because of it.

"She hit me with a soda can," Realm says, as if he's just remembering. "I mean, I deserved it, but it was a little violent, even for her. And I'm sure she's not feeling any better about things. Turns out, Arthur Pritchard knew even less about The Treatment than she did."

I take the pink-stained washcloth from his hand, wiping it under my nose to check if the bleeding has stopped. I'm relieved to see it has. "Well," I say, "we did learn about The Program's plan for mandatory admittance."

"Unless he was just saying that to get his hands on The Treatment."

Could he really lie about something so horrible? I groan, frustrated that there's no one to believe. "It's all of us," I say. "We're nothing but a bunch of liars."

Realm climbs up from his knees. "Everybody lies, Sloane. We just happen to be better than the others. It's why we're still alive."

As odd as the statement is, I think it's a reflection of our lives. We're all guilty of hiding things—it's the nature of the world today. We hide our feelings, we hide our pasts, we hide our true intentions. There's no way to know what's real anymore.

Realm reaches to tip my chin up to him, and my breath catches. He looks over my face and then smiles softly. "All cleaned up," he says. "I have to go talk to Cas about our next move. Sloane . . . you know we can't stay here."

"I'm not leaving him." I'm not going anywhere without James. I can't abandon him with The Program after us.

I slowly stand, and Realm holds my arm to steady me. I can see how frustrated he is, but after his take-it-easy speech, he can't exactly express it. I'm not sure if my brains are scrambled eggs already, but I'm going to do my best to not spur on any more memories. I move past Realm, expecting him to call out to me, but he lets me leave.

It's settled. When James gets back, we'll go. Not before. I reach my bedroom, but I pause when I step inside. My closet light is still on. I glance around, seeing nothing else out of place, and then cross to turn off the light. I wait a beat, trying to remember if I left it on—but the night has been a jumble of thoughts and I can't be sure. Either way, it sets me on edge. I climb into bed, wishing James and I had never met up with the rebels, that we'd run off on our own. But I can't rewrite history. I can live only with what's left.

\*     \*     \*

SUZANNE YOUNG

I'm half-asleep, lying in bed in the dark, waiting for James. No one has come to speak to me, even though Realm assured me that Dallas was calling all of her contacts searching for him. I remind myself that Dallas can find anyone, especially James. I'll see him soon. I know I will.

The door hinge creaks and I sit up quickly, my heart leaping into my throat. But it's not James. Realm stands there, flooded in hallway light, his skin pale against the navy of his light jacket, his dark brown hair. Disappointment rocks me, and I rub my eyes.

"Have you heard anything?" I ask, my voice hoarse.

Realm slips his hands into his pockets and shakes his head. I curse and lie back down, staring at the ceiling. If I could just talk to James—he'd understand there's nothing between me and Realm.

"Sloane," Realm says quietly, "I'm sorry. We have to leave. I'm sorry, but we do. The Program is on its way. They picked up Arthur Pritchard about twenty minutes ago. We have to get out of here."

I take a frightened breath, fear and panic tearing through me. Arthur Pritchard is gone—what if he was telling the truth? What if it's my fault that he's been caught?

"Sweetness," Realm says, striding across the shadowy room to sit next to me. "We can talk about this on the way, but we have to go."

I know Realm's right—I really do. "I can't leave him," I say. "Please don't make me leave James behind." This could end him—literally end James if The Program gets ahold of him. "Please," I try one last time.

A figure materializes in the doorway and my heart stops. At first I can't tell if it's James or a handler. I'm about to scream, but the person turns on the light. My stomach sinks.

"Dallas is waiting in the car," Cas says impatiently. He's disheveled, fidgety, and when he glances around the room, I can't help but think he's looking for The Treatment. I wonder if he was the one in my room earlier just as he goes to the dresser, grabbing the duffel bag from the top and stuffing my clothes inside.

"Sloane," Realm says, touching my knee. "We'll find him—I promise. But right now you have to come with us. If not . . . we'll make you. I'm doing what has to be done to keep you safe. I hope you believe that."

There's a sharp pinch of betrayal, and I push him away, climbing out of the bed. I pull on a sweater and then meet Cas across the room, ripping the bag from his hands. He nods to me, apologetic. Through a teary gaze, I get the rest of James's and my clothing.

I have no doubt Realm would throw me over his shoulder or drag me out of here kicking and screaming. What's worse, I know James would never leave me behind like this. He would never do this to me.

My belongings fall to the floor and I squat down, covering my face as I sob into my hands. How can I do this? How can I live with myself if something happens to him?

There's a second of quiet before Cas bends to pick up my

bag. Realm comes to put his arms around me, leaning down and whispering into my hair how sorry he truly is. I continue to cry and let him stand me up, holding on to him so I won't collapse. We walk from the room, but not before I cast one more look back over the room.

Empty.

We've been driving for hours. Stretches of highway blend together, lulling me in and out of sleep. I rest my head against the warm window in the backseat, Realm on the other side of me. There's been no word on James—good or bad, but every time Dallas takes out her phone, my hopes climb and then crash to the ground. Last time I asked her about James, she assured me that if he'd been caught, she'd know instantly. She thinks he's hiding or moping, but either way, she'll find him. I hope she's right.

Arthur Pritchard had been picked up by a group of handlers about thirty miles from our safe house. They hadn't been watching us, not that we think, but the doctor's intentions must have been reported. Someone turned Arthur Pritchard over, and now he belongs to The Program. I just hope he can talk his way out of it. He's the creator—that has to count for something.

"How much longer?" I ask no one in particular. My mouth is dry, and I'm tired of riding in the van. The other rebels have headed to Denver, although I haven't seen them since we left the Suicide Club back in Salt Lake. Cas didn't want them to come with us this time. He said we have to protect The Treatment, which means keeping it a secret for as long as possible. Of course, I'm not currently in possession of the pill, so I guess I'm keeping secrets too.

Dallas tosses an uninterested look in my direction but doesn't answer. "Cas," she says, turning to him instead. "Can we stop? My bladder is about to burst."

"Thanks for the unnecessary explanation," he replies, smiling from the driver's seat. He clicks on his blinker for the exit, and I straighten, ready to stretch my legs. Realm murmurs for her to be quick about it, and Dallas sneers, keeping her body turned away from him. This has been the pattern since we left. Whenever Realm asks her a question, Dallas directs Cas to answer him or stays silent, pretending Realm doesn't exist.

Throughout the drive I've turned over Realm's confessions in my head—every moment in which he lied to me. Realm had been in The Program more than once. He knew Roger. He remembers his life. He's had an unfair advantage our entire friendship: He can never forget.

The car bumps the curb as we pull into the parking lot of a gas station, drawing me out of my thoughts. I'm quiet as we park, and Dallas and Cas quickly hop out. I'm slow to move, but I go outside without a word to Realm, and head into the small convenience store.

Dallas is already in the restroom, and the clerk eyes me suspiciously as I loiter. I'm worried he'll recognize me from the news, and I opt to wait outside instead. I tighten my sweater around me and try to look inconspicuous. I reemerge in the parking lot, and a small blue car pulls up to the pump. I have to be more careful about being seen. I walk around the side of the building, keeping my face concealed. I wonder if James knows to stay in the shadows. I wonder if he even knows we're gone yet.

I rest against the gray siding, waiting for the others. I glance to where the van is parked, but the tinted windows make it difficult to see inside. Which is just as well—I'm sure I'd find Realm guilt-stricken, watching me. I'm not going to make him feel better right now.

"You seem a little lost."

I jump and see a guy walking over, his hands in the pockets of his zip-up hoodie. I recognize him immediately, even though he doesn't look the same. I should run, but I'm rooted in place by fear.

"Who are you?" I ask. Clearly "Adam," who I met at the suicide club, isn't who he pretended to be that night. His hair is brushed smooth, his eyes blue and clear—not the black orbs his contacts had presented. He's wearing a light-green hoodie, preppy in an Abercrombie way, not a returner way. He's also older than I first thought—midtwenties maybe. "Are you a handler?" I demand, afraid someone is about to jump out and grab me.

Adam laughs. "No, Sloane. I'm not a part of The Program— but I am interested to hear your thoughts on it." He pulls his hand out of his sweater pocket, and I flinch like he's going to

Taser me. He holds out a business card, but I can only stare at him.

"It's okay," he says gently. "I promise, I want to help."

"Well, that's the second time I've heard that in the last twenty-four hours. I didn't believe him, either." But Arthur Pritchard could have been telling the truth—after all, The Program took him. Is it possible Adam is telling the truth too?

"Why are you following me?" I ask, darting a look behind him. I expect Realm to show up at any second, but then again, I'm not sure if I want him to. Will it put him danger?

"I don't mean to scare you," Adam says. "But, Sloane . . . you have to understand—you're a big deal in my world." He offers his card again, and this time I take it. I'm caught off guard by what it says.

"Kellan Thomas," I read, then look up surprised. "You're a reporter?"

"For the *New York Times*," he responds. "Been following your story since you disappeared last month. You've taken me on a hell of a chase." He smiles. I go to hand him back his card, but he waves it off, telling me to keep it.

"I didn't tell you right away because I wanted to check your state of mind. In case you've forgotten, messing with returners is against the law. I had to make sure you wouldn't turn me in. But some laws are meant to be broken, especially ones that keep secrets. Will you talk to me, Sloane? Will you tell me your story?"

"Why? What can you do?" I'm beginning to feel anxious; Adam's—Kellan's—presence here is proving we're not that difficult to find. The Program could show up at any second. Arthur had told us the public wasn't on our side. Can Kellan possibly change that? Will he end up like Arthur if he tries?

"I'll be honest," Kellan says. "The paper's been burying my stories, and I have yet to gain access to any of The Program's procedures or methods. They operate under cloaked secrecy, and for a public health institution, that seems a bit unethical. But you and James Murphy—you're a national scandal. There've been other returners, but none with the story you have: a modern-day Bonnie and Clyde. The world is starting to root for you. I can only imagine what The Program thinks of that. I'd like to find out. Let me tell your side of things, bring some awareness to what's happening inside the facilities. What did they do to you, Sloane? What happens inside The Program?"

Kellan is watching me, his eyes wide with impatience even though he's trying to look calm. Arthur Pritchard had mentioned embedded handlers—is Kellan one of them? He could be playing both sides. I open my mouth to tell him it's too dangerous to talk to him, when I hear my name.

"Sloane?" Realm sounds frantic as he calls me a second time. Kellan closes his eyes, exhaling heavily before looking at me again.

"My number's on the card," he says. "Please talk to me. But . . . let's keep this between us. I don't want to end up in jail—or worse."

It occurs to me that I'm the "worse." I hurry past him, jogging out to the front of the gas station, where I see Realm, his clasped hands on his head as he darts a panicked look in all directions. He curses when he sees me.

"There you are," he says when I get closer. "You scared the hell out of me."

"Sorry."

Kellan asked me to keep his existence secret, but it seems that being on the run is really about deciding who to trust. I take Realm's arm and pull him close. "I have to talk to you," I murmur. He eyes me curiously and then looks around the parking lot, pausing when he sees the empty blue car.

"Not here," he says, putting his arm over my shoulders and leading us to the van. "Let's get as far away as we can first."

Cas and Dallas are already in the front seats, and as we pull away from the gas station, my heart races and I debate telling them about Kellan. But instead I look out the window to the side of the building where the reporter is probably watching us. I touch the corner of his business card in my pocket, wondering if I'll ever see him again. There's a small sense of disappointment, because even though I don't trust him, if Kellan was for real, he might have been able to help me find James.

"Dallas?" I say, earning a quick look from Realm. "Have you heard anything on James?"

She turns, but doesn't meet my eyes. "Nothing yet, Sloane." She sounds more apologetic than I would have expected. But then I remind myself that Dallas likes James. Maybe his safe return is a priority for both of us.

"Where exactly are we headed now?" Realm asks.

"Away from the city," Dallas says, speaking to him for the first time. "Middle of nowhere—center of nothing." She grins at him, her gap-toothed smile disingenuous. "You wanted us to disappear, so we are. Hope she's worth it." And then she turns around and puts on the radio, filling the silence.

Cas tells us the drive is too long and we'll have to stop. It's dark when we end up at a seedy motel a few turns off the highway. The VACANCY sign is only half lit up, and Realm heads toward the glassed-in booth to book the rooms. Dallas rolls down her window.

"Book a separate room for me and Cas," she calls coldly. "I'm not sharing a bed with you this time." Realm stops but doesn't respond. It isn't until Dallas's window is closed that he goes to the booth, talking to the person behind the glass.

"Dial it down," Cas mutters, tapping his hands impatiently on the steering wheel. "None of us wants to be in the middle of your lovers' quarrel."

Dallas turns to him. "You didn't hear what he said," she snaps. I feel my gut sink, afraid I'll be dragged into the conversation. "I fucking matter," she tells Cas, her cheeks growing pink. "He has no right to tell me I don't."

Cas reaches to put his hand on her shoulder, trying to pull Dallas into a hug, but she jerks away. "I'm fine," she says. "I wish he'd just vanish again." She glances quickly back at me. "And he can take her with him."

I want to yell that I don't love Realm and I never have. I want to remind her that James—my James—is missing, and her little pity party isn't making any of our lives easier. But it's dark, and Dallas is tired. And really . . . I don't blame her for being angry with Realm. He brings out the worst in all of us.

Once Realm raises the keys to show us the rooms are set, we grab our bags and head up to the second floor. The place is pretty dingy, with peeling yellow paint and ugly green doors. I curl my lip and Cas nods his agreement.

"It was a good choice," Realm says to Cas when he notices our exchange. "They accept cash and don't require ID." He stops in front of room 237 and uses the key—like an actual motel key with numbered chain, and opens the door. Immediately the smell of stale smoke hits my nose; the multicolored comforters on the beds are ratty and flat.

"Gross," Dallas says, looking in.

Realm holds out a key to her. "Dallas, I—"

Dallas takes the key and walks next door. She doesn't shout at him or repeat the things she said in the car. Cas looks weary as he follows her into their room, and I wait to see if Realm will go after Dallas and talk it out. But he just goes inside the room and disappears behind the bathroom door. Great. I'm starting to wonder if any of us will ever be light again, ever laugh, ever . . . live.

I close the front door and slide the chain over the lock. I'm feel like I'm in an eighties slasher flick, and I click on the lamp next to the bed. My belongings all fit inside the duffel bag, and

I open it, peering in at James's file. I can't bring myself to read it, not without James.

The door opens and Realm comes out, his expression unreadable as he goes to the opposite bed and lies down. He folds his hands behind his head and stares up at the ceiling. I lie on my side, too tired to wash my face or change my clothes.

"So," Realm says, sounding exhausted. "What happened at the gas station earlier?"

I never told anyone about the first night I met Kellan, how he knew my name. I'm not exactly sure how to frame the story. "Have you ever been approached by a reporter?" I ask.

"No." Realm scrunches his nose like it's a bizarre question. "Have you?"

I take Kellan's business card from my pocket and stretch it over to Realm. His eyes widen, and he grabs it quickly. He looks it over and then swings his legs to the floor, sitting on the edge of the bed.

"Sloane, how the hell do you know this guy?"

"I met him at the Suicide Club. He looked like everyone else . . . but he knew my name before I told him. At first I thought maybe he was a handler, like the embedded ones Arthur Pritchard told me about. But when we stopped at the gas station on the way here, he showed up. I was terrified. He gave me this card, said he was a reporter for the *New York Times* following my and James's story. He wants information on The Program. I think he can see what they're really doing to us."

Realm runs his fingers through his hair, leaving it sticking up when he drops his arm. "I don't like it," he says. "We shouldn't talk to anyone outside of the rebels. At least not yet. He could be working for The Program."

"I guess." I sit back against the pillows, thinking it over. "But we didn't believe Arthur, and he was picked up by The Program." I turn to Realm. "Do you really think they'll erase him?"

Realm considers my question for a long moment. "There's a chance this is just a stunt to draw us out," he says. "I mean, he's the creator of The Program. Could they really do that to him?"

"I hope not," I murmur. If I could rewind, I'd talk to Arthur longer, find out what else he had to say. If I could rewind time, I'd do so many things differently. My bottom lip quivers and I bite down on it. "Tell me James is okay," I whisper.

"I can't. But if James loves you, he'll find you." Realm turns to me. "I found you."

James does love me, even though Realm always tries to dispute that fact. But it's now been two days since James left—two days without a word from him. He was so angry the last time I saw him. I hope he knows how sorry I am. At that thought, I reach to click off the light, submerging the room in darkness. I lie back on the bed, curling up in the loneliness.

"Sloane," Realm says, his voice low. "Remember in The Program, when you would sneak into my room with me?" he asks. "We'd snuggle. Platonically, of course."

I used to spend time in Realm's room, talking—although I don't know exactly what we talked about anymore. I do remember what it felt like to let him stroke my hair, to let him whisper his stories near my ear.

"It was nice," Realm says. "Holding you."

I close my eyes, squeezing them tight, as if I can block out how I've missed him. Once upon a time Realm was everything to me. It hurts to remember that—because now I'm not sure if that was the real Realm. "It was nice," I say softly.

"If you . . ." He pauses, and I hear his throat click as he swallows. "If you wanted to sleep here with me, I wouldn't mind. I won't try anything either."

"I can't," I say simply. Even if I didn't know about Realm and The Treatment, I still wouldn't run to him now. I learned my lesson at his house that stormy night. I love James. It's not fair to pretend otherwise.

"The offer stands, Sloane," Realm says. "I'll always be here for you."

# CHAPTER FIVE

IT'S THE NEXT DAY WHEN WE ARRIVE AT A SMALL farmhouse outside of Lake Tahoe—and like Dallas said, it's in the middle of nowhere. It's also beautiful. Trees encase the entire property, and the small, shabby farmhouse has a charm all its own. From the peeling white siding to the enormous and inviting wraparound porch—it makes me think of a life I would have liked to have with James. Just us in the country, maybe some dogs running around. But I'm here with a group of rebels instead. Things don't always work out the way we plan.

I don't have much to carry as I make my way inside. It's a little dusty, and I cough the minute Cas pushes the door open. But I like it. I like how peaceful it is.

"This belonged to the grandparents of another rebel," Dallas says, then lowers her eyes. "But she was taken back to

The Program a few months ago. Haven't seen her since. So it's ours now." She drops her bag at her feet. "We shouldn't be disturbed."

"It's a nice place," I say, pausing to look at the framed pictures on the wall. There's an older couple, very 1970s with paisley and butterfly collars. I touch the image, reminded of my own grandparents, who passed away when I was little. Their picture hung on my wall at home.

My home. I may never see it again. I shake off the impending grief and instead walk around to explore the place, needing the distraction. I find a small room, no bigger than a walk-in closet, with a twin bed and nothing else. I decide that I like it. The window looks out over the expansive yard, a small creek cutting through the grass. I can imagine that in the mornings there might be a deer, or even bunnies, frolicking. I smile to myself and sit on the mattress, bouncing to make the springs creak.

"Hey." Cas peeks his head in my room. He looks pretty wrecked after driving all this way, and I'm sure I don't look much better. His longish hair is in tangles, dark circles under his eyes. He hasn't shaved since we left. I wonder how long Cas has been this ragged, threadbare. Maybe I was too busy to notice.

"I called dibs on the shower," he says, "but if you want it first, I'll give you this one chivalrous pass."

I grin. "No, you clearly need it more than I do." He puts his hand over his heart.

"Ouch. Well, don't plan on having any hot water."

"Such a gentleman." Cas winks, playful and flirtatious in the same way he is with Dallas. And although it should make me feel included, it only makes me feel lonelier.

I get under the covers of the bedsheets in an attempt to sleep off some of the exhaustion, listening as the shower turns on. But the emptiness of my small room becomes too much, and I go downstairs in search of life instead. I find Dallas sitting on the couch, her feet propped up on the arm as she scrolls through the screen of her phone. She glances at me.

"Did you need something?" she asks. "You have that needy expression."

I stand over her for a minute, the never-ending tension between us suffocating me. I could offer a snide comment and walk away like I usually do, but then we'll never settle this. I roll my eyes and sit cross-legged on the floor next to the couch. This piques her interest, and Dallas slips her phone into her pocket.

"I'm sorry," I say, staring at the faded rust-colored carpet. "I'm sorry I got between you and Realm—it wasn't my intention." I hear Dallas snort behind me.

"Oh, well. Society is built on good intentions, Sloane. And look how far it's gotten us." Her tone is almost harsh enough to make me leave, but I hold out. There aren't many of us left. It could be worth it to try to have a girlfriend—one person I can trust.

"If it's any consolation," I say, "I don't think he meant the hurtful things he said." I'm not trying to make excuses for him;

Realm was a total asshole. But there was something about his posture after, the way he still looks at her now, that makes me think he cares more than he'll say. I turn to Dallas, see her watching the ceiling with her jaw clenched, her bottom lip jutting out. She flicks her eyes to mine.

"That's our entire relationship," she says. "And yeah, I don't think he means to do it either, but he always does. He always has." Dallas readjusts her position on the couch, settling back with a far-off expression. "I met Realm after I ran away from home. I was in a bad place, worse than I am now. I'd been through The Program, through Roger, through my father's abuse. I packed a bag and took off on my own. There wasn't a national story behind it, not like you and James. I just disappeared, spent my nights in abandoned buildings on my way to Salt Lake. I'd heard stories of a resistance there.

"I was timid then. I'm not sure what my life was like just before I was taken, but in junior high, before the epidemic, I'd been a cheerleader." She laughs. "Can you imagine?"

I smile. "No."

She quiets for a moment and wraps her arms around herself. "Then Roger happened," she says. "When I got home, I couldn't assimilate, but I learned to fake it to get through therapy. The first chance I got, I took off. I met the rebels and they took me in. One day Michael Realm showed up. The way he acted . . . It felt like he was there for me. The way he spoke, the way he looked at me. I was scared then, but he made it better. For a while."

Listening to Dallas, I'm reminded that maybe I don't know

Realm at all. This was before I knew him. Was it before he'd been in The Program the first time? Was it before the second time? "What happened after that?" I ask Dallas, leaning my elbow on the couch.

"He left," she says. "Realm would always leave and never say where he was going. Then he'd show up again and act like nothing happened—we'd get closer, and then he'd push me away. This is the first time he brought another girl home, though. I'm not going to lie, Sloane. It hurts. I thought I'd grown immune to pain, but Realm knows just how to twist the knife to keep me from loving him completely."

Guilt falls all around me, even though I'm not the one to blame. Still, I can understand why Dallas hates me. I can't imagine how I'd cope if James fell in love with someone else.

"What about Cas?" I ask. "Have the two of you ever—"

"No," Dallas says quickly. "We're not like that. Shit, I'm not even sure what type of girl Cas likes. He's my best friend—which is how we both want it."

We sit quietly for a while, and I turn over our conversation, putting it together with what Realm has told me. I don't feel I have the full story—like there's a piece missing from their dynamic. "Have you ever talked to Realm about his behavior? Have you told him how you feel?"

Dallas's expression weakens as she turns toward me. "He said I didn't matter, Sloane. I don't think he could have been clearer than that."

I wince, Realm's words stinging even me. I don't understand

his motivation. Then again, James was kind of a jerk when I met up with him, too. "James pushed me away," I confess. "I called him on it, kind of ran off. My friendship with Realm is what made James finally admit his feelings for me. Until a few days ago, I thought we were solid. I thought we were forever." James is the connection between who I was and who I am now. Without that, I'm lost.

"We'll find him," Dallas states. "I have no doubt that James is safe. If anything, he's probably just pissed. This isn't because I hate you or anything," she says with a smile, "but I kind of see his point. You and Realm . . . You act like more than friends. I'd have left you too."

James wouldn't be friends with a girl who was in love with him, not if it hurt me. I'm ashamed of my behavior. Ashamed I wasn't mature enough to have more respect for my boyfriend. I'm embarrassed that even Dallas can see it.

"Can I ask you something?" Dallas starts tentatively. "What are you going to do with The Treatment?"

The question catches me off guard, and it takes me a second too long to answer. "I honestly don't know," I say eventually. "It's a lot of pressure. What . . . What would you do?"

"If it were me, I'd have taken it right away. I wouldn't care about Pritchard or the others. But if I were *you*"—she shrugs—"I would have given it to James." She glances over at me and smiles. "Can I be real for a second? Your boyfriend is superhot. Seriously, James really does it for me. I just thought you should know."

I laugh, tossing my head back. Above us the pipes rattle and there's the whine of a turning faucet before the water shuts off. Talking to Dallas has given me some perspective, but more surprisingly, I can see she's a good person. I haven't given her nearly enough credit. I climb to my feet, hoping Cas didn't really use up all the hot water.

"Thanks for the talk."

"Don't mention it," Dallas responds, her tone dismissive, as if she's not taking away the same bonding experience as I am. "Hey, if you see Cas, let him know I'd like to knife fight later."

"Uh . . . okay."

Dallas takes out her phone, and her change in demeanor bothers me slightly, but this could just be what she does to avoid getting hurt. I can't expect her to trust me, not yet. I start for the stairs but pause to look back at her. Dallas waves her hand in acknowledgment, a smile on her lips, and swipes her thumbs over her keypad, shutting me out.

Cas is in his room by the time I get upstairs, and I walk into the steamy bathroom, running my hand across the fog in the mirror. I study my reflection, noting that the healthy glow I had after leaving The Program is now replaced with dark circles, pale skin. I've thinned, and I wonder what my parents would think if they saw me now.

They'd probably think I was sick. They'd probably call The Program to come get me. I wonder for a moment about how it happened, but I quickly block it out. It's too horrific to imagine. Would I want to feel what it's like for my own parents to betray me?

I blow out a hard breath, trying to clear my head, and go over to turn on the shower. The bathroom is old, with a black-and-white-tiled floor and a claw-foot tub with standing shower. I don't have any soap, but I find an unopened bar underneath the sink. The minute I stand beneath the rushing hot water, I'm grateful Cas didn't use it all. My muscles, stiff from the car ride and lack of good sleep, begin to loosen, my mind slowly unraveling the past few weeks.

I start with Lacey—a place I haven't let myself go since she left. Dallas said she was back in The Program, and my only way to deal with that was to stop thinking about her. But now I can see her, both before and after her spiral. I see the note: *Miller.* Can I think of the memory of Miller? Will it spur new memories and drive me crazy? The water is beginning to cool as I close my eyes and pretend James is here with me in the shower. He says he's sorry for leaving. I say I'm sorry for lying. We're both so sorry. We're always sorry.

I work the bar of soap through my wet hair, but suddenly there's a sharp pain in my temples, a swift blow of memories smashing through the surface.

*The tile floor is ice-cold under my bare feet. I fumble with the door handle. Just as I get it open, I see the stark white corridor of The Program. Realm stalks toward the nurses' station, where Roger is standing, laughing. My wrists are sore from when the handler had me strapped down, but I'm so scared for Realm. I'm so scared of what he'll do.*

*Realm's fist connects with Roger's face, sending him over the desk and the nurse screams. I try to make my way closer, to tell Realm to stop before they take him away, but I'm so foggy. Roger drugged me.*

*"Which arm?" Realm snarls.*

*"Don't do this, Michael," Roger says. "You'll expose us all."*

*Realm punches him hard in the face again, breaking his nose, sending blood in a splatter on the white wall. "Which arm did you touch her with?" Realm demands. When Roger doesn't answer, Realm grabs the handler's right arm and twists it behind his back until it snaps, sending Roger into a fit of howls. Realm only steps back, enraged, but oddly calm.*

*Security comes rushing up, but instead of wrestling Realm to the floor, they whisper to him until he agrees, letting them lead him away. But not before he looks back over his shoulder at me, nodding, as if we have an agreement. A secret between us.*

I gasp and stumble sideways, catching the wall with my hand before I fall out of the tub. Secrets—how many do Realm and I have together? How many of them have I forgotten?

It's all too much; everything piled on breaks me, and I start to sob. I lower myself down into the tub, filled with loss and devastation. I cry under the ice-cold water, shivering but unable to get up. I'm not weak, I know I'm not . . . but this is too much. I have to let it go because it's too damn much.

SUZANNE YOUNG

The curtain slides open, followed by the squeak of the faucet turning off. I'm still crying when the warmth of a towel wraps around my shoulders, and Realm helps me from the tub. My legs are wobbly, but the minute I realize he's here, that he's touching me, I push him back.

I hate Realm for lying to me in The Program—acting as if he was just like me when he wasn't. He had his memories. He *knew* Roger. But most of all, I hate him for being here when James isn't.

I wrap the towel tighter around myself and brush the tears off my cheeks, glaring at Realm. His expression falters, concern replaced with defeat, vulnerability. "I don't want to hear it right now," I say, sounding like a petulant child. But I won't let Realm manipulate me. I feel like he already has.

"Do you know how I ended up in The Program in the first place?" he asks, taking a step closer to me.

I sniffle, surprised by the question, but also by his proximity. I move back, bumping against the sink. "You never told me," I say. "You said you didn't remember."

Realm moves, and I flinch as if he's going to touch me, but he goes to sit on the edge of the tub. "I was sixteen years old," he says in a quiet voice. "My parents were both dead and my sister was working day and night. I never saw her. I worked on and off, but mostly I smoked and drank—numbing what I could. The despair was so deep and dark that it was eating me from the inside. I started to imagine I was rotting—that if you split my skin I would bleed black cancerous blood." He met my eyes. "And so one day I decided to find out."

My breathing quickens and a slow horror starts to work through me. The confession is already too personal, too painful to hear. My eyes begin to well up.

"My sister was at her job, my girlfriend was gone—gone into The Program weeks before. I had nothing. I had no one. But I wasn't searching for peace, Sloane. I was searching for pain. I wanted it to *hurt*. I wanted to feel every inch of my death and I wanted to suffer. So I grabbed a serrated knife from the wood block on the kitchen counter, and I went into the bathroom and shut the door. I must have stood at the sink for close to an hour, staring at myself. The circles under my eyes, the disgust I felt at my own reflection.

"And then . . . I put the blade to my neck and began to saw. I watched as long as I could, watching the blood pour down over my shirt, the skin split, only to lose my place because of my shaky hand. Then I'd start again."

I cover my mouth, tears spilling onto my cheeks as the images flash through my head. "Stop," I say. But Realm looks crazed, lost in his head.

"The last thing I remember," he says, "was the thought that it wasn't black blood at all. It was red. Everything was so red. I woke up in The Program. Seventy-three stitches. Reconstructive surgery. Extensive therapy. The doctors told me I was a miracle. Do you agree?" he asks, his brown eyes wild. "Aren't I just a role model now? A fucking inspiration."

No one should suffer like that. It's too terrible to even

comprehend. I step forward and hug him, wishing I could take the pain away.

Realm's arms wrap around my waist as he holds me close, taking jagged breaths before going on. "Sometimes I wish it'd worked. I wanted to die that day, but instead I had doctors picking me apart. But that's not the worst thing I've done, Sloane. I wish it were."

I pull back and look down into his face. What does that mean? I move out of his arms, tightening my towel once again. I realize suddenly we're alone, and I'm naked other than this short white cloth wrapped around me. Realm notices my reaction and lowers his eyes.

Although my face feels swollen from crying, I put myself back together. I have to keep going, keep fighting. I may be a runaway, but at least I'm alive. I grip the glass knob of the bathroom door to leave.

"Sloane," Realm calls in a low voice. I turn to look at him. "If he doesn't come back, you still have me."

My eyes weaken. "Realm . . ."

"I love you more than James ever could," he says so seriously that I know he believes it. I can't bring myself to hurt him, say the things I should. I can only turn and leave, praying James really will come back. And wondering what it will mean for Realm when he does.

# CHAPTER SIX

**IT'S LATE. I'M LYING IN BED, CLOSE TO THE WINDOW** because I understand what Realm meant at the other house—there is a claustrophobic aftereffect of The Program. A light flips on in the backyard, and I immediately sit up, my stomach lurching with fear.

Slowly, I slide the curtain aside and peer out. It takes a second to find them, but then I see Dallas and Cas on the lawn. Dallas is laughing—a genuine emotion of happiness—as Cas has his switchblade, flipping it open and waving it around like he's from *West Side Story*. I smile too.

I slip my arms into my sweater and push my feet into my sneakers, and head downstairs. When I push open the back screen door, they both spin to face me—Cas's knife is gripped in his hand and pointed at me.

"You scared the shit out of me," he says. Dallas rolls her eyes, and I consider going back upstairs, but ultimately I'm too awake to sleep. And I definitely don't want to lie in bed and think all night.

"Do you mind if I stay out here for a while?" I ask.

"Of course you can," Cas says quickly. "I'm just showing Dallas how to defend herself. You know"—he glances back at her—"since she's so delicate and demur."

"Suck it, Cas," she says, pulling her dreads up into a high knot. "I guarantee I can put you down in less than five seconds."

Cas flips his blade closed and pulls off his jacket, tossing it to me. "Ooo . . ." he says. "I like that challenge. Wanna put down money, Sloane?"

I laugh. "I'm definitely taking Dallas on this one."

"Smart girl," Dallas says, and starts dancing from foot to foot like she's a boxer. The night is quiet behind us, the thick trees lining the property, keeping us safe from neighbors. It's cool but comfortable outside. I see the stump of a tree and go to sit down on it, completely entertained.

"All right, baby," Cas says, brushing his hair behind his ears. "If I hurt you, you'd better not hold a grudge."

Dallas nods mockingly. "Sure thing, Casanova. And if your man bits lose their ability to reproduce, I hope there are no hard feelings."

Cas drops his arms. "Hey! You can't—"

Dallas springs, sweeping his feet out from under him. At

the same time, her hands shoot forward, knocking Cas back. He barely has time to react and ends up flat on the grass, moaning. Dallas drops into a squat next to him.

"Was I too rough?" she says in a baby voice. Cas starts to laugh, shaking his head. Dallas offers her hand and helps him up. Even though she just kicked his ass, Dallas and Cas go at it again and again, nearly every time ending with Dallas triumphant.

"Want to give it a whirl?" Dallas asks me. There's a smudge of dirt over her brow from when Cas tried to reach her from the ground.

"No, thanks," I say, holding up my hands. "I think I'd rather fight Cas."

"Hey!" he calls with a laugh. Cas gets up, swiping at the grass stains on his jeans, which are past the point of return. He comes to sit on the stump next to me, smelling like earth and soap. Dallas walks over, stretching her arms to one side as she works out a kink in her shoulder.

"I meant to tell you," she says. "I got in touch with an insider. The Program is still looking for James." At the mention of his name in combination with The Program, my muscles tense. "Relax," Dallas says, reading my anxiety. "This is good news. It means he got away. James is safe, hiding out somewhere. Now it's just a matter of us tracking him down."

"He's okay?" I ask, too scared to be hopeful.

"It appears so," Dallas says. "Does that turn your frown upside down?" she teases, trying to get me to smile. My relief is absolute.

"Yes," I say honestly, blowing out a measured breath. "It certainly does." I'm weightless. Even though James isn't here now, Dallas said it was only a matter of time. And I trust her. After all this time, I finally trust her.

"I don't have The Treatment anymore," I confess. "James accidently took it. We left the pill behind with him."

Cas turns suddenly, confusion crossing his features. "Are you serious?" he asks. "You don't have it here?" He and Dallas exchange a look, and I wonder if I've made a mistake confiding in them.

"I'm sorry I didn't tell you sooner," I say. "I wasn't sure—"

"Sloane," Dallas interrupts, "it's fine. It's not like we've only been tolerating you for The Treatment." She pauses. "Okay, maybe at first. But now, hell—we're, like, almost-friends." She flashes her wide smile, and the tension evaporates. "Besides," she adds, "James will be back soon anyway *with* The Treatment. Then we'll figure out what to do next." Cas agrees, and I'm so grateful they're not mad. If anything, it might make them search for James a little harder.

"Oh." Dallas snaps her fingers and looks at Cas. "We're low on funds and I need to pay for some information. Got a connection?"

Cas grabs a bottle of water sitting on the grass and takes a sip. It hadn't occurred to me that we needed money. On the first day, Dallas and Cas collected what Realm's sister had given us. I never thought to question where else they get money from.

"I'll get us the cash," Cas says, sounding exhausted. "I haven't let you down yet, have I?" Dallas shakes her head.

"Where does the money come from?" I ask. Cas side-eyes me, and takes another drink.

"He never says," Dallas announces. "I think he's a thief, but I figure we're all allowed our secrets. And if my little klepto wants to borrow from the more fortunate, then so be it. It's keeping us fed."

"One day we'll have lobster and steak," he says, grinning behind the top of his water.

"You cook," Dallas says.

"Hell yes. I'm not going to let you burn it."

We're all smiling, but it has to be at least three in the morning by now. I say my good nights, and Dallas and Cas stay behind. I don't think they're going to fight anymore. I don't think they're going to hook up, either. It makes me like them both a little more in a weird way. Their friendship is so honest and easy, and once again I see another side of Dallas. Combined with the news that James is currently safe from The Program for now, and I almost hopeful about this whole situation.

The days pass slowly, comfortably. It's early one morning when I find Realm by the back door, a wide smile plastered across his face. It's so out of character that I actually look around the kitchen to make sure I'm not missing something. When I see it's just us, I put my hand on my hip and laugh.

"What?" I ask, returning his smile. Rather than answer, Realm takes the handle of the back door and opens it. I stare out over the yard, my eyes widening as a gentle breeze that smells like grass blows in. There are at least six deer in our backyard; one is a baby. They're so beautiful. I take a step toward them, and Realm puts his finger to his lips.

"Shh . . ." he says, turning to watch them too. I go to stand next to him, and he puts his arm over my shoulders. "It's hard to remember the good sometimes," he whispers.

The deer continue to eat out of the old garden, and the baby is lying in the grass. The property is even prettier in the morning light: green and alive. How can there be a suicide epidemic when nature can be so soft and gentle? How can anything horrible happen in a place like this? I lean my head on Realm's chest as we watch the deer, lost in a beauty we forgot existed.

"What are you guys doing?" Cas calls from behind us. One of the deer turns its head, its ears twitching. Cas stomps over to where we are, not quiet and not subtle. "Oh shit," he says, pointing to the yard. Two of the deer immediately scamper off, and the rest freeze, looking in our direction. "Should we kill one and eat it?" Cas asks.

I scoff and turn to stare at him. Realm chuckles, lowering his arm from my shoulders. By the time I look back at the deer, they're gone. Disappointment weighs me down. I liked the feeling the deer gave me; I liked feeling small next to nature.

Cas sighs and then walks back into the kitchen, reaching

into the lower cabinets to pull out a heavy pan. He fills it with water and sets it on the stove, clicking the burner to life. I think the idea of venison stew is still dancing through his head, but really he's going to cook gross processed food they got from the gas station. Cas still hasn't found money, but neither Realm nor Dallas is pressing him about it. I can see they're getting nervous, though.

Realm comes over. "Hey," he says. "Want to go for a walk? It's gorgeous outside."

I look up, feeling calm for the first time in a while. It's hard to stay angry in a place so beautiful. I agree and tell Cas to save us some food before Realm and I go out back.

The sun is shining, but the breeze is cool, and I wrap my arms around myself as we walk over the expansive lawn toward the creek, toward the woods beyond. On the other side of us is a massive mountain range, enclosing us in the safety of nature. For a minute I'm reminded of when Realm and I were both in The Program. He brought me out to walk in the flower garden with him, and it gave me so much hope. It reminded me that there was a world to go back to.

A small wooden bridge curves over the creek, and we pause in the middle of it and rest our elbows on the railing, gazing at the house and the woods. "What are we going to do with our lives?" I ask quietly. "How long do we live out here?"

"As long as we can." He lowers his head, and I look sideways at him. "We'll always have to keep moving," he says. "As long as The Program is out there, we won't be safe."

I know he's right, but to admit it crushes the contentment of the moment. I exhale, long and heavy, and then stare at the world once again—wishing it could always be like this.

"I want to tell you everything, Sloane," Realm says quietly. "But I don't know if I can."

My eyes are trained on the trees, but my heart begins to race. "Maybe it's time you try," I say. I'm not in denial; I've always known Realm was hiding something. But now, here, I'm scared of what he has to say.

Realm nods, leaning farther over the railing to study the streaming water below. "It's about Dallas," he murmurs. "I knew her before either of us were in The Program."

I pull my eyebrows together, processing his words. Dallas met him after she got out of The Program. "What?" I ask, turning to him.

Realm's expression is filled with pain, regret. "She was my girlfriend before she went into The Program. She just doesn't remember."

"Oh my God," I say, covering my mouth. How could Dallas not know? How could Realm not tell her?

"Sloane," he says, taking my wrist to pull my hand down. "After I took The Treatment and got my memories back, I sought her out. I've been trying to keep her safe."

"Why wouldn't you tell her then? Why would you pretend you'd only just met? Were you manipulating her by using things from your past?"

"No," he says quickly, but then swallows hard, looking

down. "A little. I did what I had to do, though. You didn't know her. She's not like you, Sloane."

"What does that mean?" I'm suddenly protective of Dallas, and my anger at Realm is growing exponentially.

"She's not strong. Sure, she tries to be. She puts on a show." He shakes his head. "But she's not. Dallas may think she wants her memories back, but I can tell you right now that she can't handle them. There was her bastard father, her suicide attempt. And then there was me. I wasn't exactly the best boyfriend."

"I think you're underestimating her."

"You didn't see her. I'm the reason Dallas went into The Program. I was suicidal, vicious, angry. I said horrible things. I wanted her sad—I *made* her sad. And then . . ." He stops, turning to look at the lawn as he puts his palm over his mouth, coughing a cry into it before he can compose himself.

"What did you do?" I whisper.

"I called The Program and told them to take her."

My eyes widen, and then I'm a flurry of motion, slapping whatever part of him I can hit. "You son of a bitch!" I scream, trying to wound him. He takes it all, but soon my hands begin to hurt and my arms tire. "How could you?" I whimper, heartbroken for a girl who has been through too much. More than anyone ever should. He's kept all this from her. It makes me wonder exactly what Realm is capable of. I drop down to sit on the bridge, overcome.

Realm looks at me, a small scratch—raised and red—on his cheek. "When I got my memories back," he says, "finding

Dallas was my first priority. And when I saw she was okay, I was so relieved. I'd been worried she didn't survive. Believe me, I hate myself for what I did. Right away she and I fell back into a relationship of sorts. She's vulnerable, especially to me.

"And then she told me about Roger, about what he'd done to her. And I had such guilt." He closes his eyes. "You don't understand how that kind of guilt can feel. Again I found myself taking it out on her. I can't not hurt her, Sloane. I want to protect her, but I can't even protect her from me."

"Then just leave her alone," I say. "Isn't that the best thing you can do for her? She still cares about you, Realm."

"And I'm in love with you."

My stomach twists, sickened by the words. I'm not to blame for how he's mistreated Dallas. "Don't turn this on me. You should never have told her that, knowing your past together. Knowing how she feels about you. It was cruel."

He smiles, sad and lonely. "Isn't that what you do to me when it comes to James?" he asks. "Aren't we in the same exact position?"

His words shock me, and I jump to my feet. Have I done that? Am I that cruel? I take a step back, and Realm shakes his head and reaches for my arm.

"Sloane, wait," he says. "I'm sorry. I wasn't trying to make you feel bad. I get it—that's what I'm trying to say here. I understand about you and James—you'll always choose him. I'm just saying that, on the same token, I'll always choose you."

Realm is the one who's unwell. Has he always been this

way, or is he spiraling into a depression? I step backward toward the house, yanking my arm from his. "You're crazy," I say. "Stay away from me, Realm. Stay away from Dallas."

Realm starts to follow me, but something in my expression makes him stop. Instead he leans the side of his body against the railing and watches me leave. I'm suddenly desperate to find James. I can't tell Dallas about Realm; I'm not sure I can inflict that kind of trauma on her. But I'll ask for her help in locating James. And then I'll get us the hell out of here. I start to run toward the house, running away from Realm. Always running back to James.

When I get to the house, it's quiet. The pan Cas used earlier is soaking in the sink, and there's a bowl filled with ramen noodles on the table. I can't eat anyway, not after what I just learned. Dallas isn't in the living room, but I have to find her. We have to find James and then get out of here. I head upstairs to grab my stuff, guessing that Dallas is still asleep. I climb the creaky stairs, and when I open my bedroom door, my breath catches in my throat.

James is standing at the window, staring out over the yard. I see his shoulders tense when I enter, but he doesn't turn around right away. He seems different, even though it's been only a few days. I want to see his face, but at the same time, I'm scared of what his expression will say. Is he still mad about Realm? Does he think I abandoned him?

"I saw you on the bridge just now," he says quietly. "The

land's beautiful here. A lot like Oregon. A lot like home."

I'm about to completely break down, but I sniffle hard and pull myself together. "You found us," I say, thinking back on Realm's words. He said if James loved me, he'd find me. I'm hoping that's true.

James turns, his bright-blue eyes arresting as he looks me over. "Did you think I wouldn't?" he asks. "You know me too well to think I'd give up on you. I left so I wouldn't murder your friend, but something came up. I'm just glad Dallas left a breadcrumb trail."

The moment is heavy, overflowing with emotion. My fingers are shaking so badly that I clasp them in front of me. "I was worried about you," I say.

James nods and reaches into his pocket, pulling out the Baggie. "I should give this back to you," he says quietly. "I thought about taking it, but I couldn't. See, I hesitated."

"I'm glad," I say. "I have so much to tell you, and to be honest, I doubt either of us will be taking The Treatment anytime soon." James casts a confused glance at the pill before sliding it back into his pocket. But rather than asking me, he lowers his eyes, his shoulders slumping. My stomach sinks.

"What's happened?"

James lifts his gaze. "My dad died."

I gasp, shocked beyond words. I rush forward, not caring if he wants me to or not, and wrap my arms around him. He'd already lost his mother, and now . . . his father. James is an orphan. He's truly alone in the world now. His arms are weak as they rest around my waist. I get on my tiptoes, whispering close to his ear.

"I'm so sorry, James."

James's grip tightens, and soon he's holding me, swaying with whatever grief he was holding back. I should have been with him, but instead I let Realm manipulate me. I broke James's trust. We could have faced everything together, but it's too late to take it back now.

After a moment James hitches in a few unsteady breaths. He rubs his reddened eyes and then takes in my appearance. "You look too thin," he says, sounding miserable.

"I've been a little stressed."

He nods like he can understand. Absently, he reaches to take a curly strand of my hair and twist it around his finger. "When I left," he says quietly, "I planned to cool off for a few hours, come back, and take you away from him. Away from Realm. At one point I looked up and realized I was driving back to Oregon. I just wanted to go home. I wanted our lives back. I stopped at a gas station and asked to use the phone. I called my dad."

The tears gather in James's eyes and his grief is contagious. Even though his father blamed me for James running away, he was still James's father. I murmur again how sorry I am, but James doesn't seem to hear.

"Dad didn't answer the phone," he continues. "And I got a bad feeling. So . . . I called your house."

"My house?"

James nods, letting my hair slip out of his hand. "I'm not even sure why. I did it without thinking—I just . . . knew the number. I talked to your father."

"My dad?" I squeak out. I miss my parents. Despite everything, I miss them, and knowing that James lost his dad makes me only more desperate to have mine back.

"He told me my father died last week. There wasn't a service because there was no family left to bury him. Instead the State took his body. I . . ." James starts to break but fights hard to keep his composure. "I abandoned my dad, Sloane. He died all alone."

I cover my lips with my fingers, trying not to cry. This is why James seemed different when I walked in. He's no longer cocky or confident. Over the past few days, he's lost his old life. He's had to grow up completely. His life is irrevocably changed.

"Your father asked about you," James says. "I told him you were okay, that you weren't sick. And that someday we'd come home again." I squeeze my eyes shut, tears spilling onto my cheeks. "He said he hoped so," James continued. "He asked me to take care of you until then."

I look at James again, my heart aching. "You promised that you would?"

He smiles softly. "Yeah. I told him I'd do anything to keep you safe. And I meant it, Sloane. After I talked with him, I turned the car around because I knew I could never leave you. You're all the family I have left."

The words escape me—the perfect phrases that would prove to James how much I love him. We are family. "Do you really think we'll go home someday?"

"I'm gonna try like hell," he says, shifting closer to me. He slides his palm over my neck, his thumb stroking my jaw. I ache for him to kiss me, but he's holding back.

"How did you find us?" I ask. "How did Dallas get to you?"

"I have to say"—he laughs—"she's pretty damn good. She must have had people out looking for the Escalade. First I got a note leading me to a seedy motel. I was a few days behind you. The proprietor was nice enough to tell me you shared a room with a tall, dark-haired guy with a nasty scar on his neck." James lowers his arm.

There's a rush of guilt, but I'm quick to try to explain it away. "It wasn't like that."

"I wouldn't be here if I thought it was," James says. "You're tangled up with him. I have to deal with it." James gets quiet, slipping his hands into the pockets of his pants. "At the motel," James continues, "Dallas left behind a guidebook of Lake Tahoe. From there, it was a matter of tracking the van.

"Cas let me in when I got here—acting pretty fucking surprised to see me, I must say. He showed me to your room, and when I looked out the window, I saw you on the bridge." James's eyes weaken with vulnerability. "I told you once that I wasn't a jealous guy except for when it came to Michael Realm. But that's my problem to get over, not yours. I choose to trust you."

Although I'm glad James came to a decision about his feelings, there's so much he's missed. "I've made it clear to Realm that he and I will never happen," I tell him. "He's been keeping secrets from me, terrible lies from all of us. I don't think he's well, James. All I want now is for us to run away from here."

James can't hide the relief, his mouth twitching with a smile. "We'll leave in the morning." He takes the bottom of my shirt to tug me closer. I wrap my arms around his neck, getting on my tiptoes so that our lips touch. "I give up, Sloane," he whispers against me. "I'm all yours."

There's a pain, a beautiful deep pain in my heart, and I lean in to kiss him. His lips are warm and gentle, even as his beard scratches me. His touch isn't urgent, though I'm sure we're both burning for each other. His kiss is slow and thorough and claiming. We ease back onto the bed, taking our time—something we've never done, not that I can remember. His kisses trail over my body, my heart skips a beat with his every moan. James is back—really back. And together we're about to start our new life.

By midafternoon James and I are still lying around my room as I fill him in on the events he's missed. I tell him about Arthur Pritchard, Kellan. We talk about my returning memories and the nosebleed. I even tell him about Dallas and Realm. James listens to all the stories, clearly overwhelmed with information. But he's handling it better than I thought he would. He really has matured.

"So how do you think Michael Realm is going to feel about our reunion?" he asks, motioning between us.

"I imagine he'll be heartbroken." There's a small twist of regret, but I remind myself how Realm has treated Dallas. Nothing I do to him could ever be that cruel.

"Well, in that case," James says, smiling to himself, "I can't wait to see him."

# CHAPTER SEVEN

**CAS IS THE ONLY ONE SMILING AT DINNER. WELL,** besides James, who is chewing on store-bought beef jerky like it's the best thing he's ever eaten. He showered and shaved before coming downstairs, and unlike the last time, James is perfectly content with gloating. I may have misjudged his maturity level.

James keeps his hand on my leg, casually, but still there. We sit close, and every so often he brushes his lips over my ear to whisper how much he missed me. I'd tell him to stop pouring salt in the wound, but I don't. Because tomorrow we're running away, just like we should have in the first place. I plan to ask Dallas to come with us, but I doubt she'll leave Cas. I'm going to give her the option anyway.

"So where've you been?" Cas asks, reaching to pull some jerky out of the bag on the table. Night has fallen outside, blacking out the windows and dotting the sky with stars. I plan to sit and stare up at them later, enjoy one last night in Tahoe before we leave for the unknown.

"I tried to head back to Oregon," James says. "Got spooked when I saw the billboard with my handsome mug on it." He winks at me to let me know he's joking.

Dallas chuckles. "That must be distracting for drivers."

"It was," James retorts. "Tourists lining the road, taking pictures. Traffic jams. I knew I'd be a target. Ended up camping for a day or two before I found your trail. It was pretty lonely. I found my spirit animal though." He grins. "It's a rooster."

"Shut up." I laugh, pushing his shoulder. James continues to tell ridiculous stories, leaving out everything relating to his dad. He's keeping it private, which I respect. Dallas seems brightened by James's return, and I don't feel threatened by her attention. Not like before.

Realm broods at the end of the table, and occasionally Dallas looks over at him, although she's clearly still too pissed to engage him in conversation. I hate knowing about pieces of her life that she doesn't. Can she feel deep down inside that she used to love Realm? Am I cruel for not telling her now?

As if reading my thoughts, Realm pushes his drink aside and stares at Dallas until she looks at him. "Can I talk to you?" he asks.

She scoffs. "No." She turns back to James, but Realm is quick to reach out and take her hand, startling her.

"I need to talk to you," he says again, more aggressively. At the other end of the table, Cas glares at Realm.

"Leave it alone, man," Cas says seriously. "Leave her alone." They exchange a look, one heavy in meaning, but Realm doesn't back down.

"I can't," he says, his lips pulled tight into a snarl. "And this isn't your call, Casanova. Not her, not The Treatment. Do you think I haven't noticed you searching for the pill?"

Cas stands, knocking a cup off the table and sending it to the floor with a loud clatter. We all jump, surprised to see Cas react so strongly. It's an Old West showdown, and James sits up straighter like he's ready to break up a fight.

For her part, Dallas looks utterly confused. Cas's reaction is over the top, especially since they're just friends. And I don't know what any of this has to do with The Treatment.

"Outside," Cas growls to Realm. At first I think he's calling for a fight, but Realm nods solemnly. Cas doesn't say a word to Dallas before walking out, letting the screen door slam shut behind him.

Realm pauses, but Dallas won't look at him. He rounds the table, touching my shoulder as he passes. James and Dallas don't notice. I watch Realm leave, wondering what the hell is going on. Does he genuinely want to apologize to Dallas? Is he freaking out because James is back?

Dallas curses and gets up from the table. "He's such a dick," she says, rattled. She wouldn't talk to Realm, but his attention was enough to break her otherwise good mood. Realm called her unstable, but obviously he's partly to blame for that diagnosis. There's real damage here that he has no right to tamper with. And to prove it, Dallas tosses her beef jerky on the table and storms upstairs.

James looks over at me, his eyebrows raised. "What was that about?" he asks. "Are Dallas and Cas—"

"They both say no," I tell him. "Just friends. Either way, I'm ready to get out of here. They want The Treatment, not us." At the mention, I realize we left the pill in the room. After that little exchange, I'm feeling paranoid. I want to check on it. "Let's go upstairs," I say.

James doesn't make a joke because he can see I'm suspicious. Together we go back to the room and I immediately check the small inside pocket of the duffel bag. The pill is still there, tucked inside the Baggie with Kellan Thomas's business card so I won't lose them.

"What's going on?" James asks, shutting the door before going to sit on the bed. "Have the rebels been trying to get ahold of The Treatment?"

I shake my head, trying to figure out what's making me so uneasy. "Not really, or at least, not obviously. They want to keep it safe from The Program. I assumed Arthur Pritchard was the threat, but I may have misjudged him. Now it's up to us." I think again about the doctor, hoping I'll be able to reconnect with him eventually. If he understood the risks of The Treatment, maybe he'd have another idea on how to combat The Program. Maybe there can be a happy ending in all this.

"Can I see it for second?" James asks. I lift my gaze to where he sits, and nod. I take the Baggie and crawl onto the bed. James lies next to me, and I hand him the items, resting my cheek on his shoulder. He reads the business card through the plastic and then begins tracing the pill with his thumb.

"A cure dangerous enough to kill us," he says. "What a cruel twist."

I close my eyes, thinking back on what Dallas said. She would have made James take The Treatment. Realm would have made me. They both thought it would be worth the risk, and now that James has lost everything . . . I wonder if they're right.

"I understand if you want to take the pill," I tell him. "I know you're strong enough to fight off the depression if you want the memories. Especially now that your dad is gone."

James turns to press a kiss on my forehead. "I have all I need right here," he murmurs. "And if there's a chance a doctor, or anyone, can figure out how to use this pill to save others in the future, we should hold on to it." He smiles. "How the hell did we become responsible for the fate of the entire world?"

I laugh. "I have no idea."

James slides the Baggie into the leg pocket of his cargo shorts and then turns to wrap his arms around me. He pets my hair and I reach to stroke my fingers over the scars on his bicep—the names The Program took away.

"We'll keep the pill safe from The Program," he whispers. "In the morning we'll go far away until all this has blown over. We'll even get a puppy."

"Two," I say, although I know we're just playing house again. I don't mind. When your entire life has morphed into a low-budget action movie, you fantasize about a boring suburban existence. How easy it would all be.

There's a sharp pain in my temple, and I wince and touch the spot. I'm reminded of what happened the last time a memory cracked through. But just as quickly as the pain hits, it disappears. So I don't mention it. I just snuggle next to James and drift off to sleep.

*There's a whisper of wind through the trees, rustling the leaves above us. James stands behind me in the grass, brushing his fingers through my hair as he works out the knots.*

*"I feel like I'm dating Medusa," he says. "Do you have snakes hidden in here?" He brushes my hair over my shoulder and the black curls cascade down before he leans to kiss my skin.*

*"If I did, they'd surely have bitten you by now."*

*James bites playfully at my shoulder, and I spin and push him back, laughing. He leans down to pick up a pile of leaves from the ground, eying me in a way that leads me to believe they're going to end up down my shirt.*

*"We have to get to class," I warn, taking a step back from him. "Miller will be lost without us, so no ditching."*

*James doesn't answer, only grins stupidly as he moves closer.*

*"James," I warn again, although my voice is twinged with laughter, "I will knee you so hard. Don't make me do that."*

*"You won't," he says, taking another step.*

SUZANNE YOUNG

*And just as I scream and turn to run, I feel him tackle me from behind and I fall onto the grass, leaves crunching underneath me as he proceeds to shove a handful of dirty foliage down my shirt, laughing like a maniac. But true to my word, I bring my knee up. It isn't until he howls, rolling off of me, that I regret what I've done. I curse and immediately move beside him as he cups his package, his teeth barred.*

*"Goddamn it, Sloane," he chokes out. "I think you just neutered me."*

*"I'm so sorry." I lean down and put my face near his neck, trying to hug him although he's still moaning in pain. I feel awful, even if he totally started it.*

*"You just killed all our future children," he mumbles, although his hands have gravitated to my arms as he keeps me in an embrace. I breathe against his neck, kissing him there once and whispering another apology.*

*"I didn't want kids anyway," I add. "I wouldn't want them to grow up in a world like this."*

*James is quiet for a moment, and the mood changes. The tragedy of life sinking in. "But what if I want them?"*

*I sit up and stare down at him. "You're joking, right?" I ask. When I see in his expression that he's serious, that he's completely serious, I can't talk fast enough. "James," I say, "having children when they're growing up to kill themselves is stupid. Really stupid and irresponsible. Second of all—having kids is hard. Like . . . what? I'm so confused right now."*

*James shakes his head. "I'm not saying I want to plant my seed tonight or anything—"*

*"Gross!" I slap his arm and he laughs softly. "Please don't talk about seeds of anything. I think I'm going to barf."*

*"I'm just saying," James continues, taking my hand to pull me closer. "That a little me would be kind of adorable and you should consider it. Like, fifteen years from now."*

*"No."*

*"Blond hair, blue eyes, a thirst for trouble. What could go wrong?"*

*"So many things." I let James take me in his arms. It's true that anything half-James would be cute and obnoxious, but that's not enough. My heart sinks as I consider the future—the amount of people who'll die. And how I never want to experience the loss my parents have. James must sense the despair settling in, so he hugs me tighter and kisses the top of my head.*

*"Don't worry about it now," he murmurs. "I'll ask you again in fifteen years."*

I awake with a start, the memory still as clear as if it just happened. There's no residual pain, and for a second I wonder if it was just a dream. But in my heart I know it really happened, can feel it in my soul. James is next to me in bed and I shake his shoulder.

"Sleeping," he mumbles, folding the pillow over his head.

"James." I put my palm on his cheek, and he blinks his eyes open. "I had another memory. We were playing in the grass and you were talking about having children."

He pauses, then gets up on his elbow. "I'm sorry, what?"

I laugh. "You said you wanted kids and you were so sweet. I had a memory, and right now I'm not even dizzy. I don't know, yesterday was a pretty stressful day, so it must have spurred something on. But maybe returning memories aren't always bad. James," I say, ecstatic and relieved, "we were so in love."

James smiles then, pulling me closer. I'm about to kiss him, ready to refresh his memory too, when there's a loud commotion from downstairs. I hear Dallas scream—actually scream, and both James and I bolt upright in bed.

We're still in our clothes from last night, and James pulls me from the room so quickly, I'm afraid I'm going to trip over my own feet. He staggers to a stop in the hallway when we hear voices downstairs. The true devastation hits me—The Program is here. They've found us.

James spins to face me, his eyes wide and terrified. "Back door," he whispers, and then yanks me toward the small doorway and spiral staircase that leads to the kitchen. We're halfway down when we hear the footsteps over our heads. James curses, and then we're moving faster, clumsier. I bang my elbow on the door frame as we bust into the kitchen. Behind us there's a trample of footsteps on the staircase.

James crashes through the screen door, and the morning light is bright, the air is crisp. I'm gasping in puffs of air as we escape the house, heading for the woods as our cover; it's our only chance. I'm still barefoot when my toes sink into the dewy grass and soon we reach the bridge—a bridge where I stood just this week, thinking how beautiful the world could still be. I was wrong.

"Stop!"

I glance over my shoulder and see a handler, dressed in the signature white coat, chasing us. "James!" I shout to spur him on, fear cracking my voice. James's hand is clasped tightly around mine even though he could be long gone by now if I wasn't holding him back. The second we're over the bridge, James darts to the left. We disappear into the woods, and he lets my hand go to protect his face from the branches threatening to scratch out our eyes.

We're hopping over fallen tree limbs. Branches dig into my forearms and one opens a gash on my cheek. We have to keep running.

We have to get away.

The noise behind us quiets, but then up ahead there's a flash of movement, making James and I stumble to a stop. I turn around, looking in every direction, terrified that we've been surrounded. But then I see the blond hair, and I moan my relief.

"It's Dallas," I say, and now I'm the one leading. Dallas notices us and waves us forward, but she puts her finger to her lips. The woods are dense, and I have no idea which direction we're even headed.

When we finally catch up with Dallas, she's cut up, her shirt ripped and hanging off her shoulder. "Realm?" I ask out of breath. "Cas?"

"Cas ran ahead," she says, pointing in one direction and then another, as if she's lost. "I have no idea where Realm is. He disappeared. Damn it," she says when there are shouts behind us. "This way." She motions to the right and then we're running again.

# CHAPTER EIGHT

**MY LEGS ARE BURNING AND ACHY, AND I KNOW THE** minute we stop, the soles of my bare feet will be gushing blood. Just when I think we'll never get out of the woods alive, there's a small clearing and then pavement. I've never been so happy to see civilization before.

Ahead of us is the back side of a gas station, and Dallas shouts with relief after she sees Cas there, bent over and breathing heavily. As we start toward him, a van pulls around the store, and another comes from the other side. The world seems to drop out from under me, and James and I turn back to run into the woods, but it's too late. Through the leaves we can see the white of the jackets heading in our direction, and I wrap my arms around myself, choking on a cry.

"I'm so sorry, Sloane." James breathes out. I shut my eyes

against the grief, hearing the crunch of brush under heavy boots as the handlers get closer. Hearing Dallas screaming so loudly she begins to lose her voice. I know we have nowhere left to run.

I look up at James and reach to put my palm on his cheek. Our world is falling apart, and all our dreams of normalcy were just that: Dreams. "I love you madly," I whisper.

His tears run down over my hand, and I rub them away before he grabs me and pulls me into a fierce hug. "I'll come for you," he says into my ear. "I won't let them erase you. Wait for me, Sloane." His voice is choked off by his cries, and I see the movement behind him. Slowly, hoping this is all a nightmare, I step out of his arms and see Dallas, a handler twisting her own arms around her like a straitjacket. The doors of a van are open, and three other handlers are walking in our direction, two emerging from the woods. They seem to all be converging on us at once, like a nightmare I would have thought too awful to be real.

The passenger door of the van opens, and I'm so overwhelmed by the situation that it takes me a minute to realize who climbs out: Arthur Pritchard, in a sharp navy suit. I have this sudden and crazy hope that this is all a plan to save us. I take a step toward him, ready to beg for our lives, when Roger walks out from the other side of the van. He actually laughs when he sees me, shaking his head like he can't believe it. When Dallas sees him, she begins screaming—something manic and animalistic—once again.

I can't believe Roger's here. I can't believe this is happening. I back into James, and across the lot the doctor slides his hands into the pockets of his suit.

"I am sorry for this, Sloane," he says sadly. His shiny shoes make a tapping noise on the pavement as he moves closer, keeping an eye on James.

James puts his arm in front of me, slowly backing us up, and then to the side as the handlers encircle us. We could try to fight our way out, but there are so many of them. How would that end? I look back to the woods, wondering if Realm is out there somewhere, if he can see us. If he'll save us.

"I never meant to betray you, Sloane," the doctor says. "But I had warned you about running. Ultimately, you put your trust in the wrong people."

I'm too devastated to fully comprehend his words, and I hold tightly to James as he tries to keep us shielded. Dallas is struggling to free herself from her handler, yelling for Cas, but our friend is just standing alone, watching her helplessly.

"They've come for The Treatment, Sloane," Arthur says. "I'm so sorry." Hurt crosses his features, and I can see his intention was never to harm us.

"Then why are you helping them?" I ask.

"I didn't tell them you had The Treatment," he says, "even though I knew you did. They've been embedded with you this entire time. I told The Program I could help procure your surrender today." He swallows hard, glancing back at Roger, who is just starting to focus on what the doctor is saying. "But really, I'm here to make sure you do what's right."

James stills, and I feel my face go cold. "And what's that, Arthur?" I ask.

"Don't let them get their hands on The Treatment."

Arthur has barely gotten the words out before his entire body convulses, his yelp cut off by the vibration of the Taser wires shooting volts of electricity through his body. He drops to the ground, flopping like a fish, and I scream, horrified.

James grabs my arm and we start to run, but one of the handlers catches me around the waist and tears me away, lifting me off the ground as he backs me toward a van. There is so much screaming in all directions, and Arthur's body looks lifeless, lying on the concrete in a heap. Cas is still standing there as two handlers wrestle James in the other direction, tearing us apart.

Before the handler holding me can set me down to properly restrain me, I kick him hard, sending myself headlong into the ground. My forehead ricochets off the cement, and for a moment I see stars. A warm rush of liquid travels down over my eye and I blink through it, wiping the blood away with my hand.

The handler is about to converge on me again. "Wait," Cas calls out, surprising me. I'm half-dazed as I look up, seeing him slowly approach with his hands up in surrender.

"Run, Cas," I say in a weak voice as my head spins. Now's his chance to save himself.

Watching his approach, the handler steps back, giving me

space. James is across the parking lot with a handler on each side of him, gaping in concern and terror. As Cas gets closer, he presses his lips together, looking absolutely miserable. "I'm so sorry, Sloane," he says.

I wipe the blood out of my eye again and slowly sit up. I hitch in a breath as it hits me, and fresh tears start to stream down my cheeks. "No," I say, when the crushing reality settles over me. "No, Cas."

"Just give them The Treatment," he begs quietly, as if he's the one who's pained. "Give up The Treatment and they'll let you go."

"You son of a bitch!" James yells, renewing the guard of his handlers as they wrestle him back a few steps. "I will fucking kill you!"

Cas's eyes weaken, but he shakes his head, determined to keep his focus on me. "Give them the pill, Sloane, and this will all be over. We'll be able to go home again." Tears mix with the blood on my face; I'm too stunned to speak. "We couldn't keep running," he adds in my silence. "My intel showed we had only a few days lead. They would have caught us, but I made a deal. The Treatment for our freedom."

My head is spinning, and it's not just from where I hit it. Arthur lies unconscious several feet away. Behind him, Roger watches on, a sick smile on his lips. In his expression I can see that he has absolutely no intention of letting us leave here today. I try to get to my feet but stumble to the ground again, skinning my knee and crying out in pain. I hear a scuffle

SUZANNE YOUNG

and know James is once again trying to get to me. But they'll never let him get that close again. I sit back on the pavement and look around once more. When I find Dallas, she looks catatonic.

Her eyes are wide, unfocused; her mouth is hanging open. Her arms are still wrapped around herself as a handler restrains her, but she's not fighting. She's just staring at her best friend, absolutely lost in her grief. I cry for her—the only person Dallas had let herself trust again, and this is what he's done.

Cas reads my expression and slowly, he turns to face Dallas. He tilts his head, covering his own cry at her appearance. "Let her go!" he yells out in a thick voice. "She's not part of this. You said you only wanted the pill."

"I'm sorry, Casanova," Roger says, stepping over Arthur Pritchard's unconscious body. "I'm afraid our agreement is void." Cas swings to face him, his posture hardening. "On closer look, your friends have been deemed infected. We'll be taking them all into custody at this time."

"You're not going anywhere near her, you fuck!" Cas shouts. Roger laughs, shaking his head dismissively before another handler puts his hand on Cas's shoulder, a subtle warning to stay back.

"Oh, come now," Roger says with a grin. "Dallas and I are old friends, aren't we, sweetheart?"

Cas and James both start cussing at Roger, and my stomach lurches at the thought that anyone could be as sadistic as he is. I look at Dallas and freeze. She's lifted her gaze from Cas to Roger, her lips curling, her eyes narrowing. She's coming back to life, but as what, I'm not sure. I don't think she's herself. I don't even think she's sane.

Roger isn't looking at Dallas, though. He glances around at the handlers, growing impatient at the scene. "Confiscate The Treatment and grab the girls. Put him in the other van." He motions to James. "Casanova," he adds, turning to him. "Thank you for your cooperation."

My head and heart are throbbing. We've been betrayed. Cas gave us over to The Program. How could he trust them, knowing what they've done to us in the past? A handler comes over to help me up, and I look across the parking lot at James, finding him already watching me. His face is wet with tears, his body slumped with failure.

We didn't make it. Once again The Program has won, and we're about to lose everything. James glances around the parking lot, maybe checking for one last escape, but when his gaze returns to mine, I see the hopelessness in it. His left eye has started to puff up from where he must have been hit, and I can only imagine how my blood-soaked face looks.

When I'm finally to my feet, I know our time is up. We're not even close enough to touch, close enough to talk. "Where's the pill?" the handler asks me, patting down my pockets. I'm alarmed by his touch, and then I remember: James has The Treatment. He seems to realize the same thing at that very moment.

SUZANNE YOUNG

We can't let The Program get their hands on the pill. They can't have control over the ingredients. If the pill is gone, there's still the hope that someday another brilliant scientist like Evelyn Valentine will come along and create a better one. James shrugs helplessly, as if asking if he should do it. I smile sadly, thinking it's bittersweet. If James survives this—he'll remember me. All of me.

The handler starts upending my pockets, roughly searching for The Treatment, but I block out his existence. There's just me and James, our eyes locked on each other. I nod.

As the handlers are focused on me, James slips his hand into his pocket, rifling around until he brings the pill out, a flash of orange between his fingers. He pauses one quick second, before placing it on his tongue and swallowing it dry. Once it's down, he closes his eyes, and begins to cry.

But I stop. James is safe—he's the strongest person I know. The Treatment won't hurt him. And as long as The Program doesn't kill or lobotomize him, they won't be able to steal his memories. He can fake erasure. He's the best liar I know. "I love you," I say when he looks at me again. He can't actually hear me, but he reads my lips and says it back.

"She doesn't have it," the handler searching me calls out. Roger casts an annoyed glance in my direction before turning on Cas. "Where is it?" But Cas is staring at me, and I think he witnessed the entire exchange. He confirms my suspicions.

"It's gone," he says. "Thank God it's gone."

Roger's confused for a moment, looking around at all of

us. Ultimately The Treatment isn't what brought him out here, no matter what deal Cas made. Roger calls for them to get James in the van, and the handlers grab his arms and start dragging his bucking body. I scream for them to stop, but I know it's useless. My voice gives out and I can only watch as James is sedated, looking at me one last time before his eyes slide shut.

Roger tosses an amused glance at Cas and starts toward Dallas, knowing how much it would piss him off. It reminds me of how Roger was in The Program, and how he would taunt Realm by harassing me. *Realm?* I look toward the woods again, wondering if he's there, watching. I won't believe he abandoned us. He wouldn't do that to me.

"Is she your girlfriend?" Roger asks Cas as he comes to stop in front of Dallas. She's helpless, but she looks at him with an eerie sort of calm. I'm not sure I've ever seen a more terrifying sight.

Cas ignores Roger's question and tries to get Dallas's attention. "I'm sorry," he calls to her. "I had to stop running. I was tired, Dallas. I wanted us—you—to finally have a normal life. I'll talk to them." He looks around. "I'll get you out of this. I promise."

Roger sucks on his teeth, looking Dallas up and down and evaluating her. "Oh, don't make promises you can't keep," he says to Cas. "She hates that." He grins, and I think he's the biggest monster I've ever met. But before I can imagine what horrors he has in store, Dallas reacts.

In a sudden movement she kicks out the knee of the handler behind her, spinning out of his grip and freeing her arms. She's a whirlwind of motion, and I see the glint of the metal of her knife before I realize she'd even grabbed it from her pocket. She growls like a wild animal and slams into Roger, burying the blade to the hilt in his gut.

"I hate you!" She screams a high-pitched squeal that's barely human. Roger is too stunned, or too hurt, to do more than double over. Dallas yanks out her knife and plunges it into his chest with both hands, before another handler tackles her to the pavement with a sick thud. Roger is wailing, rolling on his side as blood pools on the gray concrete.

Before they can take her away, Dallas stares down at Roger. His blood is halfway up her arms and splashed across her shirt. And she begins to laugh—not joyous or even maniacal. It's unhinged. It's crazy. She starts to pull on her dreads, yelling that she wins, she fucking wins, even as they start to drag her away.

My body shivers, my teeth chattering even though I can't feel the cold. Arthur Pritchard is slowly waking up, but they pull me past him before he's fully conscious. A handler snaps restraints on my wrists, claiming they're for my protection, although really they're for his.

A van pulls away before the others do, and I realize James was inside it. He's gone. Dallas is gone. The handler leans me against the door of the van before taking a moment to call in the incident. Although Cas isn't in custody, he's led by with a handler. He pauses, glancing over apologetically. But I don't care to hear his excuses. There's a giant hole in my chest, leaking out the remainder of my feelings.

"You killed her," I murmur in his direction, thinking of how broken Dallas is now. "You've killed what's left of her."

Cas sways with sorrow. "It wasn't supposed to happen like this," he says, pulling his arm from the handler. "They told me she'd be safe. That we all would."

"Then you're stupid for believing The Program. You're stupid for thinking they'd ever let us walk out of here. And what about Realm? What did you do to him?"

Cas furrows his brows, confused. But then my handler is back, opening the door and pushing me onto the seat. He buckles me in place, leaving me helpless with my hands bound. From outside the van, Cas watches on in horror. "I have no idea where Realm is," he says before they slam the door shut.

There's a spike of fear that Realm isn't waiting in the woods at all. That maybe Roger already found him and did something to him. I'm so overwhelmed. I'm so completely buried in despair, I don't think I'll ever find the way out.

Up front two handlers climb onto the seats. The driver reports our location, and over the scanner the operator asks if Roger is dead.

"Not sure," the handler responds. "Ambulance is in route."

"If Roger survives," I call out in a raspy voice, my entire body trembling, "I'll finish the job. I'll kill every single one of you."

The handler turns, his brown eyes wide, as the other guy

glances at me in the rearview mirror. They have the balls to actually look concerned. I rest my head against the seat, rocking with the bumps of the road, thinking I've come undone. All hope is lost now.

I'm going back to The Program.

# PART III
# NO APOLOGIES

TEENS TAKEN INTO CUSTODY

The Program is reporting that they've taken a group of teens hiding near Lake Tahoe, Nevada. The names are being withheld at this time, but there's speculation that the suspects include Sloane Barstow and James Murphy.

The two teens, first reported missing last month, have led authorities on a multistate manhunt. Exactly why Barstow and Murphy were running has never been made public, but the effectiveness of The Program has come into question.

Arthur Pritchard, creator of The Program, has stepped down amid the controversy, and his lawyer will be making a statement later in the week. He is currently unavailable for comment.

—Reported by Kellan Thomas

# CHAPTER ONE

THERE ARE VOICES, BUT I CAN'T MAKE OUT THEIR words. Not at first. My eyelids are heavy as I try to open them, letting in small slivers of light when I blink. The voice next to me is only an echo.

"Is there anybody in there?" she asks again more clearly.

My lips are numb as I turn my head lazily to the side. My head is throbbing from where I hit it on the pavement. "Help me," I whisper to the waiting nurse. I try to reach out, but my wrists are fastened down. I'm surrounded by stark white walls with the smell of bleach thick in the air. The nurse leans closer, and I recognize her from my first stay in The Program. Nurse Kell places her hand on my shoulder.

"We are going to help you," she says, an earnest smile on her thin lips. "But first we have to cure the infection." She takes a syringe from the pocket of her fuzzy blue sweater and uncaps it. "Now don't move, dear," she says, pushing up my shirtsleeve, "or this will really hurt."

I hitch in a breath, choking on it as I start to whimper. "Please, Kell," I say. "I'm not sick. I'm really not."

"That's what they all say." Her manners are sweet but firm. And when I feel the pinch and burn of the needle, I openly sob.

A handler walks in. He's tall, a bit unkempt compared to the others. He's the same one who put his hand on Cas's shoulder back at the parking lot. My heart breaks and I shake my head, trying to rid myself of Cas's memory. Pretending the past few weeks with him never happened. I can't reconcile in my mind that the guy who looked out for us is really the one who turned us in.

The handler comes over, talking quietly with Kell. When they finish, they unfasten me from the bed and drop me into a wheelchair, securing me to the armrests. The burn from the needle has turned to a tingle, and then it's like warm bathwater. A sense of calm stretches over me, even though I know logically it's not really there. The drug is numbing my panic, but it can't mask everything. I won't let it. I kick my legs, trying to buck my body out of the chair, but I'm too lethargic. I end up flopping like a fish, gasping for breath, and by the time I'm out in the hallway, I'm too tired to fight anymore. I melt into the chair, feeling the trickle of tears slide down my cheeks.

"Where are we going?" I mumble as Nurse Kell walks hurriedly beside me, her hands in the pockets of her sweater.

"To see the doctor, Sloane. They need to determine if you're a candidate for continued therapy."

My heart skips. "And if I'm not?" I ask. Kell doesn't answer me, just smiles as if it's a silly question. We're passing patients in the hallway, flashes of lemon-yellow scrubs streaking my vision. But it's the last face I see before I'm pushed through the double doors that sinks my hope.

Lacey Klamath stares at me from a chair near the window, her eyes wide and doelike. Her blond hair is styled in a short pixie cut, and her serene expression gives no sign of recognizing me, gives no hint of emotion. I almost call out to her but stop short when I see a nurse appear at her side, placing a small Dixie cup in her hand. Obediently and without complaint, Lacey swallows whatever's inside and goes back to staring blankly ahead.

When the handler pushes me through the doors marked THERAPY WING, I turn to face forward again. She's here—Lacey is here. Although I'm glad to know she's safe, it's obvious she's . . . different. I don't know what they've done to her, but I have to lock the thought away. I'll come back for her. Just like I pray James will come back for me.

They don't free my arms once I'm inside the doctor's office. I sit on the wrong side of a huge oak desk that's cluttered with papers. This isn't The Program I was in before, even if Nurse Kell is still playing the role of Nurse Ratched. Since I left Oregon, other facilities have opened up around the country. There's no way to tell what state I'm even in.

Unlike the hospital feel in the hallways, this office is homey, yet masculine. There are rows of bookshelves lining the hunter-green walls, a heavy maroon rug under the ornate chair they've fastened me to. This reminds me of someone's high-end man cave, complete with a standing globe that could be filled with liquor bottles.

Are they trying to create a false sense of comfort? Normalcy? Doesn't matter, I guess. I have to find Dallas and make sure she's okay. She's always been the one to get information for us, but now it's my turn.

Doors open behind me, and I clench my muscles. I half expect Dr. Warren to walk up, her brown hair in a cute ponytail—so nonthreatening and relatable. But the figure who rounds my chair is not Dr. Warren. I watch as a man sits in the leather chair on the other side of the desk.

He looks up after opening my file and smiles warmly. "Hello, Sloane," he says. His voice is clipped as if he's spent years getting rid of an accent. He has a manicured salt-and-pepper beard, highlighting what would be a handsome face—except for the scar that splits through his top lip. Even still, it doesn't make him unattractive, just a little edgier than the sterile doctors I'm used to. I look him over, my thoughts honest because of the drugs coursing through my veins.

"My name is Dr. Beckett," he says, and pulls a pair of thin wire-rimmed glasses from his front pocket. He puts them on, studying me. "I see they've already given you the medication." He jots something on the paper in my file. "That's unusual."

"I would say most of this is unusual." My voice is hoarse, and Dr. Beckett puts his elbows on the desk, leaning closer.

"I tend to agree, Sloane. You've already been through The Program. What could have happened to land you here twice? Has the depression set in again?"

"Are you joking?" I ask. "I'm here because I tried to get away. Because you're all a bunch of psychopaths!" My outburst is immediately met with another rush of warmth, and I curse as my head lulls to the side. I don't want to be relaxed. I want to tear this place apart.

The doctor nods his head solemnly. "Seems you've grown delusional. It's not uncommon." He jots down a note in my file. "When suicidal, patients often misinterpret the world around them. They grow paranoid. Think everyone's out to the get them. It's too bad you feel so alone. We were all really rooting for you."

"I'm sure."

"Oh, come now," he says, waving his hand. "Use your common sense, Sloane. You can't really believe we wanted you to fail. In fact, Nurse Kell personally requested this assignment. We want you to be successful. Think of your potential. You could have been such a help to the community—a poster child. Pretty, smart, flawed. The public would have embraced you as a motivational speaker. You would have convinced kids to volunteer for The Program instead of us having to seek them out. But you didn't follow your doctor's instructions. Or your handler's." He pauses, and folds his hands in front of him. "I am sorry to hear about Kevin. He was a good man. We worked together in another facility."

Although the medication should keep my calm, at the mention of Kevin I sit up straighter; the ties on my wrists squeeze in protest. "What did you do to him?"

Dr. Beckett shakes his head as if he doesn't know what I'm talking about. "Me? No, my dear. He became sick again because of you. Because of the stress you and James Murphy inflicted on him. Kevin took a dive from the St. Johns Bridge shortly after you skipped town."

It's a crushing blow, and I lower my face. Pain, sharp and jagged, rips into me before the medicine can try to mask it. Kevin isn't in The Program. He's dead. "You killed him," I whisper, squeezing my eyes shut.

"Don't be silly," the doctor says with a twinge of annoyance. "We wanted to help Kevin, but he chose another way. They do that sometimes—the sick ones. My question is"—he takes off his glasses—"what will you decide? Given the chance, would you kill yourself, Sloane? Would you go that far to keep your infected memories?"

Yes. I think my short answer is yes—but why is this the question? Why are there no other viable options? I want to be strong. I shout inside my head that I *have* to be strong, but really I start to fall apart. Kevin—my handler, my friend—is dead. The Program could have thrown him off the bridge for all I know, but even if he did jump, he did it to protect us. The Program pressured him into it. And when they start to exert that same force on me, what will I do? Everything is gone. They've changed Lacey. They'll change me. Is life worth living?

"Do we have to keep you restrained for your own protection, Sloane?" Dr. Beckett asks gently.

"Yes," I respond, defiant and angry. "Yes, you do."

Dr. Beckett exhales and then falls against the backrest of his seat. "That's too bad." He presses a call button on his phone. "Have Nurse Kell stand by with the next dose," he says, shooting me a wary look. He takes a moment to compose himself, folding up his glasses before tucking them into his pocket. I have a thought that he wears them only to appear more official. We're apparently skipping that stage of our relationship.

"We can be friends," he tells me in a soft voice, "if you want. But there is one definite to our equation: You will never, ever, leave this place with your memories. We just can't allow it. Try and understand our position."

"You're monsters."

"Are we? Or are we the cure for a worldwide epidemic? All vaccines came with an initial loss. Aren't you willing to die for future generations?"

"No. Are you willing to kill me for them?"

"Yes. Simply, the answer is yes."

I don't remember my time in The Program. Were they always this blunt? This terrifying? Or has my current situation stripped away the niceties? Part of me wishes he'd lie to me, say something to placate the fear. Then again, his honesty will keep me grounded, keep my purpose renewed.

"Now," Dr. Beckett says, "I know you've been under extreme duress. Have any memories resurfaced?"

There's a jab of grief that comes with the knowledge that I'll once again lose the pieces, lose Miller. But if I hope to get out of this alive, I'll have to play along—at least for a little while. "Yes," I say. "But not negative ones. I'll . . . I'll tell you about them, no fighting. No lying. But first you have to do something for me. I need to know that Dallas is okay."

The doctor smiles, seeming pleased that I'm willing to participate in my recovery. "Ah, yes. Dallas Stone. Seems her illness is fairly progressive. They don't expect her to survive the night without extreme measures. She's in solitary until further notice."

"What? You can't just lock her up. She's not an animal!"

"She was ripping out her own hair. She's a danger to herself and others. For God's sake, she stabbed a handler."

"He deserved it!" I shout.

"She's gone completely mad. She'll kill someone."

"Let me talk to her. Please." I yank on my restraints, wishing I could clasp my hands in front of me to show him how sincere I am. Dr. Beckett tilts his head, seeming to weigh his options. "She's my friend," I plead. "I can calm her down." Dallas *is* my friend, one I would fight for. I wish I would have realized this sooner, gotten us out that house before The Program showed up.

"You really think you can get through to her?" he asks cautiously.

"Yes." I breathe out. "I really do." Although helping Dallas is part of the reasoning, I'm more concerned with her keeping her shit together until I figure out what to do. We'll need each other to stay sane.

After a long moment Dr. Beckett nods and presses a button on the intercom—watching me as he talks. "Please take Miss Barstow down to solitary to speak with the patient. Keep them both close." When he sits back in the chair, he picks up my file and glances through it once again.

"I hope you really can talk her down, Sloane," he says, slapping the manila folder on the desk. "Because if not, you'll really hate what comes next."

# CHAPTER TWO

**THE HANDLER PUSHING MY WHEELCHAIR SMELLS** like cigarette smoke. He's the same one who brought me from my room earlier, but Nurse Kell is nowhere in sight. This small fluctuation, the fact that he doesn't smell like a Band-Aid, is a bit of hope. It reminds me of—

I lower my face, tears gathering now that the medicine's calming effects have started to wane. Kevin is dead. Lacey will be devastated. The painful fact is that it really could be my fault. If I had followed the rules, Kevin wouldn't have had to help me. He would still be alive.

There's a brush against my shoulder, and then a cloth is wiped across my eyes, over my cheeks, under my nose. I shrug away, and when I look back at the handler, he's tucking a handkerchief into his pocket.

"You're crying," he says in a low voice. "Don't do that."

I scoff, ready to tell him to drop dead because what does he care? I'm crying over a real tragedy, and he's just some asshole working for The Program. Before I can, the handler stops at a doorway with a small rectangular window and then takes a keycard from the retractable chain at his waistband. He pushes the door open, weaving his head as he tries to see inside the dimly lit room. He takes the Taser from his hip and disappears inside. I'm listening for Dallas's scream, or worse, the sound of her hitting the floor, but the silence stretches on until the handler emerges with a stony expression. He comes behind my chair again and pushes me inside the room. He unfastens my hands, giving me a stern look as warning, and then walks out, closing the door behind him.

Solitary is darker than the other places in the hospital I've seen, but it's not gloomy. The floor is covered in gray rubber tiles, and the walls have white padding. There's a small set of track lights, but there are no windows. The corners of the room are set in shadows. That's where I find Dallas, sitting on the floor with her hands bound in front of her. She's wearing bright-yellow scrubs that wash out her complexion. When she recognizes me, she smiles broadly. Her gap-toothed grin is no longer charming, not when she looks insane.

"Did I kill him?" she asks.

Has she been focused on Roger this entire time? "I don't know," I say. "Last I heard, the ambulance was coming for him." I hate the disappointed look in her eyes. What's become of us—wishing for someone's death? What has The Program done to us?

"Did they find Realm?" she asks.

"I don't know. They haven't mentioned him yet." I don't want to voice the possibility that Roger could have hurt him. This way I can hope that Realm got away. Right now he might be the only person who can save us. James will be able to remember—he took The Treatment—but he's still somewhere in The Program. I just hope he's all right.

"No one gets away," Dallas says, rocking gently. Her entire demeanor is smaller, vulnerable. "The Program will find Realm. It's only a matter of time, because somewhere in your head is a clue that will help find him. They'll get it out of you. Or me," she reasons, rolling her eyes up to the ceiling. "But probably not me because I'll be dead."

"Dallas," I whisper, leaning forward in the chair. "I need you right now. We need each other. Pull yourself together or it's over."

"It's already over."

"No." I climb down from the chair, my body still lethargic from the earlier medication. I take Dallas's hands in mine, trying to draw her back. Trying to wake her up. "We survived The Program before," I say. "We can do it again. Do you know who I saw? Lacey—she's here."

This seems to invoke mild interest in Dallas's expression. Her dark eyes widen, a slight curve in her lip. "She's alive?"

I nod emphatically, hiding my despair at Lacey's actual condition. "She is," I say. "And now we just have to hang on.

You have to hang on, Dallas, until I figure out what to do."

"I'm tired of fighting," she whispers. "Cas was right—it's too hard. I think I'd rather die."

Her sadness fills the room, fills me. I wrap my arms around her in a hug, absorbing her pain as best I can. Her hair no longer smells earthy; it smells of wet paper. Of something breaking down and dissolving. In a way Dallas is exactly where she belongs—she's suicidal, and without this intervention . . . she'd be dead. I can't let that happen.

"You have to be stronger," I say bleakly. She feels tiny in my arms, fragile. "You don't get to quit. I won't let you."

There's a click behind me, and the door opens. The handler stands there, his face hidden in gray shadows. It's time for me to leave. I pull back and put my hands on her cheeks, but I see she's not there—not really. Her eyes are unfocused, unfeeling. It's like Dallas is already dead.

*I'll save us,* I mouth, feeling the sting of tears. *Just fight a little longer.*

The handler walks over and takes my arm; he isn't rough, but firm. He sets me back in the chair, reattaching the restraints and keeping an eye on Dallas. She watches, but doesn't have any reaction. She's lost inside her head right now.

I murmur my good-bye to Dallas as the handler backs me out of the room. We're gliding through the hall, and I'm completely grief-stricken. Dallas is crazy, Lacey is erased; right now I'm the only one left standing, and ironically enough, I'm strapped down to a wheelchair. I can't wait around for James or

Realm to show up and rescue me. I'll have to gather information, explore this facility, and figure out how to get out of here. I know what The Program wants from me: complacency. I'll need to brush up on my acting skills.

"Any chance you could take me on a tour?" I turn to the handler, asking as sweetly as possible. There's a small tug of a smile on his lips as he flicks a quick look in my direction. He has hazel eyes, not remarkable or arresting like James's, but they seem kind. He's definitely more human than the other handlers I've seen—with the exception of Kevin.

"It's a little late for guided tours," he says in that same soft voice. "Maybe tomorrow."

I straighten up, disappointed but not completely deterred. I'll block out the sadness, get rid of the emotions. I was telling Dallas the truth. I will save us.

I have to.

There is quiet humming when I open my eyes. The morning sun filters in the surely sealed window of my room. I blink quickly and then turn to see Nurse Kell sitting in a chair next to my bed, knitting, of all things. I watch her, a bit disoriented, before I clear my voice to talk.

"What are you doing?" I ask.

She doesn't glance up, but the humming stops as the clicking of the metal needles continues. "I was letting you sleep in," she says. "You looked so tired yesterday."

I clench my teeth but then remember my promise to myself

the night before. I have to play along. "Yes, well," I say reasonably, "it could have been the medication you gave me."

She stops and lowers her needles. "I suppose. But maybe we won't need them this morning. Dr. Beckett would like to see you."

"Okay. But any chance I can get out of these restraints on a permanent basis? They're rubbing my wrists raw."

Kell's face flinches and she looks down toward my arms. "Poor thing," she says, examining the skin. "I'll check on your progress and see what I can do. The answer will be up to you, of course."

It's so hard to keep my sarcastic tongue from lashing out at her. Because if it was up to me, not only would I not need to be tied down, I wouldn't be in this horrible place. I want to spit in Nurse Kell's face, tell her how cruel she is. I just lower my head.

"I'll try my best." I sit there passively, but inside I'm boiling over. "Why do you do this, Kell? What's in it for you?"

She seems genuinely surprised by the question, and sets her knitting aside. "I'm saving lives. I've even saved yours once."

Does she really think that? I look her over, seeing that she does. Her round face, her short, curled red hair isn't sinister. She could be someone's doting grandmother. "You know what they're doing to us," I say, my facade falling away. "They're changing us against our wills. They're ruining our lives."

Nurse Kell's small green eyes weaken. "I know you think that, honey," she says, "but you're wrong. I've been a nurse for thirty years, and nothing, *nothing* could have prepared me for what happened when the epidemic started. I don't think you realize—"

"I lived through it," I interrupt.

"Yes, you were sick and lived through it. Which means you never saw it clearly. Those infected have thoughts that are skewed and false. I pulled a butter knife out of a fifteen-year-old's throat. That's when The Program decided spoons were a better option in the cafeteria. I got on a chair and cut the sheet a thirteen-year-old hung herself from, spirals carved with her nails into the soft flesh of her forearm." Kell's cheeks glow pink and she leans closer. "I buried two grandchildren in the past year, Sloane. So don't assume that I don't know about the epidemic. I know it far better than you do. I'm just a person willing to do what I can to stop it."

I'm speechless. She's a human being after all. "Why are you at this hospital?" I ask finally. "Why did you request to be my nurse here?"

She smiles and reaches to brush my hair behind my ear. "Because I've seen where you started—I saw the darkness in your eyes. I'm not going to give up on you until you're well again." Her expression tells me she thinks this is a noble cause and that I should be grateful. Maybe if they weren't my memories she helped erase, I'd see her good intentions.

Inside I'm screaming, *Thank you for ruining my life!* I can barely keep my voice steady when I murmur, "Thank you for saving me," instead.

\*     \*     \*

After our heart-to-heart, Nurse Kell helps me dress. I'm in a fresh pair of yellow scrubs with fuzzy slipper socks when she calls in the handler. He's the one from last night, and my anxiety eases slightly, even though I'm not entirely sure why. He could be just as horrible as all the rest.

"Asa," Nurse Kell calls to him as he pushes in the wheelchair. "Can you bring Sloane to see Dr. Beckett? He's expecting her." The handler doesn't respond, but he does take my hand to help me into the chair, an unusual show of kindness that catches me off guard.

"It'll all be better soon," Nurse Kell says as she gently straps down my wrists. Then she steps back, and Asa steers me from the room before I can respond.

The handler is gliding me through the halls once again, like a continuation from last night, but this time our pace is slower. He's taking his time. There are several patients walking freely, but none of them is Lacey. I look for her, both dreading and needing to see her. To see what's left of her.

"I want to show you something," Asa says quietly, pushing the button that opens a set of double doors—ones that don't lead to the therapy wing. I glance over my shoulder at him, trying to discern why he'd be sneaking me around. He reminds me of Realm, so I don't argue. We begin down a quiet wing where the white walls fade to a dusty gray.

"Any chance this is the way out?" I ask, trying to lighten the heaviness that's fallen on his posture. Asa doesn't look at me, only straight ahead.

"Not exactly."

My heart thumps hard, and I face front again. My ease is starting to evaporate, quickly replaced with anxiety. Asa's pace slows as we approach another set of doors. "This is where they keep them," he murmurs.

"Them?" It's obvious this part of the hospital isn't in regular use. It's quiet—mausoleum quiet—and the air smells lightly of urine. Fear is about to get the best of me and I begin to tug on the restraints, subtly at first, but then more aggressively. I don't know where he's taking me. I don't know what's happening!

And then suddenly we stop. We're in a large room—much like the leisure room, but instead of distractions and card games, there are a few scattered wheelchairs with people in gray scrubs. They're all facing a window, or in one case, facing a black-and-white painting on the wall. Several of them have a white patch over their left eye.

"What's going on?" I ask in a shaky voice.

"Doctors found that color disturbs them this soon after surgery," Asa murmurs. "Noise, too. They keep them isolated until their minds are a bit steadier."

I spin around in the chair, the pressure on my wrists enough to make me wince. "Are you saying these people have been lobotomized?"

Asa nods, meeting my gaze. "That's exactly what I'm saying, Sloane. This is what this facility does. You're one of the untreatable—this is what's going to happen to you."

The world starts to close in on me, and I search the room

once again, trying to make sense of it. Although lobotomy was always a threat, I didn't know it was definite. I never pictured it like this. I don't think I believed it could happen to me. "But I'm cooperating," I say in a small voice. "I'm telling them—"

"They're extracting the information they need, and then you'll end up here. They all do."

I blink and feel a warm tear slip over my cheek and drip onto my thigh. I'm stunned, horrified, *traumatized* by what Asa is showing me. I don't know what to do. I'm so goddamn afraid, I can't think.

"You have about a week," Asa says, "before they'll bring you down here. The longer you can hold out on the information, the more time you buy yourself. I just wanted you to know the stakes, Sloane."

A week. I have my life for one more week. How does someone process this information without spiraling into complete madness? What does he expect me to do? I can't just bust myself out. This is almost like another form of torture.

"Why did you bring me here?" I murmur, staring again at the backs of heads, the slumped shoulders, the empty souls.

"There's someone here I thought you should see."

*James.* I try and leap from the chair, searching for him, but I am immediately pulled back by the restraints as they bite into my skin. *Please, no. Please.*

Asa bends down, his cheek close to mine as he reaches past me, pointing to one chair across the room. From the profile I can see it's an old man, and I sputter out a relieved cry because it's not James. The handler turns, the bristle of his scruff tickling my skin.

"They've crushed the rebellion," he whispers. "But James and Michael Realm got away, and now any hope of ending The Program lies with you and your friends. I wanted you to know how little time you have left to figure out how."

James is okay. Oh my God, James got away. But my solace is short-lived as I stare straight ahead at the man in the chair. I recognize him. "Arthur?" I ask, my voice cracking over his name.

Asa stands and pushes me closer to the doctor. I'm in disbelief as I study him, his gray beard, his wrinkled skin. He has a patch over his eye and there's a thin line of drool from his lip to the chest of his gray scrubs.

I start to cry. "Arthur?" I call again, hoping he'll just snap out of it and look at me. But he doesn't react at all. He stares at nothing, seeing nothing. Knowing nothing. Arthur Pritchard is dead and his body is left behind to rot. "I'm sorry I didn't believe you," I whimper. "I'm sorry they did this to you." I flex my fingers as if I can reach out and touch him, but Asa backs the chair away.

"We have to go," Asa says solemnly. I watch Arthur the entire way to the door, wishing I would have done everything differently. Because what hope do I have now? What hope could I possibly have when The Program has lobotomized its creator?

# CHAPTER THREE

ASA SAYS NOTHING AS HE PARKS MY WHEELCHAIR in the center of Dr. Beckett's office, leaving me there alone. My entire body is shaking, horrified by the image of Arthur Pritchard emptied out. He's no longer a factor in our future. He has none. That's going to be me in a week unless I figure out what to do.

Is that what happened to Lacey? Was she like Arthur? Is she empty? Fresh tears threaten to brim over, but I sniffle and try to blink them away. My wrists are still tied down, so I won't have a way to wipe my face before Dr. Beckett arrives. I need a plan. And I need one fast.

The door opens behind me, and I take a deep breath and wait as the doctor comes to the other side of his desk, studying me as he walks. He looks the same as he did before, except now that I know the extent of The Program, I'm truly afraid of him.

"Hello, Sloane," he says good-naturedly. "How did your talk with Dallas go?"

Dallas. She probably has less time than I do. Who knows, they could have lobotomized her already this morning. "It went well," I say, offering a pressed-lip smile. "She's sick, but not beyond your help."

Dr. Beckett nods to himself, taking a seat as he seems to think over my words. "Is that your expert opinion?"

I don't like his sarcasm, but I hold back. "I'm not an expert, but I've seen depression. I know Dallas wants to live, deep down. I think you can save her."

"Interesting." The doctor opens my file again, his pen scratching quickly onto the white papers clipped down. "You seem to have had quite a change of heart since yesterday. What can I attribute this miraculous reversal to?"

"Nurse Kell," I lie. "She told me why she asked to be my nurse and why she's part of The Program. What can I say? It resonated."

Beckett laughs and pushes his papers away from him. "That so? Well, Sloane," he says, "you'll excuse me if I don't buy into your change right away. Authentic or not, we take therapy very seriously and we can't just accept your word for it. We have to continue, and the way I see it, you have two choices: You can voluntarily give up your memories, or we can take them. Now, I know that neither may seem like a good option, but I promise you—the first one is better."

He's right. I might have thought his threat empty, or at least had some reason to think I could outsmart him, if I hadn't seen for myself. "I'll do whatever it takes to get out of here," I tell the doctor. "On that you have my word."

"I'm so very happy to hear that. Because we need your help tracking down Michael Realm."

"W-what?" I stammer. He can't expect me to give up Realm—even if I did know where he was, he's with James. I have to protect them.

"Yes, Michael is a friend of yours from your time in The Program. Actually"—he smiles—"it says here it was a little more serious than that. Seems Mr. Realm has gone off the grid since then, but he's not really allowed to do that, you see. He's under contract."

An icy shiver trickles down my spine. "What do you mean 'contract'?"

Dr. Beckett seems taken aback. "You don't know? He didn't tell you while you were together on the run?" When I don't answer, partly because I don't want to admit being with Realm, and partly because I think I know what the doctor is about to say. Somehow—I know.

"Michael Realm is a handler, Sloane. An embedded handler who was assigned to help erase you, and then later, assigned to track you and the rebels down. Only, he must have gotten caught up in your cause, or more likely, gotten sick. We need to find him before he harms himself."

My lips work, but no words are coming out. Realm is . . . a handler? Realm . . . My eyelids flutter, and I'm on the verge of fainting as my shoulder hits the metal bar of the wheelchair. Realm helped erase me and then tracked me down for The Program? Is any of that true? Could it be?

*Realm ignores James, looking at me with a sort of reverence. "So you're happy to see me?" he asks, as if he's scared of the answer.*

*"Yes. What kind of question is that?"*

*He smiles, dropping his hand. "Of course," he repeats. "You didn't take it."*

My world breaks apart and I begin fighting my restraints. I understand now what Realm meant the first time I saw him after he gave me the pill. At one point I must have known exactly what he was. He thought I remembered that.

"No!" I scream, my skin scoring under the restraints. Tears roll down my cheeks and my throat becomes raw. I start to sob, so betrayed, so hurt. My wrists slide around in the blood as I shred my flesh under the buckle. Dr. Beckett moves around the desk to undo my restraints, and once freed, I make no move other than to cover my face and cry. "Realm," I say, moaning. "What have you done?"

My best friend helped to destroy who I was. He worked for The Program—he was never my friend. How could he be, when he had inside information on my life? My relationships? I was being manipulated the entire time. And now he's with James. What is he going to do?

I feel stupid. I feel alone. Dr. Beckett puts his arm around me in a show of support, and I turn and cry into the crisp collar of his button-up shirt, smearing blood on his sleeves. I wish I could see Michael Realm again. Just so I can kill him.

A dozen other memories want to surface, ones where Realm is kind and caring, always looking out for me. But I growl at the lies of them and push back from Dr. Beckett. He quickly grabs my arms, pinning me down.

"Stay calm," he says soothingly. But it's no use. I'm ready to tear him apart. Tear this place apart. "We will catch Michael Realm," he says, close to my face. "And then you'll be free of his lies."

I lift my chin defiantly. "How do I know you're not the one who's lying?"

Beckett lets go of my arms and sits in the chair beside me. "Don't be naive. You already knew, Sloane. Maybe you didn't want to admit it, but you knew. Michael Realm, your friends in The Program—Shepard, Derek, Tabitha. They're all part of this, Sloane."

I stare at him a moment, quickly picking through everyone I've ever known, suspicious of every friend I can remember. There's no way to know the truth anymore. There's no way to know who or what is real. "And Cas," I say. "You had Cas, too."

The doctor shakes his head. "Casanova Gutierrez was merely an informant. He's not on the payroll. We struck a deal with him—The Treatment in exchange for your freedom. At least he had a noble cause. Unfortunately, when the handlers arrived, it was obvious you'd all been infected. They told me they had no choice but to take you into custody. Suicide is contagious, after all, and you're all a high-level threat. We've let Mr. Gutierrez go, though. We try to keep our word."

I ball my hands into fists, bloodstains dotting my scrubs. I don't believe Dr. Beckett. They never planned to fulfill their bargain, just like they don't plan to let me go now. Asa confirmed it. I can't possibly take this all in; no one could. Dr. Beckett is trying to drive me insane, have me submit to The Program. Why? I'm not that special. I'm not worth this much pain and effort. What more do they want from me? They've taken *everything*!

I jump up from the chair and grab the paperweight off Beckett's desk—a cast-iron brain with its different parts highlighted. I hold it up, and Dr. Beckett slowly rises from his chair, his eyes narrowed as he darts a look from me to the raised paperweight.

"Put it down, Sloane," he says in a low voice. "I'm going to tell you only once." The door opens behind him, as if our whole conversation had been monitored from the start. Asa stands there, his face unreadable. And then he silently shakes his head. I feel myself break, crack, and fall apart. I won't get out this way—not by killing a doctor who can be replaced so easily. It's bigger than that. It's bigger than me.

I drop the brain to the floor, where it clanks loudly even through the carpet. Dr. Beckett's hand shoots out, and I push him back hard enough to make him stumble over the chair and onto the floor. I start to scream, pull my hair, before Asa rushes over. I'm losing it. I'm totally fucking losing it. Asa pins my arms to my side, locking me in his grip as he holds my body against his, immobilizing me. I continue to yell as Dr. Beckett tries to stand, and I kick out my feet, barely missing him.

Nurse Kell is fumbling with the cap of a syringe, running into the room amid the chaos I'm creating. I have only a moment to meet her concerned eyes before she stabs me in the thigh with a sedative. Soon I'm sliding from Asa's arms back into the chair, my cries fading into soft whimpers. Nurse Kell kneels beside me, wiping my face as I stare at her helplessly.

"Shh . . ." she whispers. "It's almost over, Sloane. Just a few days and this will all be over."

The words renew my cries, and I turn to my gaze to Asa who only looks through me, his jaw set hard. I'm all alone in this. And I can finally see that I always was.

I'm not sure how much time has passed, but I'm in the office with Dr. Beckett, my body slung across the chair, bandages wrapped around my wrists. My clarity fades in and out. I'm destroyed, but the medication has brought me numbness. A foggy contentment I can't fight. Dr. Beckett takes this as cooperation, and I guess it is. Except for the part where I don't really have a choice.

"Michael Realm was sent to recover you and James," Beckett says. "Unfortunately, he cut off contact shortly after leaving the facility. It wasn't until Arthur Pritchard became involved that we got a lead on your whereabouts. It's not unusual for us to keep an eye on our employees, but I must admit that Arthur's interest in The Treatment was an unforeseen complication. What did the doctor promise you, Sloane? Did you give him The Treatment?"

They don't know. I smile to myself, grateful James took The Treatment before The Program got their hands on it. I know he won't melt down—he's too damn cocky to let The Program beat him. He's with Realm now, but with The Program looking for my former friend, he's not that likely to hand James over. I look at the doctor from under my wet lashes. "Arthur wanted to undo the damage done by The Program," I say. "He was going to set us back and treat the depression the way it should have been before you corrupted the therapy."

Dr. Beckett's expression falters, and he leans closer. "Arthur Pritchard's methods failed. The Program had to evolve. And there's no guarantee The Treatment can even be reproduced. They say Evelyn Valentine used stem cells—which is illegal. Did he talk about that?"

Even through my numbness, I can feel the satisfaction. They know nothing about The Treatment, and he's hoping I can give him details. I've never been so happy to not have the answers. "I guess you'll have to ask Arthur," I say, knowing full well Arthur won't be able to tell them anything. Not after what they've done to him.

I look at a high shelf on the other side of the room, where Beckett moved his paperweight, its presence surely making him unsettled. I could have killed him. Maybe I should have.

"What do you want with Realm now?" I ask, my lips slurring my words. "You have us in custody. Even if he didn't hand us over himself, he did his job. Why do you still want to take his memories?"

Dr. Beckett folds his hands in front of him on the desk. "He's a liability," he says simply. "We're going to erase him completely."

My affection for Realm flares, even though I hate him—hate what he's done. I sniffle hard and wipe my cheek on my shoulder, refusing to give in to the sympathy. Realm betrayed me. I can't forgive that.

"Good," I say finally, even though I don't really mean it. "Good."

Asa walks me back to my room, leaving the wheelchair in the hall outside of Dr. Beckett's office. His arm is around my waist as he supports me. Once standing, the true effect of the medication can be felt, and I'm woozy and unsteady.

"Just a little bit farther," Asa says, taking a turn down my corridor.

"You should have used the wheelchair," I mumble, and reach to touch the wall so I can get my bearings. "How come I'm not restrained anymore? Aren't you afraid I'll bludgeon you?"

"No," he says. Asa gives nothing away, his face always stoic, his movements purposeful. When we get to my room, he pulls back my sheet with one arm, supporting me with the other. He helps me into the bed, and I feel the pain of all that's happened today. Asa stands for a moment, looking down at me, and I reach up my hand to him.

"Why are you helping me?" I ask. He takes my hand, and squeezes it reassuringly.

"Because Realm asked me to."

My eyes widen, and I yank my arm away from him, but Asa grabs my hand again and holds it against his chest. "Realm cares about you," he says forcefully. "He asked me to look out for you."

I don't want to listen. I use my other hand to try to strike Asa, but he blocks it easily, grabbing both of my sore wrists and making me cry out in pain. "Calm down, Sloane," he says, pinning me to the bed.

"Michael Realm is a lie," I growl, continuing to fight until Asa has to lock my hands at my side once again.

"We're all lies, Sloane," he says. "Every single one of us is hiding who we really are."

"Not like that." I start to cry again, and behind it is anger. I turn my body from side to side in the bed, fighting—against what I'm not sure. I thought Realm loved me. I was so wrong about everything. "I hate him," I say with a sob, the grief finally too overwhelming. I turn my face into the pillow. "I hate him."

I feel Asa's hand touch my head, a gentle brush through my hair. He does this until I start to drift toward sleep, a release from pain the medication can't give me. And just before I slip away, I hear Asa whisper, "Michael will be very sad to hear that."

# CHAPTER FOUR

WHEN I WAKE UP THE NEXT MORNING, THERE'S A sharp pain in my head like I've been smacked with a hammer. My hands fly up to feel for any incision, as if the doctors had given me a lobotomy while I slept. There's nothing but the knots of my hair.

My hands. I look down, surprised to see I'm no longer fastened to the bed. I hold up my arms, seeing the red marks and bruises on my wrists still there, but I'm grateful to be free. There's an ache in my chest, a deep dread. I have to tell Dallas about Realm, everything about him. From their past together to the part where he's a handler, a filthy liar. The part where I hate him.

I glance around the room, remembering how Asa took me to that awful place with the lobotomized patients to see Arthur Pritchard drooling on himself. What exactly does the handler think I can do about it? If it was that easy to escape, others would have gotten out. I'm trapped, and I'm not sure if the knowledge Asa gave me is hurting or helping me.

To keep my sanity, I run through the chronology of my life—or, at least, my life after The Program. James and I met at the Wellness Center the day after I returned. He was mean to me on and off until he became more on. He stuck up for me, including a few times when Realm crossed a line. Realm . . .

I swallow hard and shake my head to keep from screaming. I'm burning up with fury, but that kind of emotion isn't going to help. I need to think clearly. I have to figure a way out. But no sooner does the rage come that it's replaced with a shock of warmth spreading over my chest. The medication must contain an inhibitor that settles my frazzled nerves. I remember it from my first days after The Program.

Without supervision I climb down from the bed, moving slowly to test my limbs, afraid to make any sudden movements. When I'm steady, I change into the fresh set of scrubs that were laid out on my bed. I leave my room, tentative and anxious, looking over my shoulder. There are voices down the hall, and I head in that direction.

There's a waiting room, a smaller version of the leisure room. There are four other patients in there, watching the television mounted on the wall—an infomercial on The Program, it looks like—and two others sitting by the window and staring. I see that one of them is Lacey.

I smile reflexively but then temper my expression down as

SUZANNE YOUNG

I approach her. I don't want to scare her. I pause. *Can* I scare her? Will she even know what's going on? I crush the heartache that comes along with that thought.

"Hi," I say in a scratchy voice when I'm standing next to her. Lacey continues to stare out the window without any noticeable reaction to my words. I check for a scar, but I don't see one. I'm not sure how they perform lobotomies; I've never really thought to research it.

Suddenly Lacey turns to me. She drifts her gaze over my features, and her lips part slowly. "Is it time for breakfast?" she asks in a too-soft voice. Deep sadness burrows through my chest, but I try my best to smile.

"Not yet," I tell her kindly.

"Oh." She turns back to the window, her thoughts seemingly a gentle breeze in her mind, no urgency, no fear, no anxiety. I try to think of what I can say, what I can tell her to let her know that I care about her. I'm so sorry I didn't save her from The Program. I'm so sorry this happened to her.

"Sloane?" The sound of Nurse Kell's voice startles me, and I glance over my shoulder to where she stands in the doorway. Her expression is steeped in suspicion, and when she calls my name again, scolding me like a child, I know my time with Lacey is up.

"I'll talk to you soon," I say to my friend, trying to communicate in my tone that I hope to see her again. She offers one more uninterested look and then goes back to enjoying the view of the courtyard instead.

My heart is heavy as I approach Nurse Kell. I wilt under the accusation in her expression and quickly try to explain. "I didn't know where to go when I woke up," I tell her as soon as I'm close enough. "You weren't there."

She takes my arm to lead me from the room. "Asa should have left you restrained, then. Sloane, you aren't ready to interact with the other patients yet. You're a threat to them."

I turn to Nurse Kell as we walk back toward the prison of my room. "Are you going to tie me down?" I ask, finding it impossible to control the rage bubbling up. "Because I thought I was being pretty cooperative so far."

"Oh, honey," she says in a patronizing voice. "You are. But it's just not healthy for the other patients to interact with you. You're still too sick. You could start a whole new epidemic in here. Give it another week. The time will fly."

In a week I'll be lobotomized. Nurse Kell must know this, and yet she's talking to me like I should be thankful. Any camaraderie she'd tried to build evaporates right then. I gnash my teeth together, saying nothing.

"I left your breakfast in your room," she says. "I thought you'd be more comfortable there." She stops just outside my door and motions for me to enter ahead of her. I see the metal tray on a rolling cart next to my bed. The food is covered with tan plastic bowls to keep it warm. I think back to something Lacey once told me—that they put sedatives in the food. I'm starving right now—ravenous really. Can I handle a little bit of medication to get some nutrients? Is it worth the risk?

I step inside my room, walking toward the tray, when I hear the door shut behind me. I turn and hear the click of the lock. My heart dips, and I rush over to try the handle.

Kell just locked me in. I look around the room for something, anything, to pick the lock with. But The Program is careful. The sharpest thing in my room is the plastic spoon that came with my breakfast. Trapped, I go over to my bed and sit, lifting the lid to my food and finding happy face pancakes.

I stare at them a long moment, the irony—or cruelty—of them too much. And then I flip the tray, sending it to the floor with a loud clank, and curl up on my side, staring out the window.

Dr. Beckett doesn't ask to see me, and the hours alone in my room stretch on until I feel the psychosis. Murmuring to myself, imagining shapes in the wood grain of the door, I start to doubt anyone will ever come for me again, not until they're ready to take me to the gray room.

At lunch Nurse Kell comes to drop off my next meal. The minute I see her, I'm at her side, begging her to let me out. I think I might lose it completely if I don't at least get out of this room. But Nurse Kell only glances at me on her way to the overturned tray of breakfast food.

"Sorry, Sloane," she says. "You can't come out yet. I'm sorry."

The news is devastating, but it doesn't seem to bother her as she sops up the spilled orange juice that's turned sticky on the floor.

"What am I supposed to do for the rest of my time, then? Is this another version of solitary confinement?"

Nurse Kell exhales and then stands to look me over. "Dr. Beckett was called away for the afternoon. He'll see you when he gets back. For now he wants you to stay in your room and out of trouble. There's no sense in getting worked up. Now eat your lunch."

I glance down at the sandwich, surprised by how appetizing it looks. I don't remember the last time I've eaten—maybe not since I arrived here. My stomach growls in agreement. I drop helplessly on my bed and pick up my sandwich, taking a tentative bite. I wait for a chalky or bitter taste, something to prove that I'm being drugged. But it just tastes like turkey.

"Under the plate there's some paper," Nurse Kell says, coming over to shake out a napkin to lay over my lap. "Dr. Beckett thought you might want to write out some of your thoughts for your next session—to help move things along. It seems like a positive way to combat the boredom."

Bullshit. He wants information on The Treatment. On Realm. But he'll get none of that from me. "Maybe I can write to my parents," I suggest, just to see Kell's reaction. She smiles warmly.

"Well, that sounds wonderful," she says sincerely. "I'm sure The Program has already told them that you're here, but they'll probably appreciate an update from you. You've given them quite a scare."

Has The Program told my parents that they have me? It

wouldn't make much sense, not if they plan to lobotomize me. Looking at Nurse Kell, she seems honestly impressed that I'd want to write to my parents. I'm not sure she knows what happens to the people who leave this facility. I don't think anyone does.

My parents. If The Program hasn't told them, where do they think I am now? Did my father tell my mother that James had called? Do they think he's keeping me safe like he promised? If only they knew that The Program was planning to lobotomize me. Make me well-behaved. Is that how they want me?

I'm quiet as Nurse Kell finishes tidying up the room, saying she'll be back in an hour for my plates. I don't eat any more and instead find the paper and bendable pen she left for me to write with.

I move the dishes off the tray and set it up as a desk. But as I stare down at the paper, vast in white and blankness, I can think of nothing to write. Really, I think of James. And how likely it is that I'll never see him again—at least not as myself.

Closing my eyes, I imagine what I'd write to him, not daring to put it on paper. I let myself think back on the good times, some of the bad. Our promises.

*I love you,* I write to James in my mind. *In another life we could have stayed together, fought, gotten back together. Our existence wouldn't have been anyone's concern. Maybe I would have learned to swim. Maybe we would have had children.*

*James, we didn't fail each other. You took The Treatment and now you'll always remember me.* My tears drip onto the blank paper. *But I won't remember you. I won't remember how you make me laugh or make me furious with your stubbornness. James, I won't remember you.*

*But I'll always love you.*

I lie on my side, and the paper falls from the bed, swaying in the air until it lands somewhere on the floor. I'll never be able to tell James how I feel—not unless I find a way out of this. But each second that ticks by reminds me how little time I have left. No one's coming for me. Except the surgeon.

# CHAPTER FIVE

**"TELL ME YOUR LAST MEMORY OF THE FARMHOUSE,** before the handlers came to collect you," Dr. Beckett says. He's back in his leather chair, and I'm in the seat across from him, my hands no longer bound. My head is heavy as the medication the doctor gave me to calm me down winds through my body, twisting and turning and setting me at ease.

"I was with James," I say with a smile. "I had a dream about us, and I was telling him about it before we heard Dallas scream from downstairs. Then we ran through the woods." I close my eyes and tell him about the chase. About Arthur getting Tased, and Dallas stabbing Roger. He listens intently, never interrupting. But when I'm done, he licks his lips as if he's been waiting with a question.

"Where was Michael Realm during this exchange? Casanova

was there, but Michael wasn't at the farm. Do you know where he went?"

"Maybe he killed himself," I say bitterly. As the words meet the silence of the room, I immediately regret them. I don't want Realm dead. I want him to tell me the doctor is lying about all this. I want him to bring me to James.

"I'm fully confident that Michael is still alive," the doctor says. "But don't worry; you'll get your justice once we find him. Now, when was the last time you saw him?"

"In the house. He and Cas got into an argument, and they took it outside. Then James and I went upstairs and . . ." I lift my eyes to Dr. Beckett, realizing I shouldn't know that James is free. "How is James?" I ask, sounding concerned.

The doctor smiles. "He's just fine, Sloane. He's in a Program facility and being very cooperative from what I hear. You don't have to worry about him anymore. You only have to worry about yourself."

"Don't hurt him." Dr. Beckett is caught in his own lie and he doesn't even know it. I blink rapidly as if holding back tears. "Please don't hurt him."

The doctor purses his lips like he's having an attack of conscience.

"I'll send word that you asked for him. Okay?"

I nod, pretending to be grateful. I ease back in the chair and focus on the last days at the farmhouse. My conversation with James about babies, details that can't possibly help Beckett find anyone, let alone my boyfriend.

Beckett writes something down in his notes, and he's visibly agitated. I'm reminded that I have only about six days until I'll be lobotomized, unless I buy more time. That's what Asa told me. "Maybe . . . ," I start, not sure what I'm going to say next but knowing I have to do something. "Maybe I'm forgetting a clue," I say. "To where Realm is. He might have told me something, but I can't remember."

The doctor glances up, removing his glasses and setting them on the desk. "There are medications that can help make the memories more vivid," he says. "We can try them next time." He's distrustful, and I guess he's wondering the real reason to why I'm suddenly such a model patient. I'm quick to offer a cover.

"If you find him," I say, sounding braver than I feel, "I want to talk to him before you do"—I wave my hand—"whatever it is you're planning on doing to him. And then I want to go home."

Dr. Beckett nods condescendingly. "Or course, sweetheart. You'll still have to complete The Program, but after that you'll be free to go."

"Deal."

The doctor doesn't mention the lobotomy, not that I thought he would. But maybe part of me hoped he would just admit it. Then again, without the niceties, each day could dissolve into torture. I've seen Lacey, Arthur. I know what's to come. Maybe it's best to live in denial for as long as I can.

*　　　*　　　*

Dr. Beckett has me swallow a shiny red pill before leaving his office. I'm surprised when Asa isn't waiting for me, but I'm already getting sleepy so I try to hurry down the hall. I pause on my way past the waiting room.

Lacey's there, rocking gently as she stares out the window. She seems better—at least a little more with it—than she did the other times I saw her. Before walking in, I cast a glance around the hallway, and when the coast is Kell-free, I walk in.

"I like your hair," I say as my lamest and most nonthreatening opening statement ever. Lacey looks up and flashes her teeth.

"Thanks." She doesn't ask me to sit, but her posture tells me she isn't opposed to the idea. I don't remember what Lacey was like before The Program, but I have to believe she was always a badass. I wonder if that side of her will eventually come out again.

I sit on the stiff couch cushion, facing her chair, and she turns slightly as if curious about what I'll say next. I hadn't really thought that far ahead. "I'm Sloane," I say.

She smiles softly, her eyes wide as they glance over at me. In them I find no recognition, but they're not dead. Not completely. I lean closer, checking again to make sure we're not being watched.

"Your name is Lacey," I whisper. "You're Lacey Klamath and you're from Oregon."

Her smile fades, her brows pulling together as she fights to understand what I mean. She doesn't know who she is—at all—but her personality is set. It's not solely based on her memories. She'll still be Lacey. Despite the panic that's bubbling up at the thought of her never coming back, I'm trying to convince myself that she's still Lacey.

"If I could get us out of here," I say weakly, "would you come with me?"

Lacey's eyes drift past me, and a hand grips my shoulder, nearly making me leap out of my skin. I turn and see Asa standing over me, his jaw set in anger.

"You must be tired, Miss Barstow," he says coldly. "Let's get you back to your room to rest." He's right; underneath this burst of adrenaline, my body is heavily medicated, ready to crash.

I glance at Lacey once more, but she's turned away, back to rocking as she stares out the window.

I murmur a good-bye and then follow Asa. He escorts me out more like a punished child than a rebel trying to break out of a brainwashing facility. When we get into the hallway, Asa spins and I take a startled step back.

"What the hell do you think you're doing?" he demands in a hushed voice. He still smells of cigarettes, and his eyes have taken on dark circles. He's worried about something.

"You'll have to be more specific," I say, and his glare chills me.

"Do you want to be lobotomized? I'm trying to save your life, Sloane. Asking Lacey questions about escape . . . God!" He balls his hand in a fist like he wants to punch something. He takes a step away and then comes back, clearly frustrated.

"Look," he says, "I need you to be smart. Dallas won't listen and now she's scheduled for surgery."

"What? When?" They're going to turn her into one of those people. They're going to switch her off. "You have to stop them!"

"I can't," he says, coming close to my face. "She's being taken to the surgeon tomorrow. I can't compromise myself or I'll end up just like her and Arthur Pritchard."

"Then what do we do? I can't let that happen. I have to save her."

"Sloane," he says, sounding desperate. "You have to save yourself. I can't help her now, and neither can you. Just play the game. Realm is doing everything he can to get to you, I promise."

Again Realm's name gives me an odd mix of feelings that is quickly covered up by the medication. It washes over me, and in just a few seconds my mind is going fuzzy. Asa curses and then takes my elbow to lead me toward my room.

"It's the red pill. It has a sedative that works while it erases your memories," he says, continuingly checking behind us.

"What are they erasing?" I ask, although I can hear the slurring at the end of my sentence.

"I'm not sure. It depends what you told them."

"They want to find Realm," I say, just as Asa gets me into the room. "They want to know why he wasn't at the farmhouse when they came to take us."

Asa helps me into bed and then stares down. "And what did you tell them?"

"The truth." My blinking slows, making Asa appear and disappear in longer intervals. "I told him I didn't know."

Asa smiles and then my eyes stay shut. "Good girl."


I'm sitting in Dr. Beckett's office, feeling more alone than ever. I can't believe I actually agreed to take this pill—a pill that will attach to my memories, clarify them, and then target them for erasure. I never thought I could voluntarily do something like this, but right now it's my only chance to buy more time. I have five days left, maybe four. Without another thought, I swallow the yellow pill and then close my eyes, waiting for the first wave.

Across from me, Dr. Beckett's chair groans as he adjusts his position, settling in for a long session. There is a quick panic that my subconscious may really know where Realm is, but I push past the worry. I've already taken the pill—there's no more hiding inside my head. Maybe part of me thinks he deserves to be caught.

Five minutes later my eyelids flutter open. I feel calm, but unlike the sedative, it's not groggy. It's alert, clear, and peaceful. I stare at Dr. Beckett for a minute before he notices I'm looking at him. He's writing down notes in a pad, flipping between pages. He doesn't have a wedding ring; he's wearing a soft brown blazer with a T-shirt underneath—like something a hip TV star would wear to an awards show. Is he really that casual? Is this part of the image he wants to portray? He's shaved today, and it makes him look younger. He must be in his forties, but he could pass for twenties without his beard. I think he's a walking lie—a false image in his entirety.

He looks up. "Ah, I see the medication has kicked in."

I nod and settle into the chair. It's more comfortable than I remember, or maybe I'm just feeling really cooperative. "What are you writing?" I ask.

He smiles, seeming embarrassed to know I was watching him. "Decisions need to be made," he says. "Some patients are beyond our help, Sloane. I'm the one who has to make the tough calls. I'm sorry to tell you"—he purses his lips and looks away—"Dallas isn't going to make it. She's being scheduled for surgery."

I swallow hard, a mix of anger and grief exploding inside of my chest before it's washed away. "What will happen to her? This is cruel, even for The Program."

"I assure you, it isn't as terrible as you think—not for someone like her. We've perfected our techniques for a lobotomy. It's not like it was back when they were first popular. Lobotomies were for the criminally insane. They were never meant to cure patients—only to make them easier to manage. Here we have a purpose. Dallas's frontal lobe will be disconnected from the nerves that are sending her infected signals." He folds his hands in front of him in a practiced doctorly move. "We will insert a metal rod behind her eye and sever the nerves. When it's done, Dallas will have no physical scars, but she'll no longer want to kill herself."

"She won't be able to think either," I snap.

"Not true. We're not cutting out pieces of her brain; we're

rerouting the wires. The result is a calmer, less violent person. She won't remember any of the horrible stuff she's been through. Her long-term memory will be gone. She'll undergo extensive physical and speech therapy, and in three to six months, Dallas will be ready to experience life again."

"Is that what will happen to me?" I ask, my voice weak.

"It depends on if you can help us, Sloane. Tell me, where is Michael Realm?"

His mouth is lying, while his eyes give me everything I need to know. There is no other therapy in this facility. I will end up just like the others.

"I don't know where Realm is," I say.

"What was the last thing he said to you?" he asks. "What was your last conversation about?"

The memory is being sought out, and unable to lie with the medication slipping through my veins, I answer. "We were on a bridge the day before the handlers came. Realm said he understood about me and James—that I'd always pick James over him. He promised that no matter what . . . he'd always choose me. But I didn't want that."

Dr. Beckett nods. "Do you expect to see Michael again?" he asks.

I swallow hard, trying to hold the words back, but I can't. "Yes. I expect him to rescue me."

Beckett actually laughs. "That so? I assure you, that isn't actually possible. But the fact that you believe it . . . That speaks volumes. Sloane, do you love Michael Realm?"

"Right now, I hate him."

"But overall, despite how he's lied and betrayed you . . . do you love Michael Realm?"

There's the sting of tears in my eyes, a slight quiver to my bottom lip. "Yes," I whisper. "Yes, I do."

"Then we won't have to find him," the doctor says, closing the file. "He'll come for you. And we'll be waiting."

# CHAPTER SIX

WHEN I WAKE UP THE NEXT MORNING, I HAVE A
medication hangover. I don't wait for it to wear off before I'm
out of bed, pulling on a pair of clean scrubs. On the side table
is a breakfast tray, but there's no time to eat. They're loboto-
mizing Dallas today. I have to find her—save her—before they
do. I walk quickly down the hall, the room tilting in my mind
and sending me into the wall several times as I try to adjust my
balance. I have to remember the way to solitary, but the world
is hazy.

"Sloane?" I turn and see Asa coming down the adjacent
hall. "What are you doing out of your room?"

"I need to get to Dallas," I say. "You have to help me save
her."

Asa shoots an alarmed look around the empty hall before

jogging over to grab my arm, turning and leading me back toward my room. I try to pull away, but he tightens his grip.

"Let me go," I call out, but he only quickens his pace. "You're hurting me." When we get to my room, he slingshots me inside, making me stumble against the bed. He checks the hall once more before closing the door.

"Have you lost your mind?" he shouts, and then glances behind him at the door. Drawing the attention of the nurses or other handlers is the last thing Asa wants, and I test him by trying for the door again. He grabs me, pulling me to his side. He doesn't look down at me, only tips his head in my direction while he stares straight ahead.

"If you do this, Sloane, they will end you. There is no way out of solitary without Dr. Beckett's approval." His hazel eyes find mine. "And I'm guessing you don't have that."

"I can't let them lobotomize her. You have to help me, Asa."

There's a weakening in his posture, but he only shrugs. "I can't," he whispers. "Even if I wanted to, I can't. Not without compromising myself."

"Then what?" I ask. "What am I supposed to do? After Dallas, then it'll be me. Will you wait then, too?"

"No, I made Realm a promise."

"Why?" I ask, throwing up my hands. "What do you owe him that could be worth this much?"

Asa darts his gaze away, his cheeks growing flushed. "Michael Realm saved my life once, and I owe him."

"Maybe he was lying to you, too."

Asa smiles at this, turning to me. "He was. He definitely was, but that doesn't mean I'm not grateful. I would have killed myself—I sure as hell wanted to. Realm was my only friend. Real or not, he saved me. And this is how I'm paying him back. He loves you, Sloane. For all his flaws, he loves you."

"Too bad I don't feel the same," I respond. "Be sure to tell him that."

Asa flinches when his phone vibrates. He pulls it out to check a message and then takes a step backward. "I have to go," he says. "But I need you to stay away from Dallas. You have four days—you can't let them take you to the surgeon before then. Do you understand me?"

"Like I can stop it."

"Do what you can," he offers. He slips out the door, but not before I noticed the way his skin paled, his muscles tensed. Despite Asa's warning, I can't let it go. I can't just leave Dallas helpless for them to stick a metal rod behind her eye and sever her life. There has to be something I can do.

My breathing is jagged and adrenaline starts to pulsate as a frantic thought takes over. Maybe I can fight our way out.

I scan the room, looking for anything I can use as a weapon. All I see are covered plates of food and the plastic spoon that sits on the side of the breakfast tray. I wish Nurse Kell would have left her knitting needles or something sharp. I'll need a key card to get into solitary, and it's obvious Asa isn't just going to hand over his.

The minutes tick by, and all I can think about is Dallas,

whose life is about to be irrevocably changed. No one else will help her. I'm the only person who can save her. I walk over to clear off the tray of food and then pick up the flat metal pan. I'm going to have to take a key.

I crack open my door and peer out, hoping to find a nurse heading in this direction—but the hall is empty. The tray is cold in my hand and my heart is pumping blood loudly into my ears. I'll have to hurt someone, and even though I'm mad as hell, I still don't want to do that. But what choice have they left me? I'll get to Dallas, get her out of solitary, and then we make a break for it. My entire future depends on luck, on not getting caught.

I blow out a steadying breath, wondering if I've completely lost my mind at this point. Then I lean forward and whistle loudly. When I hear nothing in return, I do it again, and then there is the shuffling of feet. I curse, suddenly debating this idea, but close my door and hide behind it. The footsteps get louder, and I lift the metal tray above my head, readying the force I'll need to bring it down on whoever walks in the door.

The world is moving in slow motion as I watch the handle turn, the twitch in my arm, the shake of my breath. And then there is a side profile, followed by the back of a head with short red hair. I bring the tray down with as much force as I can. The metal connects against the hard skull with a heavy clang, sending vibrations up my arm. I see the bend of the metal and lift the tray to drive it down again, but the body falls to the floor in front of me.

It's Nurse Kell. I lower my arms and let them hang lifelessly, guiltily, at my sides. For a terrible moment I think she's dead, but then I hear a gurgle, a soft moan. I have only a moment. I have to get to Dallas.

I lean down and grab Nurse Kell's key card from her hip, and then, still carrying the tray, I rush from the room. I book down the hallway, my head whipping from side to side as I search for the right set of double doors. I expect an alarm to sound, flooding the hall with handlers, but nothing happens. Not yet.

The nurses' station is just ahead, and I stop and press myself to the wall, just out of their view. I'm not sure how to get past them, not carrying a metal tray and looking crazy. I set my weapon down on the white floor and then start forward. Therapy. I could be going to therapy.

A young, dark-haired nurse glances up as I pass. I nod to him, and he goes back to his computer as I take the turn just before the doctors' wing. Once in the new hallway, I recognize the door at the end and start running again. This is where Asa took me when I visited Dallas. I'm not sure if she's still there, but I'm about to find out.

After a quick check around me, I use Nurse Kell's key card and cautiously walk inside, seeing a series of rooms. I can't remember which is Dallas's, but she must be the only person down here because all the doors are open but one. I swallow hard, scared she won't actually be inside—that maybe I'm too late. I swipe the key card and then push the door open, my stomach in knots.

The room is awash in muted colors, and it takes me a long moment to find the figure inside wearing gray scrubs. Just at that moment, Dallas lifts her head, her eyes widening when she sees me. "Sloane?" she calls in a weak voice.

"Oh, thank God," I say, and move quickly to grab her. Dallas has dark circles that have changed the shape of her eyelids, drawing them down. She's been here only for a few days, but she looks sickly and even thinner than before. I think the isolation has been wearing on her.

"We have to get out of here," I say. "They're going to lobotomize you."

I help her up, and Dallas staggers beside me, wobbly like it's been too long since she's walked. "What?" she asks, looking over. "Lobotomy?" She uses the word like she's never heard it before. I'm not sure what sort of psychosis she's in, but I have to get us out of here.

"We're escaping," I tell her. "And if we fail, they're going to lobotomize both of us. They've already done it to Lacey, and we're next. Now move your ass!" I push her ahead toward the doors, checking behind us and sticking close to the wall. I'm waiting for an overhead alarm, flashing lights, but it's still quiet. There's terrible guilt as I wonder if anyone has found Nurse Kell yet.

When we get to the double doors, I pause, my hand against the frame. "Dallas," I say, drawing a half-glazed stare from her. "We have to run for the stairs, do you understand? Don't stop, not for anyone. Not even for me."

SUZANNE YOUNG

It takes a second, but I see the life start to return to Dallas's eyes. Suddenly she reaches out to hug me, a quick squeeze before pulling back and nodding toward the door. I swipe the card, and then we're walking, heading for the staircase, which is on the other side of the nurses' station.

But we don't make it. I'm not sure how many steps I take before I feel the sting, the surge, the overwhelming cramp that overtakes my body. The world freezes up and locks, and I'm crumbling, falling in a heap on the floor. My body quivers, tears leak from my eyes, and drool slips from my mouth. My eyes roll back in my head, and when I can finally focus again, I see the white coat of a handler, a Taser in his hand.

Suddenly someone else is there, grabbing me by the shoulders to drag me down the hall, placing me in the open before flipping me onto my back. I see Asa, staring down at me with a cold stare, not disappointed or angry, just empty. In the distance I hear Dallas screaming, calling for me. But I can't help her now.

"I'm getting a wheelchair," Asa begins, "and then I'm taking you to solitary." He looks down the hall, waiting for someone. I want to ask him about Kell, but I'm still shaking too much to talk, my jaw locked as my muscles continue to spasm.

The chair arrives, and Asa and another handler lift me and set me down. I'm slumped to the side, but no one offers any help or asks if I'm okay. I think they're going to kill me this time. I've finally crossed too many lines. I'm expecting to be driven to Dr. Beckett, but instead they turn and I'm going back where I came from. They drag me over to drop me on the bed in a room next to Dallas's. The handlers fasten me down and leave, Asa not even turning back to look at me.

There's a tapping noise, something faint at first, but the more awake I get, the louder it becomes. I open my eyes, at first startled by the unfamiliar room, until I remind myself that I'm in a Program hospital. I'm waiting to be lobotomized. The tapping stops. I turn to my right, and at first I'm too stunned to react.

"Hello, Sloane," Roger says. "I think we need to have a little chat."

I open my mouth to scream, but Roger is across the room in a heartbeat, his hand over my mouth. "Now, now," he says. "Don't make me cut your throat."

I continue fighting anyway, thrashing my head from side to side. Roger takes a step back, wincing and cupping his side where Dallas stabbed him. The minute his palm slips from my mouth and my first scream breaks through the room, his grip on my neck promptly cuts them off. I choke, my eyes widening as air is strangled out of me.

"Let's try this again," he growls as my chest starts to burn. I try to gasp, but I can't get any air in or out. "I'm going to kill your friend," he says, "but first I need to locate him. Where is Michael Realm?"

*I don't know,* I mouth, struggling against my restraints, but it's no use. Roger's weight is too heavy, his strength far outweighing mine. It feels like he's crushing my bones. He's going to kill me.

"Here's the thing, Sloane," Roger says conversationally, even as small black dots are starting to appear in the corners of my vision. I'm about to pass out. "Realm has something that belongs to me. I'm willing to trade for it, but first I need to find him. Now, you'll help me, or I'll destroy Dallas." Roger lowers his face until it's just over mine. I try again to take a breath, and fail. Roger smiles sweetly. "I will break her, Sloane. She'll wish she were dead."

His threat is enough to send me renewed energy, and I use what little strength I have left to bring up my knee as hard as I can. It strikes his thigh, knocking him off balance and sending him sideways. I start to scream, but my voice is raw, ripping at my throat as I beg for help. I choke on the air I try to take into my lungs. I watch helplessly as Roger staggers to his feet, holding his chest. He must still be healing from where he was stabbed, and I have a wild hope that his wounds will reopen and he'll bleed to death.

"I will find him," Roger says, pointing at me as he moves for the door. "Michael Realm is dead, and there's nothing you can do about it."

"Help!" I try to yell, but it comes out only as a whisper before another coughing fit starts. Roger is out the door, and I'm crying, rolling from side to side to somehow free my bonds, tearing the flesh on my barely healed wrists. "Help!" I call again, worried that he crushed my windpipe and I'll never get my voice back.

There's the sound of footsteps, and I lift my head. The door flies open, and Asa looks in. The minute he sees me, he grabs his radio and calls in a code. I try to tell him about Roger: He's going to kill Realm, do something horrible to Dallas, but he's shushing me, working frantically to undo my restraints.

More people arrive, but they never let me talk. I'm strapped to a gurney, white coats whizzing by me as I continue to struggle for breath. I'm watching for Roger's face, but he's gone. Like a phantom who came to haunt me, he's disappeared, making me wonder if he was really there at all. But at the end of the hall, just before they push me down the medical wing for X-rays, I hear one of the nurses say, "Oh my God. What happened to her neck?"

And I knew Roger had really been here after all.

I'm momentarily untied, surrounded by handlers in an infirmary while we wait for Dr. Beckett. "It was Roger," I rasp to Asa as my throat continues to ache. He nods, his shoulders rigid and his posture alert.

"Yeah, I saw him run past me. I thought he'd come from Dallas's room, but then I heard you calling." His eyes lower, heavy with guilt, and I reach to put my hand on his forearm. The minute I do, he flinches away as if I've burned him. I broke his trust by going after Dallas. I don't think he'll help me again.

The doctor walks into the room, and Asa moves quickly to pull him aside before he can talk to me. I watch, anxious to tell

SUZANNE YOUNG

Dr. Beckett exactly what happened so he can stop Roger from hurting Dallas or from finding Realm.

The doctor takes out his phone and begins talking; shooting concerned looks in my direction. Is he calling Roger? Would The Program get the police involved? After a moment Dr. Beckett hangs up, walking past Asa to stop in front of me. Absently, I touch my neck.

His smile is apologetic but warm. "Leave us for moment," he tells the other handlers, glancing back at them once. They exchange looks but then leave—including Asa. Soon it's just me and the good doctor, alone in a tiny white room. I'm starting to panic—afraid the doctor will try to hurt me like Roger did. I'm vulnerable. I'm scared.

"I must admit . . . ," the doctor begins, "I came here expecting Michael Realm. I'm disappointed he hasn't come for you. I guess he doesn't love you after all."

His barb hurts, but I move past it, focusing on what really matters. "You can't let Roger get away with this," I say after an extended silence. My voice is strangled and weak. "He's a psychopath and he's going to kill Dallas and Realm. I know he's part of the boys' club here, but even you must have limits."

"Measures are being taken."

I laugh but then grip my damaged neck to alleviate the burn. The doctors are the ones who are crazy. Not us. Not the patients. "He's going to get away with it," I say. "Just like last time." I look him directly in the eyes. "He was blackmailing patients to have sex with him in exchange for memories."

Beckett's expression falters. "Are these rumors? How do you know this?"

"I was a patient, remember?" I pause. "I was a victim."

"You retained memories?"

"Are you not getting the point? He's raping underage girls, Beckett. Who gives a shit if he lets them keep one inconsequential memory? They're losing so much more. And this should all be documented," I add. "He was fired while I was a patient."

Again Dr. Beckett looks perplexed. I can't believe this.

"Dr. Warren knew all about it," I say. "Realm broke his arm, they fired Roger and escorted him out. Why did The Program hire him back?"

"We didn't. Roger no longer works for The Program—not on a public level. And neither does Dr. Warren for that matter. Her position was terminated after you went rogue." Beckett exhales, looking weary. "Sloane, we're going to have to talk about Nurse Kell."

Guilt attacks my conscience. "Is she okay?"

Dr. Beckett tilts his head from side to side. "She's not great, that's for sure. She needed several staples to close the wound in her head. Is that how you repay someone who's been trying to help you? Do you still think you're not sick?"

"I didn't want to hurt her," I say, ashamed. "I just wanted to see Dallas. I was worried about her. What you're doing is wrong. You can't just turn us into zombies."

Dr. Beckett scoffs. "Hardly, Sloane. You've seen Lacey—the

patients are all perfectly well. Just . . . less violent. Less suicidal. Can you really not see that?"

I'll never make him understand. I think he believes this bullshit. "Leave me alone then," I say. "I don't know where Realm is, and even if I did, I would never tell you. He may have betrayed me, but at least he's not a delusional prick."

Dr. Beckett doesn't move at first, but then a wide Cheshire-like grin spreads over his face. "Poor girl," he starts in a sympathetic voice, "you really are a lost soul."

He reaches down and brushes his fingers over my cheek gently. "Sleep well, Sloane," he murmurs. "I'll do what I can to help Dallas." On cue, the door opens and two handlers come in, talking in hushed voices. Dr. Beckett gives me one last look, his expression a bit doubtful, but concerned nonetheless.

"Sweep the area, and call outside and have them search the grounds," he tells the handlers. "And keep extra security outside of solitary until the surgeon calls down tomorrow." The handlers, like mindless drones, leave with their mission.

"So that's it?" I call to Beckett's back as he starts to leave. "You're just going to sever our memories and pretend like we never existed?"

"Believe me, Sloane," he says, "I wish that's all there was to it. You can't imagine the PR nightmare you and your boyfriend have created for us. But we'll get through it. The Program will survive. Because teens will keep trying to kill themselves, and we'll keep saving them. It's the new order of things. I'm just glad I'm on the right side of the battle."

"You're not."

"Yeah, well, what do you know?" he says, annoyance cracking through his otherwise cool exterior. "You're depressed. Delusional. Your opinion means shit here." He pauses, visibly collecting himself. "I'll see you on the other side, Sloane. I think you'll be a lot more likeable then." And with that, Dr. Beckett leaves me locked in a padded cell, while he goes back to tend to The Program.

# CHAPTER SEVEN

"JAMES," I WHISPER INTO THE AIR ABOVE MY BED, wishing his name could conjure him up. Instead I can only imagine his face, his eyes so blue, the sound of his voice. James isn't really here. He never will be. I'm alone in a room, hands at my side in the most claustrophobic position in the world.

As I sit in silence, I feel my sanity wavering. I'm not sure how much time has passed since I attacked Nurse Kell—a few hours? A day? There's no way to tell. No windows. No anything. Another female nurse has come in twice to help me use the restroom. Last time she was here, she dressed me in scratchy gray scrubs, but she didn't speak to me. In fact, I could feel that she hated me. I wonder if she was friends with Kell. Once, I almost asked about my old nurse, but then thought better of it. I don't have the right to ask. I'm the lunatic who hurt her.

Now I'm tied down to a bed, calling out the name of my boyfriend, actually waiting for an answer. Time ticks by, and then, from beyond the door I hear sounds . . . heavy footsteps, not the quiet brushing steps of the nurse. Then more noise, multiple people. My pulse quickens and I smile. They came for me. James and Realm have finally come back for me.

I strain my neck, lifting my head off the bed to watch the door. I'm going to get out of here. Thoughts spin in my head, erratic and smashing into each other. I don't try to clear them. Instead I start screaming.

"I'm in here!" I yell to them. "James!" I cough, my throat still sore from Roger's attack, but I don't care. I don't want them to walk past. I hear the swipe of a card, the beep of the door. I'm almost free.

The door swings open, and it takes me a moment to process. It's not James, or even Realm. It's a guy in a white coat, comb-smoothed light hair. Behind him are two other guys, near copies of each other. The smile falls from my face. The butterflies in my stomach catch fire and turn to ash, filling me with despair.

"No," I say, shaking my head slowly. "No."

The handler betrays little emotion as he comes inside the room. He begins to unfasten the restraints, his touch firm but not painful. "We're going on a trip, Miss Barstow," he says, as if I'm unable to understand his words. "I'll help you up, and then you just have to walk with us, okay?"

"Where are we going?" I ask.

"There's a doctor they want you to meet."

I let the guy help me up, glad to be on my feet again. The back of my hair is a tangle of knots, and I run my hand over it self-consciously as we exit the room. I'm not going to see Dr. Beckett—I'm going to the surgeon. They're going to lobotomize me.

One of the handlers stays behind, guarding what must be Dallas's room. Nothing around me seems real, not the walls or the white coats. Not the smell of soap or the ache in my wrists. I'm walking through a nightmare that I'll never wake up from. Will this me—the me I am now—be trapped in a padded cell while the new Sloane takes over? I'll be waiting for James forever. A tear trickles down my cheek, and I hitch in a breath, my dry lips cracking as I begin to whimper. The fear is so completely overwhelming, so entirely encompassing, that I let myself slip back into a memory—I retreat to a safe place. A final place. I think of James.

*"Sloane," James says, his lips curved in a grin. "I think you should learn to swim."*

*"Uh-huh." I adjust the sound on the car radio, and James playfully slaps my hand away.*

*"I'm not kidding," he says. "What if we had to swim for our lives?"*

*I turn and laugh. "What, like, from sharks?"*

*"You never know."*

*"No, I'm pretty sure I'll never have to swim from sharks. I'm*

*fine with not swimming, James. I'm pretty good at skipping rocks. I'll have to show you sometime."*

*"I hate that you're scared," he says, his smile fading as his voice becomes more serious. We're on our way to meet Lacey and Kevin, on our way to join rebels. Every moment of normalcy we have has an undercurrent of fear. I don't think it'll ever go away again.*

*"I don't want you to be scared of anything," James says. "I want you to fight. Fight for everything, always. Otherwise they win."*

*I swallow hard, the unspoken "they" being The Program. "I fought for you," I murmur.*

*James lifts one shoulder in a shrug. "Yeah, well. Now I want you to learn to swim."*

*"Never."*

*James turns on the windshield wipers as a soft rain begins to patter the glass. He shakes his head as if I'm the biggest pain in the ass he's ever known. "One day," he says, "I'll find a way to convince you to listen to me."*

I open my eyes, the hallway stretched endlessly. The stark white walls begin to fade away—the color deepening to a dusty gray the closer I get to the surgeon's room. I'll never swim with James. He was right; I was too scared—always too scared. I turn from side to side, looking up at the handlers as they continue to usher me forward, moving me closer to the end of life as I know it.

I can't be scared anymore. I have to swim.

"You realize what you're doing, right?" I ask one of the handlers. "I'm not even sick. They're doing this to keep me quiet."

Neither of them looks at me, although I see the handler on my right squint slightly. I wish Asa was here; I wish he'd help me. But instead I have these two strangers with whom I'll have my last conversation before I meet the doctor. I yank my arms back, but they hold me fast.

"Keep moving," one says gently, as if I really am crazy.

"I can't believe you let yourself be part of this," I hiss at him. "I can't believe you let them destroy people. What if I was your friend? Your sister? What if I was you?"

The handler turns, his lip curled up with some sort of ready response, but I seize the moment. I throw all my weight into my shoulder and slam into him, knocking him off balance while freeing my arm from the other handler. My socks slip on the floor, but it gives me an advantage as I drop lower, missing the swinging arm of the handler trying to catch me.

I take off, sliding until I get enough traction, and then I'm through the doors leading out into the main hallway. The handlers are yelling, both to me and into their walkie-talkies. I'll never get out like this, but I refuse to let them walk me to my death. If they're going to take me, they're going to take me kicking and screaming. I won't make it easy for them.

The walls are white again and I'm running as fast as my legs will carry me. I'm not sure how far behind me they are, and I don't turn to look, afraid it will slow me down. I expect the shock of the Taser at any second, but I keep going. I'll never stop.

I take the final turn and see the backs of several security guards. The air catches in my throat, my stomach sinking to the floor. It's over. I'm about to scream, fight to the death, but they don't turn to me, and then suddenly the handlers behind me stop yelling. They listen to their handsets, glancing from me to the scene up ahead. I'm confused, my adrenaline pulsing through my veins until I hear the other voices. I realize security isn't concerned about me or the calls from my handlers because they're talking to someone, or rather, actively trying to keep someone out of the hall.

I continue in that direction, knowing I'm walking straight into the arms of security, but hoping it's my salvation somehow. I cast glances back at the handlers, who have paused, looking torn about what to do. One of the security guards raises his voice, repeating that he has no comment. *Oh my God.*

I start to jog, craning my neck around the broad-shouldered men. Another voice shouts that he will not be censored, and I recognize him. I stop next to the stairwell door, flooded with relief, overwhelming relief.

A guard steps toward him, and he comes into focus. Kellan—his dark hair, his eager eyes. "Kellan?" I say, not loud enough for him to actually hear me because my voice is still hoarse, because I'm already crying. I'm saved. The reporter won't let me get lobotomized.

Behind Kellan there's a cameraman filming the entire

exchange, even though one of the security guards keeps pushing his lens, knocking it aside. I get on my tiptoes, lifting up my tired arms to wave them and get the reporter's attention, when the door next to me opens with a loud click. Before I even have time to see who it is, a hand darts out and grabs my elbow, pulling me into the stairwell. The door slams shut behind me.

# CHAPTER EIGHT

"HOLY CHRIST, SLOANE," JAMES SAYS, PULLING ME behind him before he jams a tire iron in the metal bar of the door, securing it closed. Without another word he gathers me into a hug, pressing his lips to my forehead as we stand in the cold concrete stairwell.

I can't even hug him back. My hands are shaky as I lift them, slowly, to touch the sleeve of his shirt and then his arm—his warm skin. I look up and study his blue eyes, his shaggy blond hair, the blond beard on his jaw. He's the James from my memories. Is he just a memory?

"Are you real?" I ask, my voice wavering. I half-think I've slipped into a delusion, that I got the lobotomy and this is the resulting psychosis. But then my fingers touch the scars on James's bicep and I know it's him. I moan and fall into him again.

"I'm here," James whispers, holding me so tightly, so securely. "I'm here, Sloane. I told you I'd come for you. Now"—he leans back to see me—"we have to get out of here. Your reporter friend is running a distraction, but we have to get out *now*. Can you run?"

I nod, wiping my face, but unable to let go of James's arm. I'm afraid he'll slip away, and then someone will grab me and drag me back into the white hallway. And I can't go back. I just can't.

"What about Dallas?" I ask. "They have her and—"

"I've already sent for her," a voice says from the landing below. I look down the stairs and see Realm standing there, wearing a white jacket, his hair combed smooth. The image of it makes me so sick to my stomach that I think I might throw up. Realm as a handler. Realm as who he is.

"Once you're out safely, Asa is going to bring Dallas down," he says. "He gave me his keycard, and in the madness of everything, we were able to slip in unnoticed. It was a brilliant plan, if I do say so myself." He smiles a little, but I don't return it.

I drop James's hand and start down the stairs, my body trembling, my face hot like it's on fire. Realm's expression brightens the closer I get to him. When I pause on the landing, I look him over. His scar is still jagged on his neck, just above the collar of the white jacket. His skin doesn't look quite as pale and the circles aren't as noticeable. I'm not sure if it's makeup or just that handler-white suits him.

I slap him hard across the face. Tears spill onto my cheeks

and my palm stings. Realm keeps his face turned for a long second, and then he slowly straightens, his eyes watering.

"I'm sorry," he whispers, knowing. I lean closer.

"I don't forgive you," I growl. There's a touch on my arm, startling me, and I turn to see James.

"We have to go," he says gently, glancing at Realm sympathetically. Does James know Realm is a handler? Would he have let him come here if he did?

James's fingers slide down to take my hand again, and he nods like he's asking me to trust him. I do. He tugs me forward, past Realm, although I'm not done with him. Not yet. We trample down the stairs, Realm lagging behind. Just as we get to the exit door, we hear the stairwell door shake, clanging against the tire iron. They're coming. James squeezes my hand just before we explode out of the door, and blazing sunlight temporarily blinds me. Pebbles on the pavement are cutting into the slipper socks, but I keep going, even though I have no idea where James is leading me. An alarm sounds from the building and my fear spikes. We'll never get away. They'll never let us.

"Over there," Realm calls from directly behind me, pointing past my shoulder to the left. He could pass me—he's faster—but he's trying to protect me. On the side of the building is a small alleyway where the front of a white van is sticking out. I hear the slam of bodies against the metal door; the handlers are nearly outside. My lungs burn as I run, knowing that I'm running for my life.

There's a parking lot half-filled with cars, but we're heading for the alley. Just then I see the flash of a white coat next to the van and my entire body tenses up, making me a stumble a step before James rights me. The handler is pushing a wheelchair, stopping to slide open the back door of the van. A cry bursts from my lips because I'd recognize that blond hair anywhere. I watch as Asa loads Dallas into the back of the van, her body limp and uncooperative as if she's heavily drugged. In the distance I hear the start of sirens, and I know I don't want to stick around for the police to arrive.

Even though The Program is wrong, I'm not taking the chance the authorities won't believe me. In the chaos, I could end up back inside the facility while they sort things out. I'm not so naive as to think The Program wouldn't do everything possible to keep me quiet.

"You have to run faster, Sloane," James says, gasping, looking once behind us and then renewing his speed, practically ripping me off my feet. The handlers must be closing in, and it's as if I can feel them breathing down my neck. Dallas once said it was impossible to break someone out of The Program— they've tried. James told her she must be doing it wrong. I sure as hell hope he's figured out the right way.

We round the corner and Asa is already in the front seat, the engine running. He tears off his white jacket, pulling on his seat belt and revving the engine. The back is still open, and we're so close to being free I'm sure we'll make it. *We have to make it.*

I hear the gear shift and for a wild second I think the van is going to leave us behind, but I feel someone take hold of the back of my shirt and launch me forward. I'm completely off balance as I stumble, slamming gut-first into the running board of the van. There's a commotion all around me, a flurry of grabbing hands making it impossible to tell what's happening. And then I'm moving. Gravity rolls me inside the van and the door slams shut, locking me inside.

Realm collapses next to me, and we're shoulder to shoulder. The van tires squeal, spinning out as we fishtail and shoot forward. My lungs burn and my side aches. I may be injured internally, but my adrenaline is rushing too hard for me to properly analyze my condition.

"Thanks, man," James says, his cheeks flushed and his hair matted down with sweat. I turn and see he's looking at Realm. Realm gasps for breath next to me but lifts his hand in a half-hearted salute. Realm is the one who pushed me into the van. I turn away from him, unable to look at his face—even though he just saved my life.

"Sloane?"

I smile, recognizing the voice, and I force myself up, groaning at the severe pain in my side. I push Realm's hand away when he tries to help me. Dallas is in the back, a seat belt across the chest of her gray scrubs. She's not wearing a patch, and I can't contain my relieved laughter. She hasn't been lobotomized.

I want to get to my feet and hug her, but the van is racing forward at a breakneck speed and I can't get my bearings. James has moved to the passenger seat, talking with Asa and giving him directions. The handler, my friend, is now a fugitive, and I can tell by the lack of color in his cheeks that he knows that.

There's another sharp pain in my side, and I lift the corner of my gray scrubs to check for an injury. There's a dark purple fist-size bruise with dark magenta in the middle. I swallow hard and quickly cover it, trying to remember which vital organs are on my right side.

"Realm, help her onto the seat," James calls from the front, drawing my gaze. When he sees my expression, he furrows his brow. "You okay?" He checks with Asa before coming to gather me from the floor, using the seat to hold him up. I don't answer and let James move me, biting down hard on my lip to keep from screaming at the pain of being jostled. Realm skirts around us, taking James's spot in the front.

I'm folding in on myself and slide in next to Dallas. James is concerned, but he's also checking out the window to look for cops—or worse, handlers. I catch the reflection in Asa's driver's-side mirror and immediately freak.

"They're following us!" There's a black car close behind, racing through the traffic. When we turn, it turns with us. Overwhelming fear bubbles up.

James quickly follows my gaze to the black car behind us and then takes my hands to calm me. "It's Kellan," he says. "It's okay. It's just Kellan." I meet James's eyes, surprised. Certainly confused. "I had his business card," James adds. "He helped us break you out."

I check the car again, but the windows are too tinted for me to see the driver. There's so much happening, I'm not sure what to ask first. I rest my head against James's chest, happy to have him back, happier to be free. I can't help but wonder for how long, though.

"Where are we going?" I ask, wrapping my arms around James, sighing after his hand brushes along my hair. I tense when Realm is the one who answers.

"We're going to Oregon," he says quietly. I force myself up, glaring toward the front. Is he crazy?

"They'll be waiting for us there. I can't just show up at my front door. My parents turned me in to The Program!"

"It's our only choice."

"Oh, now I'm supposed to trust you? You're a handler— you've always been a handler. You let them take me!" Tears threaten to spill, betrayal attacking me all over again. Even if I forgave everything Realm did before, he didn't get us out of that farmhouse. He found us for The Program—and he disappeared when I needed him most.

Realm lowers his head, not daring to look back at me. "I didn't *let* them take you. I just didn't have the power to stop it. Cas told me about his deal, but all of us would have been screwed if I didn't leave when I did. I got James." He turns to me, his jaw set hard. "I got him for you, so yes, you should trust me."

James pulls me closer, murmuring that Realm is right. But it's not enough for me. I'm angrier than I thought possible—

about Realm being a handler, about the farmhouse. . . . But that's not all. There's a touch of a memory in the back of my head, and I turn to Dallas, sure it has to do with her. But nothing surfaces. I look back at Realm. They erased it. The Program erased part of the reason why I'm angry with him; I can feel it. What more could he have possibly done? I refuse to forgive him for crimes I can't even remember—I'm not that kind.

"So we go back to Oregon," I say, agitated that The Program got to any of my memories at all. "And then what? How long before they come for us again?"

Asa glances at Realm, obviously having the same concerns. I realize how shitty this must be for him. Whatever debt he had to Realm is paid off, but now his life is ruined. He's on the run with a group of half-crazed rebels.

"I don't know," Realm says solemnly. "But you're not going home. We're going to Oregon to meet someone—a friend. Probably the only one we have left."

"Who?" At this point, I can't imagine anyone would want to fight with us, not even for him.

Realm smiles sadly and turns to face front again. "We're going to see Dr. Evelyn Valentine."

# CHAPTER NINE

**THE FARMHOUSES IN THE OREGON COUNTRYSIDE** still look the same, and nostalgia builds the closer we get to town. I've spent my life driving through these pastures, grown up hiking and camping with my family—my brother. Even though I can't remember, I've spent them with James, too.

My eyelids are heavy as I battle against sleep, but my side is stiffening, pain radiating from the bruise. James is in the back of the van talking to Dallas, but her one-word responses do little to placate our fears. She's unwell—severely unwell. There's an unspoken agreement between all of us to keep watch over her. And to make sure she doesn't leap from the moving van.

Realm has been talking on the phone with Kellan, but he's not offering much information. The conversations sound grim though, all ending in "We'll see." I would have thought our faces would be all over the news and scanners, but The Program must be trying to cover this up. There's not even an Amber Alert issued for us.

The seat shifts as James grabs the corner and climbs up to sit next to me. The movement renews my pain, and I grind my teeth to fight back a cry. I'm not quick enough to hide it, and James leans in close, turning my face to his.

"What's wrong?" he asks seriously. He notices how I'm favoring my right side, and his eyes flip accusingly to mine. "You're hurt?" Realm immediately turns from the front, and I know a spectacle is about to begin.

"I banged the side of the van pretty hard," I say through dry lips. "I'm not going to lie, it fucking hurts. Asa," I call to the front with a weak smile, "happen to have anything to fix that?"

My handler glances in the rearview mirror. "Some shots of Thorazine. You can expect to sleep if I hit you with one though."

I shake my head. We may have to outrun the threat for right now, but if I fall asleep, I'll be helpless. I can't take the risk. I don't think I'll ever sleep again.

"Let him give you the shot," James whispers, leaning in closer. He slides his palm gently over my bruise to check it, and I wince. "I can't kiss the pain better."

"I'm sorry I pushed you," Realm says quietly. "I did this."

I swallow hard, looking over at him. There's a rush of affection, but I quickly squash it, refusing to let him in even a little bit. Because if I do, I don't know how much of me he'll take.

"Don't be stupid," James says to him, not unkindly. "You saved our lives. Now, Asa. Can you pass me back the needle?" I look pleadingly at James, but he shakes his head definitively. "I won't let anything happen to you. I promise."

We stare at each other, knowing he's promised before. Maybe this is how we go on: making promises about things beyond our control to offer one more moment of hope. Hope—like Arthur Pritchard offered us, is sometimes enough to survive on.

So I nod, pushing up my shirtsleeve to give him access to my upper arm. Asa gives him the needle, and James looks all sorts of nervous as he takes off the cap and holds it up like he's about to stab me. If my side didn't hurt so badly, I'd laugh.

"Hold on," Realm says, climbing back and snatching the needle out of James's fist. "Jesus, you're not trying to break through her breastplate." Realm slides in between us, and this close to him I'm struck with grief. He's taken off the handler's jacket and is wearing a cotton T-shirt underneath instead. But his hair is still combed to the side, and I think he looks handsome. I hate him more for it.

"Here," he says quietly, unable to meet my eyes this close. He runs his fingers over my muscles, warm and gentle, and then grips the underside to lift my arm. "Take a breath," he whispers, too kindly. Tears well up, and I press my lips together to keep from crying. I don't want him here—I don't want the pain and regret. I don't want to love him and hate him at the same time.

There's a pinch and a deep burn as he injects me, and I

cry out. But it's not the needle hurting me, and Realm knows that. When he removes the tip, I cover my face and continue to cry—cry for all I've lost in the past few months. The ways I've been violated and betrayed. They were going to lobotomize me! Nothing will ever be right again. So I cry.

Realm gets up and James slides over, whispering I should let it out, as he helps me lie across his lap. I curl against him, my side still aching, and hiccup a few more whimpers. The Thorazine slowly works through me, coating me in contentment. This time I don't fight against the calm.

"We'll be at Evelyn's in an hour, and Sloane can rest there," Realm announces from the front, pausing before going on. "So long as the doctor lets us in."

There's the loud scrape of the metal door opening, and I'm startled awake. My side doesn't hurt anymore—it feels stiff and full, and I imagine for a second that my midsection has hardened like petrified wood.

"Let's get her to the back," a woman's voice says. The sound is raspy with a light German lilt. It must be Evelyn Valentine. Strong hands slide under me, lifting me from the seat, and my head falls against James's chest. I'm trying to wake up, but I can keep my eyes open for only a few seconds at a time as I battle the Thorazine.

"Is she suicidal?" the doctor asks.

"No." It's Realm who answers from next to me. I blink my eyes open and see the wood shingles of a small cottage as we approach the entryway. There are vines crawling up the sides like the house is trying to stay hidden in nature. "She's upset, though," Realm adds. "We almost didn't get to her in time. The other one, Dallas, she needs your help."

The doctor sighs, mumbling something I don't understand. I turn my head lazily to find her, but the scene is bouncing wildly as James carries me. It's hard for me to catch my breath.

"Hello, dear." Then she's next to me: a tall, slender woman with glasses. She's somewhere in her sixties with shaggy brown hair and a mole on the side of her nose. She smiles; her teeth are yellow and crowded, but her expression is genuine. I like her immediately.

"Don't try to talk," she says with an impatient wave of her hand. "You need to sleep off the drugs. I'm going to have a look at your side first, just to make sure you haven't injured anything too badly."

"Will she be okay?" James isn't trying to be brave. He's a wreck, and if I wasn't the one being carried, I would want to hold him and tell him I'm fine, just so he wouldn't have to be so scared.

"Oh, I think so," the doctor says, and I feel her brush back my hair. My body shifts as James turns sideways to fit us through the doorway. We're swallowed in darkness. The windows are covered, and from above us a light flicks on. "It looks like a nasty hematoma, but I'll poke it a bit just to make sure." She pats my arms to let me know she's joking. "All right, put her in there."

Cool sheets come up to meet me as James sets me on a small twin bed. I'm groggy, achy—but mostly I'm terrified to be alone with anyone but James. I grab his shirt to prevent him from leaving my side. He sits next to me on the bed, taking my hand and holding it to his lips.

"All but blondie out," the doctor calls, shooing Realm and Asa from the room. "Now get that awful color off of her," she says to James, and he begins to work my arms out of the gray scrubs. Evelyn kneels next to me, checking over my side before actually poking it and making me moan. She apologizes, but does it again in a few other areas. When she's finished, she walks to the dresser and pulls out a bright pink T-shirt, handing it to James. "Help her into this this," she says. "I can't bear to put her back in gray."

"Is she okay?" James asks, his voice strained.

"Contusion, bruising. She'll be tender for a few weeks. So far as I can tell, most of her damage will be emotional." The doctor takes a small wooden chair and sets it next to the bed, sitting down. Once I'm dressed, she runs her gaze over me and James. "I am so sorry for what you've gone through. But perhaps you can fill me in a few things. Like how the hell Michael Realm found me."

I lag against him James, widening my eyes a few times to wake myself up. "When we were taken from the farmhouse," James starts, "Realm was in the van I was loaded into. He was dressed as a handler, him and Asa, and they brought me to some sketchy-ass motel near the facility. Asa was off the books on the pickup, so The Program had no idea he was involved. Basically my entire existence at the site was covered up because I went off the grid. Realm saved me."

There's an ache in my heart, because I'm not sure what James could tell me that would make me forgive Michael Realm. I honestly don't.

"I had the business card of a reporter," he continues, "and Realm and I met with him. We asked for his help, promising to get him the story of his career—but not until Sloane was free." James shrugs. "Realm offered you up, Evelyn. He said he could get Kellan an interview with you if he helped us."

The doctor's good nature slips momentarily as she looks toward the door where Realm is waiting on the other side. Realm told me once that Evelyn cared about him. But if she was hiding from The Program, did he have the right to turn her over? Does he have the right to do any of the things he does?

James goes on. "Kellan had the idea to walk into the facility and cause a stir. He'd tried to get in before and knew security would show up to strong-arm him out. Once that happened, Realm and I were going to slip in. Of course, we didn't expect Sloane to try to break *herself* out, but I guess we should have." He smiles, but James hasn't recovered, not from the idea of losing me. I can't remember my last time in The Program, but if it weren't for James and Realm—I'd be gone. The real Sloane Barstow would be dead, and I don't know if there is a way to feel whole again. To ever feel safe.

"And the other girl?" Evelyn asks, crossing her arms over her chest. I can't read her expression, whether she's all business or truly pissed.

"Dallas is one of us," James says. "But she's been violated. I don't think she's okay, no matter what she looks like on the outside. Realm thought you might be able to help her, too."

"Michael Realm seems to think a lot of things," Evelyn says. "Please, go on." She's definitely pissed. I'm happy the Thorazine has begun to fade, or maybe my adrenaline is working it through my system quicker, because I half-expect the doctor to kick us out.

"The plan was to get Sloane and Dallas out and head here," James says. "Realm's known your location for a long time—said it's why he's been staying in Oregon, to be closer to you. He'd been waiting for the right moment to show up at your door. I guess this was it."

Evelyn is quiet, and in the silence, I glance around at what must be her bedroom. The light is dim, but it's quaint. There are pictures on the walls—landscapes of forests in clumpy oil paints, and the sheets of the bed are a deep green. It's humble here, and it occurs to me that we've just shattered what was left of her life. She's harboring fugitives.

"I knew my time would come," she says solemnly. "And if I can save a few more kids on my way out, so be it. Once The Program learns of my location, you can expect them to converge on this place. You can't stay long."

"But if you talk to Kellan," James says, leaning toward her, "you can tell him your story. We can take down The Program. Realm thought you'd know how."

Evelyn smiles briefly, tugging her red sweater closed around her. "Michael always did think too highly of me. Truth is, The Program will eliminate me long before the government can offer me any protection. And I'm too old to run any longer. Too tired. I have a lot of secrets in my head. Ones I'll never forget." She tilts her head, looking over James. "I suspect you're the same?"

In the craziness of escape, I'd forgotten. James has taken The Treatment—he knows everything about us, about himself. Oh my God. What does James know?

"I wasn't a doctor," he says. "My secrets are small compared to yours, I'm sure."

Evelyn leans forward, looking concerned. "Are you well?" she asks quietly. "Were you able to hold off the depression?"

James shifts uncomfortably. "I had help," he says. "Between Realm and medication, I was able to fight off the worst of it. I stayed focused on Sloane and making sure she was safe. But it wasn't easy. I think I'm past the worst of it though."

Evelyn nods. "Not everyone was so lucky," she says solemnly. "You'll have to be prepared. The memories will continue; some may be harder to take."

"I understand the risks. But right now we don't have time to dwell. You were kind to let us in, but I need to know, Evelyn, can you end The Program?"

The doctor rolls her eyes toward the ceiling, like she's trying to stop tears from slipping out. "I don't think Michael's left me another choice. And I have no delusions about how far The Program will go to keep me quiet." She sniffles hard and then leans back in her chair, crossing her legs.

"Did you know I never had any children of my own?" she asks. "When the epidemic began, I didn't have the same investment as some of the other doctors. That's not to say I wasn't horrified—I was. But as much as I researched, I couldn't find the source of the outbreak.

"The closest I got was a small school outside of Washington, where three girls poisoned themselves at a sleepover. They were among the first, and other than being friends, there were no genetic markers or links. One of the girls—sixteen—had been on antidepressants since she was nine. She'd been diagnosed with a myriad of conditions, and was prescribed medications to help her function at school. In the end, I believe the medication cocktail is what led to her suicidal thoughts. Now, what she said to her friends, how they came to want to die—that's the real mystery. Because after that day, the outbreak pushed outward.

"News stories, articles, copycats. It all happened so quickly that it no longer became the focus of *why* teens wanted to kill themselves, just how to stop them. It was a worldwide psychosis. At least, that's what I believe. There are other scientists with different theories, of course. All seems moot now—now we have The Program," she says with a flourish of her hands. "And wouldn't that just save us all."

I'm absorbing all of Evelyn's words, putting them together

with what I've seen and experienced. I can't say I completely buy into her notions—I won't downplay the outbreak to a fad. But maybe there are some kernels of truth in there.

"I took a shine to Michael," she says nostalgically. "He has such a good heart, such a fighter. But he can also be cruel and manipulative—and that was after he'd been stripped of his memories. The Program didn't save him—it made him worse. I knew then it wasn't the answer. I began playing with formulas and came up with a way to return the memories. I gave The Treatment to Michael, Kevin, Roger, and Peter." Her eyelids blink quickly as she fights back the start of tears.

"Peter didn't make it. Despite everything I did to get him through, he didn't make it." Her voice chokes up, and I have to look away. "He would have survived if I hadn't given him The Treatment. I killed him. I vowed to never take that chance again.

"But . . . ," she says, shrugging sadly. "The Program learned about The Treatment, and my contract was up. I wasn't about to stick around for a lobotomy, but I did what I could to protect my patients. I destroyed the files, the formula. There are no pills other than the one Realm kept. I don't suppose he told you who it belonged to?"

"No," I say. The doctor scoffs softly, ready to continue, and it strikes me whose pill Realm stole. Roger—all this time, Roger was looking for his Treatment, and it was with Realm. He must have figured it out.

"Can you make more?" I ask. I think of Dallas, wondering if her past would help or hurt her.

Evelyn shakes her head slowly. "Oh, I would never do that. Bringing back all those dark thoughts at once? I may as well kill them myself. Arthur Pritchard had that idea, and I told him it was a mistake, The Treatment was a mistake. He didn't believe me."

Arthur Pritchard, alone in a gray room. "They lobotomized him," I say quietly, earning a look from James. "I saw him in the Program."

Evelyn's shoulders sag slightly. "Well, I'm sorry to hear that. I truly am. But the fact remains, The Treatment won't save everybody. It was the testing of a naive scientist, when all along, I should have been preventing The Program from erasing memories in the first place.

"You asked me if I knew how to stop them"—Evelyn levels her gaze on James—"and the answer is no—I don't know how to make the world believe. But if your reporter can find the studies The Program buried, I believe he'll have his answers. The Program is the reason the epidemic is spreading. The pressure, the attention—it's causing a whole new outbreak it hopes to contain by resetting the world. The Program is breeding suicide."

# CHAPTER TEN

IT'S LATE BY THE TIME EVELYN FINISHES TALKING, and she tells us we can stay in her room to rest while she checks on Dallas and the others. It feels sort of creepy to be lying in her bed, but at the same time, with James next to me, I just want to sleep for a few hours. We don't say much, just a few relieved murmurs about being back together. I have so much to ask him, but with all I've learned in the past few hours, I don't think I can contain another thought.

I'm not sure how much time passes when James moves next to me, saying I slept like the dead, and I'm stirred awake. It's dark, but he clicks on the light, flooding me in unflattering hues. I glance down at the pink T-shirt and gray pants I'm wearing, and take a moment to familiarize myself with where we are.

It comes in a wave, and I'm quickly out of bed, wincing when I put pressure on my side. I check the bruise again, and James sticks out his bottom lip, seeing the colors. He comes to hug me gently. I promise I'm okay—even though it hurts like hell—and kiss his lips before leading us from the room.

We don't have to go far. I stumble to a stop, putting my arm out to stop James from passing me. Evelyn is at her round kitchen table with a bright light pointed at her. Kellan sits close by with his cameraman, recording their interview. Realm and Asa are standing off to the side, and Realm meets my eyes before looking away. James and I stand and listen as Evelyn Valentine tells the world about The Program. She's matter-of-fact, and at times maybe even a little cold, but she's believable.

When they take five to reset the camera, I slip past them in search of Dallas and find her alone in the living room, staring at a blank television screen. Evelyn has gotten her out of the gray scrubs too, and Dallas sits in an oversize Seattle Seahawks T-shirt, more out of place than I've ever seen her. She glances over when I sit next to her.

We don't say anything. Her lip quivers before she smiles widely, flashing the gap in her teeth. I put my arm around her and she leans into me, sniffling back a cry as we both stare at the blank television—we're bonded but too damaged to talk about what we went through.

"Sloane," James calls softly. I look over to see him in the doorway, perfect—at least for me. I kiss Dallas on the cheek, making her laugh, and then get up to meet James. Dallas's laugh isn't a sound I thought I'd hear again, and it gives me a small sense of home. I take James's hand and lead him back into the kitchen.

Evelyn is done with her interview, exhausted as she mumbles about making tea. I go to help her, turning the stove knob until the burner catches fire, and I set the kettle on top. There's a touch on my elbow, startling me, and I turn to see Asa.

"I wanted to say good-bye," he says in his quiet manner. In regular clothes I think he looks just like anybody else—average and normal. There is nothing sinister about this handler, not when his eyes are so kind.

"Good-bye?" I repeat. "But we've hardly had a chance to talk. I know nothing about you."

Asa smiles, looking around sheepishly. "No offense"—he motions to the cameraman—"but I want to keep it that way. There's a girl back in San Diego I'd like to go check on. Then I plan to lie low while this shit hits the fan. I truly hope you all make it. I really do."

"I know." I lean in and hug him, careful of my injured side. I can't blame Asa for not wanting to get involved. If anything, it proves how smart he is. My former handler makes his rounds, carefully avoiding the reporter, and slaps hands with James and hugs Realm. And just as quickly as Asa slipped into my life, he's gone, having played his part in my rescue.

The night is long, and James and I opt out of a filmed interview in exchange for a written statement—mostly because we don't want our faces out there any more than we have to.

Realm refuses to talk at all, and Kellan doesn't even approach Dallas. He got everything he needed from us and Evelyn. The doctor isn't kind when he thanks her, ready to leave. I see her anxiety continue to ratchet up, her expectant looks at the door, the wringing of her hands. But she doesn't ask any of us to go—not yet.

I offer to walk Kellan out, and it's just the two of us when we get to his car. It's close to midnight—the stars blotted out behind the canopies of the trees. There are crickets and frogs and so many noises around us, we could never feel alone.

"I'm sorry," Kellan says. Surprised, I look up to meet his eyes, noting again how they're not the dark black I saw the first time I met him at the Suicide Club.

"For what?"

"Not coming sooner. James told me how close you came to—"

I swallow hard and look away, stopping his statement. "But you came," I say, pressing my lips into a smile. "In the end, all that matters is I'm not there now."

"We have them, you know," he says earnestly. "I'm going to find the studies, and those combined with Evelyn's statements, the eyewitness accounts—The Program can never survive this PR mess. I assure you, Sloane. They'll never take anything from you again."

I hope Kellan is right, and at this point I believe in him. He chased me around the country, helped save my life—I have to believe he's a good reporter if he can do all that. The cameraman comes out from Evelyn's house with his gear, nodding a good-bye to me, and Kellan and I exchange one last hug. I watch as he climbs into his vehicle, ready to finish his big story. Before he pulls away, he rolls down his window.

"Sloane?" he asks. "If The Treatment was still around—if Evelyn made more . . . would you take it?"

I digest his words, rocking back on my feet. The pain of my time in The Program is still so raw, and yet, I think it's just the tip of the pain I've endured in the last few months. What could getting it all back bring me?

"I don't think so," I tell him sincerely. "Sometimes, Kellan . . . I think the only real thing is now."

He smiles at my answer, although his brows pull together like he's a little confused. I wave to him and he drives away, leaving the rebels behind. Leaving us to each other.

The house is quiet when I go inside. James is curled up on the living room floor, talking quietly with Dallas while she lies on the couch above him. I like the picture—him being sweet to her, protecting her. James is different since he took The Treatment. More thoughtful in a way that proves we belonged together all along.

There's a clink of a cup and I follow the sound into the kitchen, uneasy when I find Realm at the table all alone. Evelyn's bedroom door is closed, and Realm glances over his shoulder when I walk in the room. Despite my urge to walk right back out, I take a seat across from him, daring to look him in the eyes.

"I told you once that I wish you hated me," he says. "Is it too late to take it back?"

I don't want him to be funny; it only makes it hurt more. I bring my hands into my lap, squeezing them into fists in an attempt to control the emotions threatening to burst through. "Why?" I ask. "If you were a handler in The Program—if you were the one who erased my memories—why pretend to be my friend? Why continue even after I returned?"

Realm swallows, his eyes watering and downcast as my words hit him. "I was doing my job. I fell in love." He looks up. "I did what I could to keep you. But the simple answer: I'm selfish. I thought I could make you love me back—that without James you would. I thought I could wear you down."

"I did love you."

Realm smiles sadly. "Not like that. Never like him." Realm's gaze drifts past me to the living room. "He's not bad, you know. I kinda like him. And I was wrong: I could never love you the way he does. That kid is absolutely nuts about you."

I laugh, bringing my hands to the table as the anger fades. There's more between Realm and me, instances I'm sure I can't remember. I don't want to. I want to leave us here—make a truce. I say good night, even though his eyes plead for more time.

James grins when he sees me, patting the carpet and telling me he saved me a spot. We plan to leave first thing in the morning. Evelyn is lending us a car so we can hide out somewhere in town, and Realm is taking Dallas to Corvallis, where she says she has a cousin who'd be willing to help her out for a while. We don't know if Evelyn and Kellan have done enough to free us, but for the first time, we're close to an ending. And there's solace in that.

"We have to leave."

The voice cuts through the room, and I'm on my feet, still blurry with sleep. I find Realm in the doorway, reddish-brown smears on the sleeves of his shirt. I let out a horrified cry, and both Dallas and James jump up, disoriented and confused.

"Oh my God! Are you okay?" My first thought is that Realm is hurt, and I search for a source of his injury. But when I find none, I look past him toward the bedroom. The blood belongs to someone.

Realm is detached, licking the corner of his mouth as if he's not exactly clear what he's going to say. "Evelyn killed herself last night. She . . . uh, she didn't want to go back to The Program. She left a note." He takes a crumpled piece of paper out of his pocket. He doesn't even look at it though; he stares through it. "She didn't want them to ever get their hands on The Treatment. And she didn't want them to get us. She . . . she said she was protecting her brain from the scientists."

I stumble backward, and James catches me around the waist and eases me back onto the couch. I want to run in and check on her, but I know Realm would never leave her side if there was hope of reviving her. I see the devastation and guilt in

SUZANNE YOUNG

his eyes. Next to me Dallas begins to weep, and James quickly takes her arm.

He sniffles back his own tears. "Realm's right. We have to go."

"We should call an ambulance," I say. "Something!"

"No," Realm says with a shake of his head. "I'm sorry, but it's too late. I've called Kellan and told him already; he'll send someone when we're clear. Now, James, grab the keys hanging by the door; car's through the garage. I'll meet you out front."

"Realm . . . ," I start to say, but he's already disappeared back into the kitchen. I hear cupboards opening and closing, the sliding of drawers as Realm gathers supplies. Evelyn Valentine is dead. She didn't have to kill herself; she could have come with us. But ultimately her fear was too great. She was right—The Program has become the epidemic.

The next moments take on a dreamlike quality; Dallas cries, and James pulls her along while he shouts for me to hurry. We load the car and wait for Realm. He walks out the front door, pausing to lock it. He stands there, his back to us, staring at the house. I choke up, thinking Evelyn was probably the closest thing he had to a mother other than his sister. He doesn't talk to us when he gets inside the car, only sits at the window, staring out, carrying a brown leather case.

I never asked what he took from Evelyn's house that day. But I imagine Evelyn Valentine was a piece of his past he wasn't willing to forget.

THE FALL OF THE PROGRAM

Once cloaked in secrecy, The Program project has been suspended indefinitely by the US government. Reacting to an interview confirming a system-wide cover-up, Congress moved swiftly to shut down all facilities until further notice.

As more details emerge about the procedures used in The Program, public outrage grows. One handler, Roger Coleman, was arrested on several counts of statutory rape and is awaiting trial. Coleman is accused of soliciting sex from underage patients in exchange for memories, and is facing up to sixty years in prison if convicted.

The scandal originally broke after a taped interview with the late Dr. Evelyn Valentine (a former employee) was leaked. She confirmed The Program's knowledge of a study indicating their role in the epidemic, substantiating claims of a cover-up.

Since the closure, all patients have returned home and will be provided with follow-up care. But, as of now, the long-term effects of The Program remain to be seen.

—Reported by Kellan Thomas

SUZANNE YOUNG

# CHAPTER ELEVEN—SIX MONTHS LATER

**I ROLL DOWN MY WINDOW TO LET THE WARM AIR** blow through my hair. James switches between radio stations, but all we hear are updates: The Program is dead, doctors and nurses testify in front of Congress about the lobotomies and the drop in suicides. Kellan Thomas is a household name—the rogue reporter who got the scoop of the century. He found the studies, and his interview with Dr. Evelyn Valentine was broadcast on every major news outlet. He never even used the story he collected from me and James.

The epidemic continues, but shortly after The Program received a cease and desist order while under federal investigation, the outbreak calmed—much like Evelyn had thought it would. Suicide hasn't vanished, not entirely, but every month brings better statistics, and hopes are high.

James's phone vibrates in the center console, and I look down just as he reaches to click ignore. Michael Realm. After all that's happened, James and Realm have forged a friendship I try not to get between. I've never been able to trust Realm again, and I don't know if I ever will. But my boyfriend is allowed to be friends with whomever he chooses—even if said friend once had me erased.

"I thought he was out of town," I say. "Wasn't he making some bad choices down in Florida?"

James pulls the car over to park in front of a pasture with cows milling about so he can quickly type out a return text. "I hate when you use your disapproving voice," he tells me. When I don't laugh, he sets down the phone and tugs me closer, resting his forehead against mine. "Be nice."

"Shut up," I mumble.

James smiles and then leans back to watch me. "That's not very nice. Come on, baby. Life is good." He runs his fingers between mine over and over as he talks. "*We're* good. I don't want to ruin it with talk of Michael Realm."

"Says the person who's now his best friend forever."

"Not true." Tingles races up my arm at James's touch, warming my body. "What I am is grateful," he says. "He got me out of The Program; he helped me get to you. He was grilled by those investigators and he didn't once mention our names. We owe him. Not to mention that, without him, you would have ended up lobotomized—"

I pull my hand from his and cross my arms over my chest.

"Yeah, I got it," I say, still uncomfortable talking about my last hours in The Program. Even when I was questioned by authorities, I told them I was too drugged to remember the final details, the escape. I told them to defer to Program records, which I knew had probably been destroyed by then.

James is quiet for a moment, letting my anger pass as it always does. Then he starts in on my new favorite pastime since escaping the control of The Program: recall.

"There was this one night," he says in that far-off voice he reserves for memories, "where you and Brady were about ready to throw down. I told you both that you were being stubborn, but I was, of course, ignored." He rolls his eyes, but I'm smiling, the thought of my brother settling over me like a blanket.

"What were we fighting about?" I ask.

"What else? Me. You didn't want me to stay the night because Lacey was coming over, and you said I was too obnoxious to play nice with others. Brady said Lacey was a lawsuit waiting to happen and that I was the safer bet. It got kind of ugly."

"Who won?"

James laughs. "Me, of course."

I lower my arms, grinning at the way the memory plays across my head. I don't remember any of it, but I love when James tells me the stories. I love that he has them. "And how did you pull that off?" I ask.

He licks his lips, leaning a little closer. "I promised to be sweet. I may have had a little twinkle in my eye when I said it."

"Hmm," I say, reaching to take the fabric of his T-shirt in my hand to pull him closer. "I know that look. So, what? I just gave in? That doesn't sound like me."

"It wasn't at all like you," he whispers, pausing just as his lips brush against mine. "That's how I knew you loved me. And that's why I started leaving you notes. I told myself I wanted you to talk me out of it, but really, I just wanted you to talk to me."

I kiss him; it's playful and easy—we have time now. There's no one after us. We're free.

My phone rings from my back pocket, and James groans, trying to grab it from my hand when I take it out. He's still kissing me as we both fumble for the phone, and when I finally pull away to check it, I see it's my mom. "She has impeccable timing," James says, and then drops back into the driver's seat with one last mischievous glance in my direction.

I laugh and answer. "Hi, Mom." James shifts the car into gear, leaving the pasture behind as we continue down the peaceful, winding road toward our destination. "What's up?"

"Hi, honey," my mother says, her voice distracted. "I can't remember what you told me—was it mac 'n' cheese you wanted me to pick up? That stuff is horrible for you."

"I know, but I've been craving it. I haven't had it in forever." *Not since I was on the run with the rebels,* I think. I'm trying to convince myself I can handle memories of that time, even though my subconscious quickly tries to wipe it away.

"Your dad still wants pork chops, so I'll make that junk as a side dish. Oh, here it is." The phone rustles, and I tap my nails on the door.

"Anything else?" I ask, wanting to get back to James.

"No, that's it," my mother says happily. "Tell James I said hello. Make sure you're both home by six." I agree, and as soon as we hang up, I look sideways at James.

"I wish she'd stop trying so hard," I say, although not unkindly. When I first returned home after the scandal broke, my parents were overwhelmed with the attention from the press and then the horror of the stories broadcast on the news. It's taken months of therapy—normal therapy with normal doctors—for me to stop blaming my parents. Then they had to stop blaming themselves. We're finally in a good place, I guess.

"At least she's trying," James says, continuing to stare straight ahead. My parents helped him buy a small stone at the cemetery to keep his father's remains. Although it alleviated some of his guilt, James is still haunted by the fact that his father died alone. But we all have our crosses. Now James is at my house, staying in Brady's old room. Soon it'll be just us, because despite how much my parents kind of annoy me, I told them I'd stay a year. I realize I've missed them. I missed who they could be.

The sun glitters in the sky, but James stays quiet, maybe thinking about his dad. I don't like when he falls silent, bothered by things I can't remember. Sometimes he cries out in his sleep—an aftereffect of The Treatment—as a tragic memory floods back in. He'll be quiet for a few days, but eventually we talk it out. It's not always easy to remember—I can see that now.

"Tell me another story about us," I whisper.

The corner of James's mouth twitches and he flicks a glance at me. "Clean or dirty?"

I laugh. "Let's try a clean one."

James seems to think for a moment, and then the smile fades to something softer, sadder. "There was this one weekend where we went camping with Lacey and Miller."

At hearing the names, I feel a sharp twist of grief. But I need to hear their stories. James checks to see if I'm okay with him going on, and I nod to let him know that I am.

"So Miller, he was crazy about Lacey—I mean, the kid thought she walked on water. So you, being the insistent little matchmaker you are, thought camping would be a perfect double date. Which could have been the case if Lacey wasn't completely allergic to nature. She was miserable, and Miller was like, 'Oh, you don't like mosquitos? Me either! Oh, you think beans are gross? Me too!' It was painful to watch! So finally I pulled the kid aside and gave him some advice."

"Uh-oh."

"I told him he needed to play a little harder to get. Only he didn't quite understand the concept. He spent the rest of the night ignoring her. The next morning Lacey cornered you, crying, asking what she did wrong."

"How did it all work out?" I ask. I can't remember Miller, not the way James does. I never really will. But hearing about him, it makes me feel connected to myself. Miller's like a favorite character in a childhood story.

"Well, you little charmer," James says, "you went to Miller and told him to stop being an asshole. You had no idea I'd talked to him at the campsite. He went back to Lacey and apologized, she gave him a hard time, and then eventually they met up without us and became blissfully happy." James smiles. "Miller never ratted me out, either. He let you think he was an idiot. But really it was me."

"I can't believe I didn't guess that. I must have been blinded by your good looks."

"Who isn't?"

James pulls up to the empty spot near the grass and parks the car. We sit a minute, both of us feeling so much after the memory. "I wish I could remember," I say, and look over at James. "But I'm glad you do."

"I won't stop until you know every second of our lives," he says simply. "I won't leave anything out. Not even the bad stuff."

I nod. James has made that promise every day since we left Evelyn's house. Sometimes he repeats stories, but I don't mind. When we visit Lacey, we tell her some of them, and although she smiles, I'm not sure she really gets it. But she was well enough to finish school, take some college classes. Her therapist even thinks she'll get feelings back one day. So we don't give up. We never give up.

"I got you something," James says, trying to fight back a smile.

"Is it shiny?" Really, I just want to taunt him a little.

"Not really."

I furrow my brow. "Uh . . . is it flesh-colored?"

He laughs. "No, that's for later." He reaches into his pants pocket, but pauses, arresting me again with his gorgeous blue stare. "Do you remember the dream-slash-memory you had the day we were taken from the farmhouse? The one about my seed?"

"Ew, no." I don't remember anything about the day we left the farmhouse, not anymore. "I hope to God you're talking about farming."

James takes out a plastic bubble, the kind you get from a gumball machine. There's a flash of something pink and sparkly inside. I bite my lip, giddy with the smile trying to break through.

"That looks shiny," I say.

"I'm a great liar. Anyway"—he pops the top, taking out a ring—"you knew after that memory we loved each other madly—I think you even said I was sweet. Now I remember how I felt that day. Even then, even with everything going on, I knew I'd never let you get away."

"Don't you dare make me cry," I warn, but I can already feel the burn in my eyes.

James takes my hand and slides the ring onto my finger. "I've given you a ring twice before," he says, "and trust me, both times were way more romantic than this. But I'll keep giving them to you—same Denny's, same ring." His smile fades into a look far too serious for a sunny afternoon. I reach to put my palm on his cheek, leaning in to kiss him.

"I've lost you too many times, Sloane," he murmurs between my lips. His hand slides up my thigh, pulling it over his hip as he lays me back on the seat. His kisses are sweet but also a little sad. I try to change the mood entirely, and James quickly pulls back, laughing.

"Hey, now Miss Handsy," he says, nodding toward the windshield. "Are we going to do this thing or what? You still have all your clothes on."

"I think I'd rather stay in here," I say, grabbing his belt. He playfully swats my hand away and then wraps his arm around my waist, pulling me close.

"Let's go," he whispers, kissing me in a way so sweet and tender, I can't help but trust him. James climbs out of the car, and I take a steadying breath and stare out at the river. This is the first place where James kissed me, both times. I take my towel from the backseat, and with my heart thudding, I open the door.

James is standing at the top of the bank, and when he turns, his eyes are crystal blue in the sunlight. "Come on, chicken," he says. And I smile.

"I don't know," James says, holding my wrist as he draws me farther into the water. "I think the problem is that you still have on far too many clothes." I roll my eyes, my lips trembling from the ice-cold of the river water.

"You say that every time, and I'm still not convinced that's the problem. Now shut up and do something impressive before I go to wait in the car," I say in a shaky voice. As if on a dare he'd love to take, James grins and then dips underwater, coming up to brush back his hair.

"Don't move," he says, pointing at me. He begins the swim out to the dock, and I cross my arms over my bikini top as I watch him. His strokes are strong and majestic, and before he even climbs out of the water, I am already duly impressed. I whistle.

James glances over, winks, and then does a backflip into the water. I clap when he surfaces, stopping a moment to admire the new ring he so subtly put on my left hand. James starts swimming in my direction; his mouth occasionally dips below the water.

"That can be you," he says as he gets closer.

"Baby steps."

"Toughen up." When he's in front of me once again, James wraps his cold arms around me, lifting me half out the water as he kisses me. His lips are slightly cooler than mine, and it takes only a minute before my fingertips dig into the skin of his back, pulling us closer. Making us downright hot.

"Later," he says between my lips. "I think you're just trying to distract me."

I laugh and give him one last peck before he sets me back down into the water. He blows out a dramatic breath, tossing me a look of mock disapproval, and then he reaches out his hand to me.

"Grab on," he says seriously. I take his hand and let him

begin to pull me deeper. "Kick your legs. Scissors, Sloane. Think of them like scissors."

I do as he says, both of us patient—and soon my fear begins to melt away. My fear of the water. My fear of drowning. My fear of death—of life. It's in these quiet moments since The Program that I've found the reason to go on. It's not James. It's not my parents or my friends.

I've found me. After all this time, after all that's been taken and destroyed, I've found my way back home. I haven't gotten any more flashes of my old life. The stress of The Program or running no longer cracks the surface of my psyche. I've accepted that, enjoying James's stories in place of my memories.

And Realm, for as much as I still distrust him, has restarted his life at his old cabin. The last time he saw Dallas, he told her the truth about them—which I had forgotten from the day at the farmhouse. None of us has seen her since, but she does occasionally send me postcards from Florida. All the last one said was *Don't tell Realm.*

Roger is in prison—but not for his attack on me or Dallas. Tabitha, one of the embedded handlers from The Program, pressed charges, admitting that when she was first a patient, Roger had assaulted her, too. Turns out, there were a lot of girls willing to step forward. Roger will be serving fifteen to twenty in an Oregon penitentiary and is awaiting charges relating to his role in The Program.

None of the handlers or nurses has been prosecuted yet. Dr. Warren never resurfaced, and Dr. Beckett lawyered up.

Nurse Kell didn't report me for attacking her, although the guilt still eats away at me. I wish I could tell her I'm sorry—but I've never had the chance. Maybe one day I will.

I haven't heard from Cas, but Realm has spoken to him a few times. They've both agreed to leave Dallas alone, let her start over. Then again, I never believe anything Realm tells me anymore.

"All right," James says, his hands supporting my weight as he takes us deeper. "I'm going to let you go, but you'll be just fine."

My breathing starts to become erratic, and I'm so terrified I'm not sure I can do it. "James," I say, about to ready to grab him. He leans forward, his lips near my ear.

"Fight, Sloane," he whispers.

I swallow hard, measure my breathing, and then give him a quick nod before I start to lap my hands. They're uneven at first, large splashes of water coming over my face. But then I feel James's hands leave me, the water rushing past. James is beside me as we both head for the dock. There are a few moments when I think I won't make it, that I'll drown here just like Brady did. But I don't stop.

When I reach the dock, I grab on, laughing wildly. It's taken me all this time, all this loss, to realize what really matters is *now*. Not our memories. Now. And right now I'm here in the river where my brother died. With James. Swimming.

# EPILOGUE

THE APARTMENT'S TOO BRIGHT WHEN DALLAS walks out of her bedroom, blinking against the sunlight. She runs her palm over her short pixie cut, momentarily missing her long dreads. Her roommate left the coffeemaker full before she took off for work, and Dallas murmurs her appreciation as she fills a cup and drinks it black. Dallas's shift at Trader Joe's doesn't start until noon, and she plans to spend the morning doing absolutely nothing. A plus of no longer being on the run.

She glances at her short nails, which she's been biting obsessively. It's a side effect—a way to process the trauma without actually freaking out and murdering anyone. She also goes to counseling—real therapy now that The Program is gone—to deal with some of her anger issues. Of course, she doesn't always tell the truth—not about the parts that still hurt. And she plans to skip today's session; she has an actual date later tonight, and frankly, that's more important.

At the thought, Dallas smiles, sipping again from her coffee as she takes out her phone to scroll through her messages. One of the other cashiers—Wade—asked her out last night. He doesn't know about Dallas's past, doesn't even know she's been through The Program. It's sort of a taboo now. No one talks about handlers. No one asks about the past. She's not sure if keeping secrets is healthy—she suspects her shrink wouldn't think so—but she likes that she's able to start over here, in Florida.

The few messages on Dallas's phone are from Wade. He has a dry sort of humor that she enjoys. He's not like the other guys she's dated, but maybe that's why she likes him. He's safe, kind of boring. Kind of good. Dallas swallows hard and sets her phone down.

Aside from her hair, there are a few other things that Dallas misses. She misses her friendship with Cas—even though it hurts to remember sometimes. Despite his involvement with The Program, she still believes he was her friend. She has to believe it. She even misses Sloane, who, although annoying, turned out to be tougher than she ever imagined. And one of the best friends she's ever had. She sends Sloane postcards once in a while, just to let her know she's alive. But she doesn't want her to show them to anyone. Especially Realm.

At his name, Dallas quickly stands and drains the rest of her coffee, eager to push the thought of Realm far from her head. She goes about cleaning the kitchen and then slips her arms into a robe to go check the mail from yesterday.

The air outside the duplex is humid, and even the early-morning sunshine is bright. When she first moved here, Dallas loved the sunshine. It made her feel alive, healthy. Now she's used to it, and it's beginning to lose its charm. She thinks about Oregon some days—visiting Sloane and James. But she never does.

Resting on the wooden slats in front of the mailbox is a small leather case. Dallas takes a quick glance around her quiet street, her heart thumping, before she picks it up. The mailbox lid is lifted by a few oversize flyers, and she crumples them in her hand and heads back inside.

Her paranoia will never really fade. She knows that much. Dallas drops the junk mail into the trash and then sets the case on the kitchen table. Her fingers shake as she reaches inside, and when she pulls out a picture, she stumbles sideways into the chair. It's her, a picture of her before The Program. Soft blond hair, a hoodie—a normal girl. And next to her is Realm. Smiling.

There are other pictures, and tears fall over Dallas's cheeks as her entire past unfolds in front of her. She frantically sorts through all the photos, the notes. She has no idea how any of this stuff was saved, but she figures they're probably not hers at all. They're Realm's.

The last thing Dallas finds in the case is a postcard much like the ones she sends to Sloane. It's from Florida, from her very town, and has a bright-orange sunset streaked across the sky. Dallas's breath catches in her throat when she looks down at the message scrawled across the white background. It's not signed, it's not addressed. It holds only two words, two words that cut through Dallas and make her dissolve into sobs; heavy, aching sobs that both break her down and build her up. The doubt that's haunted her, the self-hatred, eases slightly, and she knows now she can heal.

Dallas wipes her cheeks and stands. She's going to get ready for work and pick out her outfit for her date tonight. She's going to do everything she wants to do. She's going to accept that good things can happen to her.

Dallas closes the leather case, set to store it away in her closet. She looks at the message one last time, memorizes it, and then leaves the postcard on the table before she walks away.

*You matter.*

# TURN THE PAGE FOR A PEEK AT THE THRILLING NEW STORY FROM SUZANNE YOUNG:

# THE REMEDY

**IT'S TIME TO SAY GOOD-BYE. I SIT IN THE ARMCHAIR** closest to the door and fold my hands politely in my lap. The room is too warm. Too quiet. My mother enters from the kitchen, her left eye swollen and bruised, small scratches carved into her cheeks. She limps to the plaid sofa, waving off help when I offer, and eases onto the patterned cushion next to my father. I shoot him an uncomfortable glance, but he doesn't lift his head; tears drip onto his gray slacks, and I turn away.

I begin to gnaw on the inside of my lower lip, waiting in silence as they consider their words. This intervention-style farewell is hardly the format I imagined, but the moment belongs to them, so I don't interfere. I cast a longing look to where my worn backpack waits near the door. Aaron had better not be late picking me up this time.

"Are you sure you can't stay another night?" my father asks, gripping his wife's hand hard enough to turn his knuckles white. They both stare at me pleadingly, but I don't give them false hope. I won't be that cruel.

"Sorry, but no," I say kindly. "This is where we say good-bye."

My mother pulls her hand from my father's, curling it into a fist at her mouth. She chokes back a sob, and I watch as the stitched wound on her cheek crinkles her skin.

I reach for my own tears, trying to appear sympathetic. *You'll never see your parents again,* I think. *Isn't that sad?* But all I can muster is a bit of blurry vision. It seems a little heartless, even to me, that I can't mourn their loss. But I've only known these people for two days. Besides, the clips on my hair extensions are driving my scalp mad. I reach a fingernail in between my red strands and scratch.

My mother takes a deep breath and then begins her rehearsed good-bye. "Emily," she says in a shaky voice. "When you died, my life ended too." A tear rolls slowly down her cheek, slipping into her dimple before falling away. "I couldn't see beyond my grief," she continues. "The counselors told me I had to, but I could only replay those last minutes in the car. This horrible loop of pain—" She chokes up, and my father reaches to rub her back soothingly. I don't interrupt. "And then you were gone," my mother whispers, looking at me. "I loved you more than anything, but you were torn away. I tried . . . I tried so hard, but I couldn't save you. I'm sorry, Emily."

I'm a barely passable version of Emily—different eyes, smaller chin. But my mother is grieving, and through her tears I'm sure she thinks I look identical to her dead daughter. And maybe that resemblance pains her even more when we're this close.

"I love you too, Mom," I say automatically, and flick my gaze to my father. "And thank you, Dad, for all you've done for me. I was very happy. No matter what, I'll always be with you"—I put my hand on my chest—"in your hearts."

The words are dry in my mouth, but I stick to the script when I can't personalize my speech in some other way. Ultimately, this is what they wanted to hear—or rather, what they needed to hear to have closure. They wanted me to know I was loved.

My phone buzzes in my pocket, but I don't ruin the moment to check it. We're past deadline and it has grown dark outside, but I won't leave until I'm sure my parents will get through this. I wait a beat, and my mother sniffles and wipes her face with her palms.

"I miss you, Emily," she says, and her voice cracks over my name. "I miss you every day." The first tears prick my eyes, the honesty in her emotions penetrating the wall I've carefully built. I smile at her, hoping it lessens her ache.

"I know you loved me," I say, going off script. "But, Mom . . . this wasn't your fault. It was an accident—a terrible, tragic accident. Please don't blame yourself anymore. I forgive you."

My mother claps both hands over her mouth, relief hemorrhaging as her shoulders shake with her sobs. This is it—her closure. She needed relief from her guilt. My father climbs to his feet and motions toward the door. I stand to follow him, but pause and look back at my mother.

"I'm safe now," I continue. "Nothing can ever hurt me again. Not one thing." I turn to leave the room, my voice barely audible over her cries. "Good-bye, Mom."

My assignment is complete.

I follow my father to the front door, and when we reach the entryway, I rummage through the shredded middle pocket of my backpack and pull out a sweatshirt. I yank the Rolling Stones T-shirt off over my tank top and hand it to my dad . . . or, rather, Alan Pinnacle.

For the past two days, I've been wearing his daughter's favorite clothes, eating her favorite foods, sleeping in her bed. I'm the Goldilocks the bears took in to replace the one they lost, even if it was only to say good-bye.

Alan looks down at Emily's black shirt and pushes it in my direction. "Keep it," he says, staring at the fabric like it's precious. I widen my eyes and take a step back.

"But it's not mine," I say quietly. "It belonged to your daughter." Sometimes parents become confused, and part of my job is to keep them grounded in reality. Martha sits on the couch, staring toward the window with a calmed expression, but I worry that Alan is having an emotional breakdown.

"You're right," he says sadly. "But Emily isn't coming home." He holds up the shirt. "If this is still being worn, in a way, her spirit will be out there. She'll still be part of the world."

"I really shouldn't," I say, although if I'm honest, that T-shirt was my favorite part of this assignment. But we're not supposed to keep artifacts of the dead. It opens up the possibility of lawsuits against the entire grief department, claims of unprofessionalism.

"Please," he murmurs. "I think she would have really liked you."

*It's just a shirt,* I think. *No one's ever been fired over a shirt.* I reluctantly take the fabric from his hand, and Alan's face twists in a flash of pain. Impulsively, I lean in and kiss his cheek.

"Emily was a lucky girl," I whisper close to his ear. And then, without waiting to see his expression, I turn and walk out of Emily Pinnacle's house.

The night air is heavy with moisture as I step onto the wooden slats of the front porch; cool rainy wind blows against my face. The headlights of a car parked down the road flick on, and my muscles relax. I'm glad I won't be hanging around for a ride; Aaron usually sucks at being on time. I reach into my hair and begin to remove the extensions, unclipping them and then shoving them into the bag on my shoulder, where I stuffed the Rolling Stones T-shirt.

The car pulls up, and I hold my backpack over my head to protect myself from the rain. I throw one more glance back at the house, glad neither parent is looking out the window. I hate to break the illusion for them; it's like seeing a teacher at the grocery store or a theme-park character without its oversize head.

I open the car door and drop onto the passenger seat of a shiny black Cadillac. It reeks of leather and coconut air freshener. I turn sideways, lifting my eyebrows the minute I take in Aaron's appearance. I pretend to check my nonexistent watch. "And who are you supposed to be?" I ask.

Aaron smiles. "I'm me again," he says. "It was a long drive. I didn't have time to change clothes."

This was one of those rare moments where Aaron and I were on assignment at the same time—a mostly avoided conflict. It was probably a good thing that I was running late tonight. I scan my friend's outfit, holding back the laugh waiting in my gut. He's wearing a dark brown corduroy jacket with a striped button-down shirt underneath. Although Aaron's barely nineteen, he's dressed like an eighty-year-old professor. Sensing my impending reaction, he steps on the gas pedal and speeds us down the street.

"Twenty-three-year-old law student," he explains, turning up the volume on the stereo. "But his real love was math." He shoots me a pointed look as if it sums up his assignment completely. "The counselors are really pushing my age, right?" he asks. "Must be this sweet beard." He strokes his facial hair and I scrunch up my nose.

"Gross," I say. "You're lucky Oregon celebrates its facial hair; otherwise you'd be out of work." Aaron's smooth, dark skin disappears every No Shave November, but that ended five months ago. I'm partners with a Sasquatch. "When are you getting rid of that thing?" I ask.

"Um, never," he says, like it's the obvious answer. "I'm looking fine, girl."

I laugh and flip down the passenger-side mirror. The light clicks on, harsh on my heavy makeup. I comb my fingers through my still-red shoulder-length strands. Emily's hair was ridiculously long, so I had to wear itchy extensions. I'm glad to be rid of them.

"Too bad," Aaron says, motioning to my reflection. "I liked your hair long."

"And I like that special blazer. You sure you can't keep it?"

"Point made," he concedes. We're quiet for a moment until Aaron clears his throat. "So how was it?" he asks in a therapist's voice, even though he knows I hate talking about my assignments. "You were super vague on the phone," he adds. "I was getting worried."

"It was the same," I answer. "Just like always."

"Was it the mom?"

"Yeah," I tell him, and look out the passenger window. "Survivor's guilt. There was a car accident; the mother was driving. After arriving at the hospital, the mom ran from room to room, searching for her daughter. But she was DOA." I swallow hard, burying the emotions that threaten to shake my voice. "All the mother wanted was to apologize for losing control of the car," I continue. "Beg her daughter for forgiveness. Tell her how much she loved her. But she never got the chance. She didn't even get to say good-bye. Martha had a hard time accepting that."

"Martha?" Aaron repeats, and I feel him look at me. "You two on a first-name basis?"

"No," I say. "But I'm not calling her Mom anymore, and it seems cold to call her Mrs. Pinnacle." When I turn to Aaron, he looks doubtful. "What?" I ask. "The woman washed my underwear. It's not like we're strangers."

"See, that's the thing," he says, holding up his finger. "You *are* strangers. You were temporarily playing the role of her deceased daughter, but by no means are you friends. Don't blur the lines, Quinn."

"I know how to do my job," I answer dismissively. My heart beats faster.

Although all closers take on the personality of the dead person, I'm the only one who internalizes it, thinks like them. It makes me more authentic, and honestly, it's why I'm the best. "Don't be judgy," I tell Aaron. "You have your process; I have mine. I'm completely detached when it's over."

Aaron chuckles. "You're detached?" he asks. "Then why do you keep souvenirs?"

"I do not," I respond, heat crawling onto my cheeks.

"I bet you have more than hair extensions in that bag."

I look down to see the edge of the T-shirt peeking out. "Not fair," I say. "The dad gave that to me. It doesn't count."

"And the earrings from Susan Bell? The flashy yet clashy belt from Audrey Whatshername? Admit it. You're a life klepto. You keep pieces of them like some whacked-out serial killer."

I laugh. "It's nothing like that."

Aaron hums out his disagreement and takes a turn onto the freeway. It'll be at least forty-five minutes until we're back in Corvallis. I hate the away assignments, but our town is fairly small, and we don't have nearly as many deaths as Eugene or Portland. But being away can mess with your head. Nothing's familiar—not the places or the people. A person could forget who they really are in a situation like that. It's high risk, and the return is always more difficult after being cut off completely. But it's our job.

Aaron Rios and I are closers—a remedy for grief-stricken families. We help clients who are experiencing symptoms of complicated grief through an extreme method of role-playing therapy. When a family or person experiences loss—the kind of loss they just can't get over, the kind that eats away at their sanity—grief counselors make a recommendation. For an undisclosed sum of money, clients are given a closer to play the part of a dead person and provide them the much-needed closure they desire.

At this point I can become anyone so long as they're a white female between the ages of fifteen and twenty. I'm not an exact copy, of course, but I wear their clothes and change my hair and eye color. I study them through pictures and videos, and soon I can act like them, smell like them, *be them* for all intents and purposes. And when a family is hazy with grief, they tend to accept me readily.

I stay with them for a few days, but never more than a week. In that time, my loved ones get to say everything they needed to but never got the chance to, get to hear whatever they've told the counselors they needed to hear. I can be the perfect daughter. I can give them closure so they can heal.

I'm saving lives—even if sometimes it's hard to remember which one is mine.

"So what have I missed?" I ask Aaron. When he called me earlier to set up my extraction, he tried to talk, to reconnect me to the outside world. But I was with the family when my phone buzzed, so I fed Aaron some bullshit excuse to get off the line. Now I'm desperate for a reminder of my real life. I rest my temple on the headrest and watch him.

"Not much." He shrugs. "Deacon's been texting me non-stop. Says you're not answering your phone."

"Well, he's not supposed to contact me when I'm on an assignment," I point out. Our guidelines state that we only consort with our partners or our advisors while on assignment to keep us from breaking character. But the fact is, I could have responded to Deacon's texts. I just didn't want to.

My eyes start to sting and I check around the front seat and find a bag of open trail mix stuffed into the cutout below the stereo; salty-looking peanuts have spilled into the cup holder. My father will kill Aaron for bringing those in here. And for dirtying up his Cadillac. We always use the same car for extractions. It serves as a reminder of our real life, something familiar to bring us home.

I hike my backpack onto my lap and start rummaging through until I find the case for my colored contacts. Although

I'm not deathly allergic to nuts, they irritate my eyes and make my throat burn. Aaron's usually pretty good about not eating them around me. I guess he forgot this time—which is understandable. Assignments tend to leave us confused. At least for a while.

"I think Deacon's worried you'll run away without telling him," Aaron continues. "It makes him crazy."

"Deacon never worries about anything," I correct, resting my index finger on my pupil until I feel the contact cling to it. "And I don't know why he's asking you. If I planned to run away, you wouldn't know either." I remove the film and place it back inside the case before working on the other eye.

"Yeah, well, he worries about *you*," Aaron mutters, clicking the windshield wipers off now that the rain has eased up. "And whether you admit it or not," he adds, "you worry about his ass all the time too."

"We're friends," I remind him, reliving the conversation we've had a dozen times. "Just very good friends."

"Whatever, Quinn," he says. "You're hard-core and he's badass. I get it. You're both too tough for love."

"Shut up." I laugh. "You're just mad we get along better than you and your girlfriend."

"Damn right," Aaron says with a defiant smirk. "It ain't cool. You two—"

"Stooooop," I whine, cutting him off. "Change the subject. Deacon and I are broken up. End of story." I stuff my contact case back into my bag and drop it down by my feet.

The traffic has faded from the freeway, leaving the dark road empty around us.

"I'm not saying you should hate each other," Aaron continues. "But you shouldn't want to bone every time you see him either."

"You have serious problems, you know that, right?"

"Mm-hmm," he says, nodding dismissively. "Yeah, *I'm* the one with problems." He whistles out a low sound of sympathy, looking sideways at me. "You've both got it bad," he adds.

"No," I tell him. "We're both better off. Remind Deacon of that next time he's checking up on me." Aaron scoffs and swears he's staying out of it. He won't, of course. He thinks we're still pining for each other. And . . . he may not be entirely wrong. But Deacon and I have a very platonic understanding.

Deacon Hatcher is my ex-boyfriend turned best friend, but more importantly, he used to be a closer. He gets it. Gets me. Deacon was my partner before Aaron, almost three years side by side until he quit working for my dad eight months ago. He quit me the same day. The breakup may have wrecked me a little. Or a lot. Deacon and I had shared everything, had a policy of total honesty, which isn't exactly easy for people in our line of work.

I hadn't even known he'd ended his contract with the grief department when he told me we were over, said he'd moved on. I assumed he meant with another girl, so we didn't speak for over a month. I'd been blindsided, betrayed. Only thing left for me was closure, and I was damn good at it. I absorbed more of my assignments' lives, their families' love. I rebuilt my self-esteem with their help, their memories. Then my father assigned Aaron as my new partner.

The next day, Deacon showed up at my front door, saying how sorry he was. Saying how desperately he missed me. I believed him. I always believe him. But every time we get close—the very minute I fall for him again—Deacon cuts me off, backs away and leaves me brokenhearted by the absence of his affection. Whether it's his training or his natural disposition, Deacon *is* charming. The kind of charming that makes you feel like you're the only person in the world who matters. Until you don't anymore.

I'm tired of the push and pull that continues to crack and heal over the same scar. I told Deacon that I was done letting myself be vulnerable to him, that he was ruining me. The thought seemed to devastate him. So Deacon and I agreed not to get back together, but acknowledged that we couldn't stay away from each other either. Best friends is the compromise. It lets us go to the very edge of our want without actually going over. And that works for us. We're totally screwed up that way.

From the center console Aaron's phone vibrates in the cup holder. He quickly grabs it before I do, and rests it against the wheel while he reads the text. After a moment he clicks off the screen and drops his phone back into the cup holder. "Myra says hello," he says, glancing over. "She's *super* excited for you to be back."

"I'm sure," I say, flashing him an amused smile. Aaron's

girlfriend is barely five feet tall, with wide doelike eyes and a red-hot temper. She used to hate me—which, under normal circumstances, could be understandable. I spend *a lot* of time with her boyfriend. We're over it now and the entire situation became a running joke between me and Aaron. And although Myra might still hate me a *little*, she's one of my closest friends. But everything will change soon. This is Aaron's last month as a closer—his contract ends in four weeks. After that, he and Myra are going to run off and live some deranged life in one of the Dakotas.

"Any chance I can talk you into dropping me off at home first?" I ask Aaron in a sickly sweet voice. "I've been dreaming about my bed for the entire weekend. Emily had a futon."

Aaron whistles in sympathy. "Sounds tough, Quinn. But I already called Marie to let her know we're on our way." He smiles. "And you know how much she loves late-night debriefings."

False. Marie absolutely hates when we come by after dark.

I exhale, dreading our next stop. I just want to go home, tell my dad good night, and then crash in my bed. Unfortunately, none of that can happen until we register our closure and confess our sins. Our advisor, Marie, has to interview us before we're allowed to return to our regular lives. There are procedures in place to make sure we don't take any grief home with us, take home the sadness. It's the old saying: misery loves company. Yeah, well, grief can be contagious.

# ABOUT THE AUTHOR

SUZANNE YOUNG is the *New York Times* bestselling author of the Program duology. Originally from Utica, New York, Suzanne moved to Arizona to pursue her dream of not freezing to death. She is a novelist and an English teacher, but not always in that order. Suzanne is the author of *The Program*, *The Treatment*, *The Remedy*, and *A Need So Beautiful*. You can visit her online at www.suzanne-young.blogspot.com.